pob

FLASHBACK

OTHER BOOKS AND AUDIO BOOKS
BY J. MICHAEL HUNTER:

Wrongly Accused

FLASHBACK

a novel

J. Michael Hunter

Covenant Communications, Inc.

Cover images: Moon II © Nikolaos Vasilikoudis coutesy of stock.xchng, City Sunset Pano 04 © Falk-Henning Schaaf coutesy of stock.xchng

Cover design copyrighted 2008 by Covenant Communications, Inc.

Published by Covenant Communications, Inc.
American Fork, Utah

Printed in Canada
First Printing: July 2008

14 13 12 11 10 09 08   10 9 8 7 6 5 4 3 2 1

ISBN-10 1-58911-508-1
ISBN-13 978-1-58911-508-6

To my mother, Faye St. Clair Hunter.
And to my grandmother, Veatrice Falls St. Clair.

Acknowledgments

I appreciate my wife LeAnn's continual support and encouragement. I would like to express gratitude to Jennifer James Spell for again providing me with excellent editorial advice. I would also like to thank the people at Covenant for giving me another opportunity to publish, especially Kat Gille and Linda Prince for all their help.

A safe but sometimes chilly way of recalling the past is to force open a crammed drawer. If you are searching for anything in particular you don't find it, but something falls out at the back that is often more interesting.

—J. M. Barrie, *Peter Pan*, 1902

1

Laura woke suddenly, her eyes searching the shadows for the stairs—for the body—but they were gone. She listened but heard only her pounding heart and her erratic breathing. Feeling as if the dream had sucked all the air out of her, she struggled, gasping for breath.

She cowered under the bedcovers, trying to stop the panic attack she felt coming on. After all this time, the dreadful dream was back. Moving the blanket up over her mouth and nose, she stared into the darkness, too afraid to get out of bed. As the dream began to replay itself in her mind, she closed her eyes in an effort to shut it out, then immediately opened them again when the images became more vivid. She forced herself to reach out and turn on the lamp on the nightstand, and with the darkness gone, she was finally able to breathe a little easier.

A knock sounded at her bedroom door, and Laura froze. Then she heard her roommate, Megan, call out, "Are you all right, Laura?"

"Come in," Laura invited when she had found her voice.

Megan opened the door and walked in. "Are you all right?" she asked again. Megan's short blond hair was messy and her robe on inside out, but she was a welcome sight. Laura sighed heavily and sat up, moving to the side of the bed. "Just a bad dream."

Megan frowned, her brow furrowed with concern. "It sounded pretty bad—you screamed."

"Did I?"

"I'm worried about you. Do you want to tell me about the dream? Maybe it would help." Without waiting for a response, Megan sat down in the corner chair beside Laura's dresser.

Though they had been roommates for almost a year, Laura had never told Megan about the recurring dream that had haunted her, because she'd stopped having it not long after Megan moved in. Laura had seen no need to bring up the dream in conversation, plus she had feared that talking about it would cause a recurrence. "It's hard to explain," Laura muttered.

Megan shrugged. "Dreams usually are. You probably can't even remember it very well."

"I wish I couldn't," Laura replied. "But I've had the same dream many times, more than I can count." She paused, waiting for Megan's reaction.

Megan yawned and sat up a little straighter. "What do you mean?"

Laura hesitated again. "I mean . . . I had this dream frequently when I was little, and also after my mom passed away. But it stopped again months ago—until tonight."

Megan rubbed her eyes and leaned forward with interest. "Wow. What's it about?"

"Falling," Laura answered flatly. "Falling down stairs."

"Oh," Megan said nonchalantly, waving her hand toward Laura. "Falling dreams are common—I have them too, and they wake me up sometimes."

"Do you die at the end of yours?" Laura asked with a tremor in her voice.

Megan's expression immediately became concerned again. She crossed her arms and shivered. "What do you mean?"

"In the dream," Laura explained, "I run down a long, dark hall, then suddenly I fall down a flight of stairs—and I fall for what seems like forever. At the bottom of the stairs, I can see myself lying there. It's like an out-of-body experience in which my spirit looks down at my body. The eeriest part is that I see a person crouching over my body, a person wearing a hooded cape. That's when I usually wake up."

Megan's frown deepened. "That's bizarre. How often did you say you would have this nightmare?"

"Several times a month, and, like I said, it started when I was a little girl. It stopped for a while, then began to happen again when my mother died. But I thought I'd finally gotten over it this time—I hadn't had the dream for several months . . . before tonight."

The mention of her mother brought a flood of emotions. Laura's father, John, had died of a heart attack when she was a child. After John's death, Laura's mother, Sarah, had attended secretarial school and then gotten a job working for a lawyer. She had raised Laura as a single mother, helping pay her way through college so she could obtain a teaching degree. Laura had taught kindergarten for about a year when her mother had died of cancer, and the dream had started again.

Laura's bishop had introduced her to Megan, who was renting a studio apartment over a garage while working part-time and attending City College. The bishop had suggested that it might be financially beneficial for Megan to move in with Laura, who couldn't afford to live alone after her mother's death. A convert of only a few months at the time, Laura was grateful for not only the financial assistance but the spiritual strength Megan contributed.

"What do you think the dream means?" Megan asked.

"I wish I knew," Laura responded. "After my mother died, I went to see a grief counselor for a while, and I told her about the dream."

"What did she say?"

"Well, at first she said that falling is often symbolic of a person's fear of failure. I'd lost my mother—I was on my own for the first time in my life—and the fall symbolized my fear of not being able to handle things on my own. I had no idea what would happen if I failed, but the idea was dark and foreboding, just like the hooded figure. The counselor also said the hooded figure might represent death. It had taken my mother from me—it had changed my life. She said I viewed death as something fearful and awful, dark and menacing—something hovering over me like the hooded person."

"Makes sense," Megan affirmed with a shrug.

"It did until I told her that I'd had the dream—the exact dream, mind you—over and over again when I was a child. I told her that this dream had been with me for as long as I could remember, that I almost felt like I'd been born with this dream inside me. She didn't know how to explain that, so we moved on to other topics like my anxiety attacks."

"I took this class once," Megan started, "where the professor said that recurring dreams weren't dreams at all. He believed they were memories passed on to us from someone else."

Laura's eyes widened. "Are you serious?"

"Yeah. He called it genetic memory theory or something like that. The idea was that experiences are imprinted on our DNA and passed from one generation to another."

"What do you think of that?" Laura inquired.

"I don't buy it," Megan replied. "I'm more inclined to believe dreams connect the past—the individual's past, not their ancestral past—to the present. Whatever is bothering you has to do with your own life, not something that happened to your ancestors. Is there something that's happened recently that might explain why you've started having the dream again? You said it had stopped again a few months ago, right?"

Laura hesitated.

"What?" Megan pressed.

"Well . . ." Laura opened the drawer of the side table and slowly pulled out an envelope. "There *is* this." She handed it to Megan.

Megan looked at the return address. "A law office in Virginia. Are you in some kind of trouble?"

"Read it," Laura urged.

Megan took out the letter and read quickly, then exclaimed, "Wow, Laura! I can't believe this. How long have you known about this?"

Laura looked down at her pajama-clad knees. "A week or so," she answered softly.

"What? And you've been keeping it a secret?"

"Well, I needed to think about it," Laura explained. "I mean, I'm not sure what I'm going to do about it."

Megan jumped up from the chair. "Do about it? What do you mean? Of course you know what you're going to do about it! If I had a letter from a lawyer saying that I'd just inherited a plantation and millions of dollars, I know exactly what I'd do!"

"What would you do?" Laura asked.

"I'd be on the next plane to Virginia asking, 'Where's my money?'" Megan replied with a chuckle.

Laura stood and walked over to the dresser, then looked at herself in the mirror. Her long, chestnut hair was mussed from the bedsheets, and her face looked even paler than usual. People had always told her she was a pretty girl, but she'd always had a hard time accepting the idea. She'd struggled with fears and anxiety for what seemed her entire life—all twenty-four short years of it.

For most of her life, Laura's mother had tried to shield her from any situation that could cause discomfort. When Laura began living alone after her mother's death, she had realized that such overprotectiveness had probably caused her tendency to have panic attacks. Her mother had referred to her as a "nervous child," but she hadn't outgrown her anxiety by the time she reached eighteen. After high school, Laura had somehow managed to ride the bus to St. Louis's City College every day and had eventually received her teaching degree. After graduation, she found a job at the elementary school just a few blocks away from her mother's apartment. She never had to travel far from home, and that was just the way she wanted it.

Laura glanced at Megan. "I guess I'm a little attached to my comfort zone," she confessed, realizing that it sounded inadequate and perhaps even a bit immature.

"A little?" Megan quipped.

Laura smiled. "Okay, I'm a lot attached to my neighborhood. I mean, I know everyone in the neighborhood and at work, so I feel safe here. I have everything I need—I don't really need a mansion or millions of dollars."

Megan laughed. "What are you going to do, tear the letter up and forget that it ever came? Do you want to spend the rest of your life asking 'what if'? Laura, as your friend, I feel I should tell it to you straight: It's time to get out of your comfort zone. Destiny is calling. You're going to Virginia, and I'm going to make it my personal goal to make sure of that."

"We'd better get some sleep," Laura mumbled. "Maybe we can talk about this again tomorrow."

2

Laura sat at her desk in front of an empty classroom. The school day was finally over, and she was exhausted. Unable to go back to sleep after the nightmare, she'd been preoccupied all day. Her students had even commented on it. She couldn't put the letter from Virginia out of her mind. Her mother's only sister, Laura Buford, had died and left her namesake niece millions. The bequest included a mansion on a tobacco plantation of several thousand acres in the Blue Ridge Mountains. Laura could have it all if she agreed to move to Virginia and live in the mansion for three years. And that was the problem: she would have to leave St. Louis.

Laura massaged her temples. She wanted to go home, but first she needed to prepare the classroom for the next day. The afternoon sun glared through the west windows, making the room uncomfortably warm despite the air conditioning. Such were the hazards of teaching summer school, Laura decided as she walked over to pull down the shade. That's when she saw the man in the silver Mercedes.

The sun reflected off the car's windows, so Laura couldn't be absolutely sure it was the same balding man she'd noticed before, but she was pretty sure it was the same car. It was parked across the street from the school.

Laura tried to remember the first time she'd seen the Mercedes. She seemed to recall noticing it near the neighborhood market when she'd picked up a few groceries last week. At the time, she had assumed the man was waiting for someone who was in the store, and she had only noticed him because he was driving her dream car. But two days later Laura saw the car again, with the same man behind the wheel, when she came out of the city library. At that point she had wondered if someone—perhaps an elderly lady who needed a driver—had moved into the neighborhood. But then she had noticed the same car parked on her street as she walked to work that very morning, and she had seen someone inside it. Now it was parked across the street from her school, and she was sure it was the same man inside.

Laura's heart began to pound, and she pulled down the shade. *Calm down, Laura,* she thought. *Don't let your imagination run wild on you. He could have a perfectly normal reason for parking outside the school, and he might just coincidentally end up in the same places you do.*

Rubbing her throbbing temples again, Laura realized she was just tired and being silly. She quickly prepared the classroom for the next day, cleaned off her desk, grabbed her purse, and headed out.

As she walked out of the school into St. Louis's sweltering summer heat, she dug through her purse for her sunglasses. She couldn't find the glasses and dug deeper, looking into the bag's dark crevices as she made her way down the street. Customarily she walked to and from work unless she had too much to carry, in which case she had Megan drop her off if it worked with Megan's schedule. The school was so close that Laura felt silly driving unless it was absolutely necessary.

After checking her purse again without any luck, Laura realized she must have left her sunglasses at the school. Turning abruptly, she saw *him* and froze. Her heart pounded, and sweat sprang to her palms and forehead.

He stood at the crosswalk she'd just crossed, obviously following her, and he seemed startled to find her suddenly facing him. He was tall and thin, almost gaunt, a balding man of about fifty with lines etched so deeply in each cheek that they almost looked like scars. Dark circles underlined his deep-set eyes, the resulting shadows making his expression almost eerie. She didn't know him—other than having caught sight of him here and there in his silver Mercedes—yet she was sure by the look on his face that he knew her. But how? And what was she to do now that she was face-to-face with him?

Laura gasped involuntarily as she realized that the man must know her habits—what time she went to work each day, her lunch hour, her trips to the grocery store and the library. And yet she didn't understand why he should care to know all this. She wondered what motivated stalkers in the first place. Possibly she'd passed him on the street or in the grocery store—perhaps she had innocently spoken to him. Maybe she'd smiled faintly at him as she normally did when she inadvertently made eye contact with a stranger as they passed. She meant to be polite and friendly, not encourage anyone's attention.

Could her shy smile have caught a stranger's eye? Maybe he was lonely, looking for companionship. She was young enough to be his daughter—perhaps he'd lost a daughter, and Laura's large green eyes reminded him of her. For that matter, she could look like a deceased wife or old girlfriend. No matter how innocent she tried to make it, she knew he could be a mentally or emotionally disturbed individual, or worse, a psychopathic rapist or murderer.

As all these thoughts passed quickly through Laura's mind, the man turned and walked away. She didn't dare return to the school for her sunglasses—she had to get home as quickly as possible. Turning on her heel, Laura headed toward her apartment.

Breathing rapidly and walking quickly, Laura turned back every few seconds to make sure the man wasn't following. Her quiet neighborhood had taken on a gloomy hue in the late afternoon sun, the great oak trees and weathered Victorian mansions that lined the street casting long shadows across the crumbling sidewalk. Except for the occasional vehicle passing, the old neighborhood was quiet until Laura heard a voice—her voice. She was muttering prayers out loud. "Please let me get home safely. Don't let anyone hurt me."

The words came in raspy breaths—she was nearly hyperventilating. Glancing back over her shoulder again, Laura thought she detected a flicker of movement, but the sidewalk was empty, and she decided it must have been a breeze disturbing the leaves on the trees that lined the block. She should stop, pull out her paper bag, and start breathing into it, Laura realized. She should start her mantras. *You're okay. Inhale slowly. Calm your mind and soul.* What were the rest of them? That was the problem with panic mantras: she could never remember them when she most needed them. By the time she realized she needed them, her mind was racing so fast, she couldn't remember anything other than pure, unadulterated fear—panic so intense it seemed to run through her veins like poison. It didn't matter, though, because prayer came more naturally now than mantras, and prayer actually worked every time. Glancing over her shoulder, Laura again thought she saw a flash of movement, and this time she told herself it was probably a cat or a squirrel. She knew that anyone who could see her would think she was acting strange, and that they might call the police and have her checked out. The police would approach carefully, not knowing exactly what they were facing— for all they knew she could be a strung-out junkie with a knife or a gun.

Off—Off—Officer. It's okay. I—I—I'm not on drugs. This evil-looking guy is following me, maybe trying to kill me. He—He's been following me around town. No, don't shoot. I'm reaching for my brown paper bag—really.

She laughed at her own thoughts, then lapsed into silence as she realized how hysterical she sounded. Her heels beat on the sidewalk, echoing like gunshots against the worn housefronts.

She tried to refocus her thoughts and began naming the residents she knew in each building. *Cooper up, Hillstead down. Breathe, Laura, breathe! Miriam and Dylan. A bunch of guys.* The largest houses in the neighborhood had been turned into apartments, and young professionals had purchased and restored the smaller homes. The rectangular apartment building where Laura lived had been squeezed in between two huge Victorian homes years before, its brick façade standing out among the many wood-framed houses. Six apartments made up the two-story structure—three on the first floor and three on the second. Laura lived on the far right end of the first floor.

Finally reaching her door, Laura fumbled with her keys and then dropped them on the cement with what sounded to her like a loud clang. As she picked up the keys with trembling hands, the metal tinkled and pinged like a wind chime. She forced the house key into the lock, looked back over her shoulder, and pushed the door open.

Once inside, Laura slammed the door, locked it, and fastened the deadbolt. She'd left the air conditioner on that morning, and the apartment felt cool. Leaning back against the door, she closed her eyes, gulping in air. As she uttered a silent prayer, she tried to slow her breathing. A sharp pain racked her chest, but she felt herself calming down. The grief counselor had taught her the technique, and it worked. *I'm home. I'm safe,* Laura told herself.

3

Laura opened her eyes and looked gratefully at the apartment that had been her home for twenty years. She stood in the living room, her back still braced against the front door. In front of her was a narrow hall with doors to two bedrooms and a bathroom, and to the left was the kitchen. The place hadn't changed much in all the time she'd lived there. When Megan had moved in, she had commented that the place looked as if it had been sealed in a time capsule for two decades, but that since she was into the 80s, she liked it.

Should I call the police? Laura wondered. *What would I tell them— that a man was following me?* The police would ask if he'd approached her, spoken to her, or threatened her in some way. Reminding herself that it could just be a coincidence that they were in the same location several times in a row, Laura decided to ask Megan's opinion when she got home.

As Laura scrutinized the small apartment, she had to admit that it looked outdated and worn. Nothing except the carpet had changed since her parents had moved in during the mid-80s. The couch and loveseat were cornflower blue with peach flecks, and those colors were mirrored in the calico rabbit on the floor. A large oak-laminate book-shelf held a stereo—complete with a turntable—and a small collection of books.

Laura didn't own many books, not because she didn't read but because she tended to check them out from the library. She did, however, own a set of Barbara Michaels' suspense novels. When she purchased them for fifty cents each at a library fundraiser, she had already read them all, but she couldn't bear to see them discarded.

"Why are you selling these?" she'd asked Tom London, the elderly, bearded librarian, as he stood between book-laden tables at the fundraiser.

"No one checks out Michaels anymore," he declared. "Mary Higgins Clark has succeeded her, and even Higgins Clark is on her way out."

"But these are classics!" Laura exclaimed as she began stuffing the books into her shopping bag.

Tom smiled. "You're one of the few remaining devotees of Gothic romance."

"Romance?" Laura replied quizzically. "These are mystery novels—suspense."

Tom chuckled. "I guess they're whatever you make of them."

Laura had started reading Michaels in high school, and perhaps she had become a bit obsessed with the series. She used to daydream she was in one of Michaels' scenes, and there was always a dark, handsome man in the picture. The man had to have dark hair, as that somehow resonated better with a brooding disposition, and he had to be brooding—to have some dark secret that made him interesting in an almost psychotic way. In the end, his secret would always be revealed, and he and his heroine would be freed from the chains that held them to a dark past, free to join each other in a blissful future.

Laura wished she could turn her current situation into a Michaels' novel. She imagined herself running down the street, the stalker chasing her. Suddenly a dark, handsome stranger would appear, and she'd run into his arms. "Save me! He's obsessed with me. He wants to carry me off to his mansion!" The good-looking stranger would sweep her up in his arms and carry her to his own mansion, which was actually more akin to a small palace, because he was really a European prince. Indeed, her imaginary prince would be living incognito in St. Louis to avoid being forced into marriage by his parents, but he was required to marry in order to inherit the throne. Now in love with the lovely though anxiety-ridden Laura McClain, he could return to claim his rightful place in the kingdom with his beautiful new princess.

After focusing her mind on such pleasant thoughts, Laura felt her heart slow to a normal rhythm. She finally pushed away from the door and tossed her keys into the basket on the table beside the loveseat.

Then she took off her shoes and picked them up. Walking past her large freshwater aquarium, she stooped to glance in at the tropical fish that gathered near the top, some sticking their puckered lips above the water's surface, and informed them that she would feed them momentarily. She then risked a peek out the front window and, seeing no silver Mercedes, closed the curtains, being careful not to knock over the odd assortment of antique bottles filled with plants and other trinkets lined up on the floor beneath the window.

Since her childhood, terrariums had been a hobby of Laura's. Whenever she found a yard sale in the neighborhood, she would search for unique old bottles. Sometimes she found unusual little things—usually stashed in a shoebox most garage-sale shoppers overlooked—to go in the bottles. She filled the bottles halfway with potting soil, inserted the plants, and then added various curios. Many of the jars had wide mouths, but for narrow-mouthed jars, she used plastic terrarium tweezers to situate the plants and other objects.

Entering her bedroom, Laura placed her shoes on the rack at the bottom of the closet, then closed the closet door. Perhaps it was a compulsion, but she couldn't stand to see a closet door or a drawer left open. Her bedroom was always neat, in spite of its mismatched décor. Her mother had given her the pink quilt on the bed, so she still used it even though it was almost threadbare. In contrast, the desk that held her computer and printer was aggressively modern, made of brushed nickel and frosted glass. A photograph of Laura and her mother hung on the wall above the desk. Laura was twelve years old in the picture, and it was one of the few formal photographs her mother had sat for.

After crossing the room to the vanity, Laura sat in front of the mirror. She took off her clip-on earrings and stopped to look at herself, noting that she could have used a little more makeup under her eyes today. The sleepless night—the dream—had taken its toll, and she looked haggard. In addition, the news about her aunt's estate had been bothering her for more than a week.

Virginia. As far as Laura could recall, her parents had mentioned the place only once or twice in her presence. It was almost as if Sarah and John McClain had appeared from the fog when they arrived in St. Louis before Laura was born. At the time, John had sold insurance, and a promotion had brought him to St. Louis—or so her mother had told her.

Brought on by the stress of his job, a heart attack killed Laura's father before she turned eight. She and her mother had continued living in the same apartment. After her mother's death, Laura had made only necessary changes. She could have moved into the master bedroom, but she had seen no need to do so. This bedroom was not that much smaller, and it had been easier to get rid of most of her mother's things to make room for Megan's belongings than to move her own things as well.

As far back as Laura could remember, her mother had been efficient and driven, never wavering from her goal of helping her daughter make it safely through life. In fact, Sarah McClain had been so stubborn that no one could stop her once she made up her mind. Laura sighed as she supposed it was that determination that had helped her mother survive widowhood and poverty.

Laura knew her mother had loved her; after all, she had sacrificed a great deal to make sure Laura received an education and started a successful career. Sarah had held an odd assortment of jobs while she worked her way through secretarial school, ending up with a decent job as a legal secretary. All of her extra money went toward a savings account for Laura's college education. Sometimes Laura had felt as if her mother expected someone or something to break down the door and take her daughter away. Laura attributed this defensive mode to her father's early death. Sarah probably lived in fear that she'd lose Laura, too, and Laura often wondered what her mother would have been like had John McClain lived.

Laura still had vivid memories of her father—always polite but aloof. Laura remembered that she could never tell what he was thinking and that she would get exasperated at his reserve. Now that she was older, she wished she could have gotten inside his brain and seen what made him tick—what he wanted from life. She thought he'd loved her, and yet she hadn't understood him and doubted he had ever understood her. But he was gone, and the chance to get to know him in mortality was gone as well.

For her entire life, Laura's parents never talked of their pasts, and they seemed to avoid questions about themselves. Whenever Laura inquired about her mother's childhood or young adulthood, a wall went up, and eventually Laura just let it go.

Laura stared into the mirror, looking beyond her own image to the closed closet door. Suddenly she froze in horror. The door was closed now, but when she had first entered the room, she had put her shoes in the closet without having to open the door. While she could have left it open that morning, she couldn't remember the last time she had done so, and she was quite certain she had closed it today.

Slowly she stood, her heartbeat speeding up. She stepped over to the bedside table and soundlessly opened the top drawer, then sighed with relief that her diary was there. But the relief vanished in a heartbeat when she realized that the ribbon was not in place over the diary's cover. Perhaps it was paranoia or superstition, but she always placed a silk ribbon across the top of the diary in such a way that she would know if it had been moved. As an adolescent who suspected that her mother was prying in her diary, the idea made sense, but Laura knew that as an adult, it was an odd habit.

Nonetheless, as Laura stared at the diary, her heart pounded in her chest. Someone had been reading her diary while she was at work! That morning, before leaving for the school, Laura had quickly recorded her dream before going to work, after which she distinctly remembered replacing the ribbon. She always replaced the ribbon. *There's no way Megan would*—Laura stopped herself before she even finished the thought. Megan couldn't have been the one snooping through her diary: Megan had left the apartment before Laura that morning.

Laura looked up, her eyes darting from side to side as she wondered if whoever had invaded her privacy was in the house right now. She wanted to run out of the bedroom and out of the house, but she was immobilized by a fear so intense she could not make her muscles move. Maybe he was hiding in a closet or behind a door, or maybe he was in the bathroom behind the shower curtain. What if he pounced on her as she ran through the living room? She conjured vivid images of her stalker—his pale face with deep crevices, his dark, deep-set eyes. With an experienced predator, she knew she wouldn't have a chance.

Suddenly Laura realized that he might be hiding in her bedroom. Maybe he was in the closet, behind her clothes, so she hadn't seen him when she'd put her shoes away. Maybe he had reached for her but she had closed the door too quickly.

Standing by the bed, Laura shifted her gaze toward the floor. Perhaps the stalker was lying under the bed, waiting for her to move closer so he could reach out and grab her. With that thought, Laura darted for the bedroom door, hitting the doorframe hard with her shoulder and then stumbling into the living room as she tried to catch her balance. The front door loomed before her. Just moments ago, the bolt and lock had represented security. Now they stood between her and the outside world. She thought the intruder would get her before she made it out, but she still managed to pull at the bolt with one hand and turn the lock on the doorknob with the other. She was going to make it out! She flung open the door and plunged out, but immediately she banged into something.

"Laura, what on earth?"

When Laura saw Megan's surprised face looking up at her from the ground, she burst into tears. "There's a man in the apartment!" she screamed. "He followed me home from work and got here before me."

"Laura, that makes no sense. Now calm down."

* * *

Laura sat on the couch in her living room, her hands shaking and her heart still beating frantically. Through the wooden dowels separating the kitchen from the living room, she watched Megan in the kitchen.

Megan removed a carton of lemonade from the refrigerator and poured two glasses. She set one on the table in front of Laura and then sat on the loveseat across from Laura with the other.

As she had bravely searched every corner of the apartment, Megan had looked at Laura like she was a paranoid, hysterical ninny—at least Laura thought so. Even Laura thought her own explanations— the open closet door and the diary ribbon—sounded preposterous.

Yet she was glad Megan had shown up when she did. She had no idea what she would have done once outside in her bare feet. Her car, which she rarely drove, would obviously have been useless without the key. Maybe she would have run down the street and knocked on someone's door. Maybe she would have run to a nearby park and hidden until she felt safe to go back—but who knew if she would ever have found the nerve to return. More likely she would have found a phone and called Megan to come and get her.

Laura smiled faintly. "I guess you can see now why I could never move to Virginia."

Megan sat forward on the loveseat and set her lemonade on the table. "Laura, don't be silly. You were up most of the night, so you're tired, and you know how your anxiety increases when you get really tired. It was an anxiety attack—and you actually handled it quite well."

Blood rushed to Laura's cheeks, and she looked down, uncertain how to respond. Megan was probably right. Her tiredness had caused her overactive imagination to conjure up things that simply were not happening. "Still. I'm not ready for a big change like Virginia—not yet."

"No one is ever ready for a big change like this. Major life changes don't usually wait for people to be ready. We dive in headfirst and do the best we can. We make mistakes—and we learn."

Laura stood and walked to the window, noticing that Megan had opened the curtains. "You really think I can do this?"

"I'm absolutely certain, Laura. Just remember who you are."

Laura looked intently at Megan. "Sometimes I'm not quite sure who I am."

"Perhaps this experience will help you figure that out."

A flicker of movement outside the window caught Laura's eye, and she turned and studied the street. Two large oaks stood between her apartment and the sidewalk. Was someone hiding behind one of the trees? Had someone darted from one to the other? More likely a bird had flown from one to the other. Laura frowned, then turned back to Megan. "I suppose a trip to Virginia is one way I could get away from the man I think is following me."

Megan stood and walked to Laura. "Oh, no you don't. This isn't about running away. This is about discovery—finding out about yourself and the family you don't know. Maybe it will be like coming home."

4

She ran, the darkness pressing against her like a potent force ready to envelop and consume her. She could see a gentle glow ahead, but as she reached it, she fell, and her body dropped into nothingness . . .

Laura jolted forward, and her eyes flew wide open. She heard a gasp that must have come from her own mouth. Glancing across the aisle of the bus, she saw an old man staring at her, smiling curiously.

"Fall asleep, did ya?"

Laura rubbed her eyes and wiped her sweaty forehead, then ran her hand across the top of her head to rest on her braided ponytail. The air in the bus felt muggy, and Laura's jeans and cotton shirt clung to her damp body. As she stretched, she peered out the window at a hollow of farmsteads and orchards where the meadows rolled in the distance to misty, purple-blue mountains.

The flight from St. Louis to Washington DC had only taken about two hours, but she'd been on this bus for several hours. Heading into a tree-coated wilderness speckled with an occasional gas station or diner, Laura wondered what she had gotten into. She already missed civilization, with its shopping centers, grocery stores, and drugstores, not to mention dentists, doctors, and hospitals. Not that she liked to go to these places, but she liked to know they were there when she needed them.

Suddenly the bus slowed and then pulled onto the shoulder of the road and stopped. As the doors opened and someone exited the crowded vehicle, Laura looked out the window. Shaking her head, she wondered where the person was headed—she could see only a highway and lots of trees.

"May I sit next to you, young lady?"

Laura turned from the window. The short and stocky elderly woman standing in the aisle had obviously just gotten on the bus.

"Sure," Laura replied awkwardly. No one in St. Louis had ever asked to sit next to her on the bus; if a seat was empty, you just took it.

The woman threw a bulky bag on the overhead luggage rack as if it were a potato sack, then lifted herself into the seat as the bus pulled back on the road.

"Hattie O'Donnell," she declared, extending her hand toward Laura.

Laura hesitated before grasping it. "Laura McClain."

"Where are you headed, Laura McClain?" She had a pleasant southern drawl.

"Bufordville."

"That's where I'm headed myself. My sister Lettie married a boy from Bufordville. Well, he's dead and gone, but I visit Lettie once every few weeks. She's getting feeble these days, I tell you. Never know when she'll up and die on me, and that'll make me the last of the Hansen girls. I was the baby, you see."

Hattie paused and eyed Laura appraisingly. "I don't recognize you, and from that accent of yours, I assume you're from up north."

"St. Louis," Laura revealed.

"That's out by the Mississippi, ain't it? I had a cousin who went on one of those steamboat cruises once, the ones they have out yonder. You ever been on a steamboat cruise?"

"Uh, no, but I toured a steamboat once when I was in grade school."

Hattie gave off something halfway between a huff and a snort. "Funny how we never take advantage of what we have in our own backyards. There's lots of things right here in Virginia I've never bothered to see."

During the awkward silence that followed, Laura gazed out the window. Now that the pleasantries were over, she hoped Hattie would perhaps nap or read or otherwise keep to herself.

"Who're you visiting?"

No such luck, Laura thought. "Actually, I'm moving to Bufordville."

Hattie's mouth fell open, her expression incredulous. For several seconds, the old woman appeared to be speechless, but she finally managed to croak, "Why would you want to do that?"

Laura smiled, restraining a chuckle while wondering why someone *wouldn't* want to live in Bufordville. "My aunt died and left me her house in Bufordville." As soon as she said the words, Laura wished she hadn't.

"Who was your aunt?" Hattie asked, her eyes narrowing.

"Laura Buford."

Hattie covered her mouth with her hand. "My goodness! Such a young and pretty thing as yourself being burdened with that place. And I notice you're not wearing a ring. Not that it's any of my business, but do you know much about tobacco?"

Blood rushed to Laura's face as she saw that Hattie's loud voice had drawn some of the passengers' attention. The last thing she wanted was for anyone to notice her, but then she realized that Hattie could perhaps give her some information. "You knew my aunt?" Laura asked carefully.

Hattie smiled. "Well, I wouldn't say *that*. I mean, not personally. In these parts, everyone has heard of Buford's Bluff. It's the largest plantation in the valley—I think Lettie said it's over eight thousand acres. I used to come here years ago and attend the annual Harvest Moon Festival. Needless to say, I was a young girl then, but it was quite a festival, and it was held on harvest moon night. The dinner could beat all dinners. The festival was romantic too, with dancing and courting and all kinds of carryings on. It's too bad they stopped having it . . . too much of a burden, I suppose."

"Forgive my ignorance, but what exactly is a harvest moon?"

Hattie leaned toward Laura and tapped her arm. "It's nothing more than a reason to have a party . . . and for some people to get drunk, if you know what I mean. Of course, it didn't start out that way—at least, I don't think it did. Let's see, there's the snow moon in February and the strawberry moon in June—I love strawberries—and the cold moon in December. I can't remember them all. It was a way of keeping track of the months long ago. But the harvest moon was special—I remember my papa explaining it. The harvest moon somehow lasted longer than the other moons, and it has something to do with autumn and the change in seasons. That extra dose of light came in handy for farmers who were working long days to harvest their crops in September."

"So the Bufords always hosted the harvest festival for the town?" Laura asked.

"A lot of people in the area worked for the Bufords at some time or the other, so I suppose in a way it was like having a company party. Of course, the whole community was invited—that's the way hospitality works here in Virginia, but you probably know that."

"Actually, I don't know much about Virginia at all. This is my first time here, since my parents moved to St. Louis before I was born."

"Are your folks still living there too?"

"Actually, they've both passed away," Laura answered with a twinge of sadness in her voice.

Hattie sighed. "Oh, I'm so sorry, dear. I know a bit of loneliness myself. My Harold has been gone for ten years, and I go to bed each night longing to tell him about my day. I want to tell him when I'm sad and when I'm glad—I want to tell him everything. Sometimes I find myself talking to him." Hattie bit her lip, lost in thought for a few moments, and then added, "I guess some people would say that's crazy."

"I don't think it's crazy at all," Laura said reassuringly. After all, she still talked to her mother sometimes. As the weeks raced by from the time Laura had called her aunt's lawyer to the day she stepped on the plane for Washington, she had thought a great deal about her mother, wondering if she would've approved of her daughter's decision. Laura wasn't sure she herself approved. She had turned her car and apartment over to Megan, and she had arranged for a year's leave of absence from her teaching job. She had some money in a St. Louis bank account, so if things didn't work out in Virginia, she could return home as if the whole incident had never happened.

The dream that had plagued Laura for so long had come less frequently during those intensely busy days of preparation. However, she had dreamed of her mother several times, and she wondered if her mother disapproved of her moving to Virginia. Sarah McClain had chosen not to return to Virginia, even after her husband died and there was no reason to stay in Missouri. As far as Laura remembered, her mother had never even gone back to Virginia on a visit. Sarah had mentioned her childhood home a few times, but it seemed almost painful for her to think or talk about her sister Laura or about Buford's Bluff.

Laura turned and gazed out the window at the mountains covered with a dreamlike lavender mist. These were the famous Blue Ridge Mountains, and Laura knew she should appreciate their beauty. But instead, her thoughts kept going back to her parents.

Eventually the turmoil of emotions brought on by her mother's death had finally started to settle down, and the wounds began to heal. Then the letter from Virginia had arrived, tearing the wounds open again, and Laura felt as if she had been left bleeding.

She wasn't quite sure when the anger had begun to creep up on her. At her father's funeral, she had sat with her arms stoically crossed, warding off the outside world. She had kept her composure at her mother's funeral as well, never giving in to her inner turmoil. At the cemetery she hadn't let anyone see her pain, though she'd stood wondering if her security might disappear into the graves that had swallowed up her parents.

In retrospect, Laura realized that the anger had probably begun to simmer with her father's death, but she first noticed it when she returned to the apartment after her mother's funeral. As she sat alone in total darkness, tears running down her cheeks, she realized she was all alone. That was when the anger had started to temper her grief and shock. How could her parents abandon her like this? She had counted on them, and now they were both gone! And though the anger brought guilt along with it during those first terrible weeks, the anger may have been the only thing that had kept her functioning. The anger had resurfaced as she was trying to decide whether to go to Virginia. Her mother had chosen not to introduce her to Aunt Laura and wouldn't tell stories about her family. Laura had begun to feel resentful that so much had been kept from her.

But now, that was all behind her. She respected her mother's choices and hoped her mother could have respected hers. She recalled a conversation she'd had with Megan, but now it wasn't Megan she pictured across from her in the apartment. It was her mother. "This is about discovery—finding out about yourself and the family you don't know," she imagined her mother saying. "Maybe it will be like coming home."

5

"You're home, Laura."

Laura opened her eyes. "Home?"

Hattie was gently shaking Laura's arm, so she sat up and looked out the partially open bus window. The odor of cigar smoke wafted in from the outside. A small white building attached to the bus station featured a revolving red-and-white-striped electric barber's pole, and men sat smoking on benches out front while an assortment of faces gazed out the barbershop window. Apparently, this was downtown Bufordville.

A small crowd had gathered in front of the Greyhound bus station, and some of the spectators stood on their tiptoes, trying to peer in the bus. A lady with a large straw hat and thick oblong glasses stuck her face as close as she could to the partially open window next to Laura. "Eleanor?" she asked hoarsely. Startled, Laura leaned back.

Laura felt like she was in a foreign land, surrounded by strangers. But somehow she would make the best of things. In fact, she planned to be happy here in Bufordville, whatever it took.

She glanced back at Hattie, who gave her a reassuring smile and stood to get her belongings from the overhead rack. Noticing the elderly woman struggling with the large bag, Laura lifted it down for her and followed her off the bus. A white two-story house with a wide front porch filled with rocking chairs and a few benches stood on the other side of the station. A sign over the door indicated that the place was a boardinghouse. Honeysuckle and morning glory covered the porch rails, and bees buzzed around the fading blooms.

Using her hand to shield her eyes from the bright sunlight, Laura looked across the street. A row of redbrick buildings stood against a backdrop of rolling mountains speckled with orange and yellow. Maple and poplar trees grew from round holes in the concrete sidewalks, and on a hill in the distance stood a water tower with *Bufordville* painted in huge black letters.

Hattie was by now hugging a gray-haired woman, who Laura assumed was her sister, Lettie. Laura was turning to survey the view in the other direction when a handsome older man in a dark suit approached her.

"Laura?"

"Yes?"

Tall and lean, the man had a fine-boned face and full, wavy white hair combed back neatly. He gave off an air of sophistication and dignity, though Laura thought his white goatee made him look a bit like Colonel Sanders. "You're your aunt's image," the man said in a deep, pleasant voice with just a hint of Southern drawl. "Beauty does run in the Buford family."

Laura's cheeks warmed as he reached out his hand. "I'm Roger Ballister, your aunt's attorney." As Laura took his hand, he shook hers firmly.

Suddenly Hattie ran to Laura and grabbed her other hand, shaking it vigorously. "If you need a friend, Laura McClain, give me a call. I'm staying at my sister's house—Lettie Larsen."

"Thank you, Hattie. Have a good visit." Hattie released Laura's hand and hurried back to her sister.

Roger smiled. "I see you make friends easily. Your aunt was that way too."

Laura felt her smile fade. "I'm afraid I'm not usually that way, Mr. Ballister."

"Please call me Roger. My car is right over there on the street. Let's get your luggage."

Roger and Laura carried her bags to his gold Buick, where the luggage fit easily into the large trunk. He opened the passenger door for Laura and sauntered around to the driver's side. Swallowing hard, Laura felt the sense of doom she always experienced when confronted with a social situation. Riding in the car with her aunt's lawyer would be like standing in the elevator with a stranger, only worse. An elevator ride was usually over in seconds, although it sometimes felt like it took much longer. Laura wasn't sure how long it would take them to get to Buford's Bluff—but she just knew the ride would be excruciating.

Her palms were sweaty and her throat was dry, and it occurred to her that she should have found a water fountain in the station. After all, she would need to speak. She took a deep breath and began silently rehearsing her positive mantras. *I'm a valuable individual with an intelligent mind. I don't have to impress anyone. I need to be myself because I'm a worthy person.*

When Roger got in and slammed his door shut, Laura couldn't recall a single mantra. In fact, in that moment, all she could remember was that her name was Laura and that she came from St. Louis.

Roger drove slowly down the street, and Laura peered out the passenger-side window, turning the back of her head toward him. Bufordville was charming in a run-down, weathered sort of way, Laura decided as they passed the city library and a general store. In the back of her mind she could hear Roger talking, but his words seemed faint, and she could barely hear them above the sound of the motor.

As she tried unsuccessfully to focus on what the man was saying, Laura recognized the onset of a panic attack. She felt trapped, and she glanced over at Roger to see if he had noticed her shaking. But he was still talking, apparently assuming she was listening. What should she tell him?

Excuse me, Mr. Ballister. I need you to take me back to the bus station so I can get the heck out of Bufordville. You see, I'd feel a lot safer back in St. Louis in my own apartment with Megan. As Laura tried to take deep breaths to calm herself, the car approached a railroad crossing with flashing red lights. Roger stopped the car just in front of a fading white line on the pavement, then glanced over at Laura and smiled. She forced a smile apologetically. Roger had finally stopped talking, and Laura knew that her silence had revealed her inattention. The quiet was momentarily broken by the wail of the train whistle, and then a headlight appeared down the track, followed by a few empty, rattling railcars and a caboose. Laura wasn't sure if the Buick was swaying or if she was about to faint.

When they started across the now-clear tracks, Laura cleared her throat and said, "I don't mean to be rude, but I just realized you've been talking and I haven't heard a word. I'm just overwhelmed at being here, I guess. I've never been out of Missouri until today."

Roger smiled. "Oh, my dear, no need to apologize. I can certainly understand—I was just babbling on about the town history anyway."

Laura knew she needed to attempt conversation, so with great effort she forced herself to vocalize the first question she could think of. "Why didn't my mother help Aunt Laura run the plantation?" Laura inquired, her voice cracking a little. "I mean, it was the family business for generations, right?"

Roger didn't answer immediately, appearing to mull over the question. "Well, your mother met your father. He was an independent sort, and I must admit that Laura Buford was a bossy lady. Your father and mother moved to St. Louis to find their own way. Your aunt Laura was unhappy about it, but she accepted what had to be. She was quite a bit older than your mother, so she was used to taking care of things without troubling her little sister."

He hadn't told her why her parents had moved so far from Bufordville, but she assumed there must have been a disagreement between her mother and her aunt. Roger obviously didn't want to disclose the actual reason—perhaps he didn't know.

"Why did Aunt Laura leave the place to me?" Now that she'd spoken, the conversation would be easier. The first sentence was always the hardest.

Roger started to speak, then paused for several seconds. Finally, he glanced over at Laura and began again. "You're her only living relative, Laura. She didn't have any children, and your mother was her only sibling. You're her namesake, and she felt a special closeness to you. She believed you could keep this plantation alive."

Laura shot an incredulous look at him. "She didn't even know me."

He smiled back at her. "But she knew the Buford bloodline."

Remembering with a start that she hadn't yet inquired about her aunt's death, Laura abruptly asked, "How did she die? She wasn't very old. Let's see . . . my mother was thirty-two when she had me, so if she were alive she'd be fifty-six. How much older was Aunt Laura?"

"Ten years."

"That would make her sixty-six."

"Yes, your aunt Laura was sixty-six when she passed," he stated with a sad smile. Laura realized a few minutes too late she could have questioned Roger without all the mathematical tricks. She felt her face warming again.

"Heart failure," Roger said.

"What?"

"Your aunt died of heart failure. She always had a bad heart."

"Oh. That's too bad."

As they headed north, the car coasted down a hill, and a vast river stretched out before them. "That's the James River," Roger explained, "and there's Buford's Bluff, your new home."

Through the trees, across the river, Laura caught a glimpse of a large white house. The road wound down the hill, where they eventually crossed the river on a long metal bridge. A variety of barges and boats sailed on the river beneath them. "An active place," Laura remarked with some surprise in her voice.

Roger smiled. "Oh, yes, Buford's Bluff is prosperous. They ship the tobacco from the plantation down the river to the big cigarette factories in Richmond."

"I don't know much about the tobacco industry," Laura admitted, wondering how she would tell Roger she found tobacco positively repulsive. She decided to worry about that later, after she settled in and learned about her aunt's business.

"Tobacco seeds are planted in seed beds in late winter and covered in plastic," Roger declared, apparently willing to give Laura her first lesson in the family business. "When the plants get big enough, field hands move them into the field. When the plants bloom, toppers lop off the tops so the plants can grow heavier. When the plants are mature, the stalk cutters cut the plants down and leave them on sticks in the fields for a day or two until they're wilted."

"Is that what those tepees are?" Laura queried, pointing to what looked like the silhouette of an Indian village on a far hillside.

"Yes, those are stakes of wilting tobacco. Pretty soon the curers will hang the wilted plants in the curing barns to air cure. Those are the sheds you can see over on the horizon there."

Laura studied the shacks standing guard on a hill of reddish mud that looked freshly plowed. "So the tobacco goes from the curing houses to the cigarette factories?"

"Well, Charlie Osborne, your plantation manager, hauls the tobacco on barges down to Richmond, but it takes a while for the tobacco to be made into a finished product. Freshly-cured tobacco has a sharp aroma and a bitter taste. The factories place the tobacco in storage barrels for aging and fermentation before using it."

"It sounds like a complex process," Laura said. "I don't know if I could ever understand it."

"Don't worry. Charlie will teach you all you need to know," Roger assured her.

Laura's stomach churned. "I see."

In truth, she only wanted to understand it as far as she absolutely had to. Even before she'd heard of the Word of Wisdom, she'd considered smoking to be a filthy, terrible habit, and based on what she'd heard, the tobacco industry wasn't exactly squeaky clean either. In a way, she was surprised places like Buford's Bluff still existed, and she wondered again why she was even here. Part of it was the money of course—having that kind of money offered protection. But Laura felt guilty that the money came from tobacco, from selling something that caused irreparable harm to others. Sighing to herself, Laura decided she would stay at Buford's Bluff for the required three years, sell the place, and buy a nice house in the St. Louis suburbs, a place with a security gate. She would also donate a substantial amount of money to help fund research into cancer and heart disease, in memory of her parents and her aunt.

The other less obvious but even more compelling reason for coming to Virginia was curiosity. She wanted to know why her parents left Virginia, since she knew there had to be more to it than employment. And it was like Megan said: perhaps she could learn something about herself here by learning about her family.

"There she is," Roger exclaimed, slowing the car as they came up the hill.

Looking up, Laura gasped. This couldn't be her house, yet it was— or would be if she could stick it out long enough. As she studied the beautiful white-columned mansion crowning the hill like a Greek temple, her pulse quickened. The front porch faced the river, and Laura made out the faint outlines of furniture on the porch—she suspected wicker. She could imagine sitting there in the evenings, looking out across the gracious lawns sloping south to the water.

"Do you like what you see?"

"Oh, yes," Laura affirmed. "I can almost see Scarlett O'Hara standing on that porch."

Roger laughed. "Well, I'm afraid you won't find Rhett Butler waiting for you at the house—just Agnes, the housekeeper and cook, and old George, the gardener and handyman. They're the only staff left. Your aunt used to have an entire team, but she cut back several years ago. By then, I think the servants bothered her more than they helped her. She said that in old age, one only has time for the ultimate simplicities."

Laura's stomach flip-flopped, and perspiration broke out on her forehead. She'd never had anyone work for her, and she had no idea how to act around so-called servants. She wondered why were they still at the mansion, since no one had lived there since her aunt died. *Maybe they come with the place,* Laura thought with a mental groan. *Oh, what will I say to them? I don't want to order them around!*

As if he could read her thoughts, Roger advised, "Don't worry, Laurie. Agnes and George are like family, and they'll treat you with the same respect they did your aunt."

Laura didn't like being called "Laurie" by a perfect stranger; she had only allowed her father to call her that. It seemed oddly informal for Roger to use a nickname for her when they had barely just met. Perhaps he thought it would put her at ease, she thought wryly to herself.

Low-hanging weeping willows bordered the road to the house. As the car climbed the hill from the river, willow fronds occasionally scraped against the hood. Laura made a mental note to find out if the gardener trimmed these trees or if it was hired out. If the willows kept growing they would eventually be a traffic hazard; besides that, it was a bit too dark under the trees for her liking.

Closing her eyes, Laura could hear her heart pounding, and she noticed that her palms were wet. *Great,* she thought. *My claustrophobia is kicking in now.* As she felt warmth on her face, she opened her eyes and saw that they'd left the shadows behind. They passed a handsome stone building between the driveway and the mansion's west side, and Laura asked, "What's that?"

Roger smiled. "The horse stables—Buford's Bluff's pride and joy."

"They're huge," Laura exclaimed.

"Yes, they are quite large. There's a museum inside that houses the medals and trophies your aunt's horses have won. There's also a spacious banquet hall for receptions and parties."

"In the stables?"

Roger chuckled. "Like I said, those horses were Buford's Bluff's pride and joy."

Following the circular driveway, Roger drove around to the back of the house. Laura noticed that a small entry porch covered the back door. Just then the door opened, and a tall, stern-looking woman with a long nose came out and stood a few steps above them. She was wearing a black dress and had her black hair pulled back tightly in a bun. In spite of the dark hair, the woman looked about sixty years old. Laura realized this must be the housekeeper, Agnes. As she felt the older woman's gaze boring through her, she wasn't so certain she would be able to last three days here, let alone three long years. Then again, as the potential owner of Buford's Bluff, perhaps she would be allowed to let Agnes go and hire new staff. For now, though, she would leave things as they were. After all, Agnes had probably been at Buford's Bluff for decades, and she might have just the information Laura needed.

6

Roger broke the tension. "Miss Agnes Hayes, this is Laura McClain."

Agnes stretched out her hand, and her long, crooked fingers grasped Laura's tightly. "It's a pleasure to meet my new mistress," Agnes stated in a surprisingly soft voice. Laura smiled but thought the title "mistress" seemed a bit old-fashioned.

"I'll have George bring your things from the car," Agnes said, stepping aside.

"Oh, no," Laura returned, "I only have a few bags. I can—"

Roger gently grabbed Laura's arm. "George will be upset if you start doing his job for him. Let's have Agnes show us around the place, okay?"

Embarrassed, Laura felt her face flush. *Apparently,* she thought, *I'll need to learn a lot more than how to run a tobacco plantation.*

Still holding Laura's arm, Roger guided her from the rear entryway through a dining room and into a large parlor. Victorian furniture wasn't Laura's favorite, but it certainly fit the style of the mansion. Roger released her arm, and Laura moved to the fireplace, her eyes transfixed by the beautiful portrait that hung over the marble mantel. Agnes stepped to Laura's side and said quietly, "Your aunt, the late Miss Laura Buford."

Roger approached them and looked at Laura. "As I mentioned earlier, you do favor her."

Laura admired the image. Her aunt's eyes were green, with full lashes and thick brows that matched her dark hair. She was fair-skinned, but had a rosy blush on her high cheekbones. The red lips were thin but curved upward above a slightly pointed chin. But there was more than mere beauty in Laura Buford's features. Her countenance exuded charm and confidence, and her niece felt a flood of regret that she had never even met her.

"Your aunt was tall and slim like you," Roger pointed out.

"The resemblance is remarkable," Agnes added.

"Such an enormous room," Laura burst out suddenly. She walked to the glass doors that overlooked the front of the mansion. "Nice view of the river."

Relieved that the others had curtailed their remarks on her physical appearance, Laura turned to face the room again. She noticed several large, leather binders on a small table nearby and stepped over to investigate. Lifting the cover of one binder, she saw old black-and-white photographs. Next to this table was a lower table that held an assortment of terrariums, and Laura looked at them admiringly.

"Your aunt loved to fiddle with those bottle gardens," Agnes explained.

Laura squealed involuntarily. "I actually make terrariums myself. Maybe we really are alike—I mean . . ." As her voice trailed off, she squatted and gazed through the glass at the woodland scenes with miniature pinecones, driftwood, empty shells, acorns, and lichen-covered pebbles. One terrarium even featured a tiny reflecting pool made from pebbles and water. In one bottle that contained miniature animal figurines, a Venus flytrap opened its mouth wide; Laura decided her aunt definitely had a sense of humor.

As they left the parlor and walked into the front foyer, Laura gasped. "Wow!" A colossal mahogany staircase dominated the entry, its stairs covered with an Oriental carpet. Laura bounded up the first several steps before she caught herself and turned back. "May I?"

Roger smiled. "Why of course, my dear. It's your house now. Or it will be before too long."

Agnes scowled, but Laura made up her mind to pay her no heed, remembering an experience she'd had as a new college graduate back in St. Louis.

* * *

Laura had arrived early for a job interview, hoping to make a good impression. But Mrs. Wilson, the principal, seemed perturbed by her appearance.

Mrs. Wilson had stepped out of her office to speak to Laura, giving her a perfunctory glance up and down. "Miss Whittaker, the assistant principal, is conducting the interviews for the kindergarten job. She's still at lunch and won't be back for another fifteen minutes. You're early."

As Laura took a seat near the secretary's desk, the secretary called into Mrs. Wilson's office on the intercom. "Mrs. Wilson, Miss Whittaker just called. She's stuck in traffic and will be late."

After several seconds of silence, Mrs. Wilson came out of her office, clearly even more irritated. "That's okay, Joyce. I think I can take care of this interview. It should only take a few minutes."

As a shy, socially awkward individual—at least around adults—Laura had been used to being overlooked and undervalued, but no one, to that point, had ever dismissed her with such blatant rudeness. She sensed a pending disaster as Mrs. Wilson looked at her and sighed.

"Come into my office, young lady," Mrs. Wilson ordered with a patronizing smile.

Said the spider to the fly, Laura thought.

Mrs. Wilson had been right—it took her only a few minutes to reduce Laura to mere mush. Oddly, she never could remember Mrs. Wilson's exact words, and she told herself she'd blocked them out because the experience was so traumatic. Nevertheless, Laura did manage to hold back the tears when she walked out, and the secretary had stopped typing and given her a sympathetic glance.

She walked out to the lobby and sat on a bench by the school's front door, feeling numb and wondering what to do next. How would she tell her mother? She'd catch the city bus and ride around for hours trying to muster the courage to tell her. Or she could lie and say it was a good interview but that the other applicants all had several years' experience. Of course, she didn't want to lie, and besides that, her mother would know the truth as soon as she saw her anyway.

Suddenly the school's front door swung open, the rush of air blowing Laura's hair. "Miss McClain?"

She glanced up to see a pretty young woman standing there, her blond hair disheveled. It'd been a windy day in St. Louis.

"Yes?" Laura responded weakly.

"I'm sorry I'm late—there was an accident on the interstate. I'm Miss Whittaker, the assistant principal, but please just call me Jill." Jill sat down next to her. "I suppose we could move to my office, but I would rather avoid Mrs. Wilson's wrath, if you don't mind."

Laura smiled, lacking the will or perhaps the courage to tell Jill that Mrs. Wilson had already interviewed her. She decided she would talk with Jill for a few minutes—let her go through the motions. Then she would leave and never see Jill or Mrs. Wilson again.

It took Jill Whittaker less than twenty minutes to repair the damage inflicted by Mrs. Wilson. Jill had the rare talent to build people up, to make them feel important and needed. This time Laura remembered almost every word of their conversation. They'd discussed children, especially the struggles of inner-city children and how they needed love and acceptance as much as they needed math and reading. Laura remembered smiling and even laughing as she talked with Jill.

A week later, when she got the call offering her the job, Laura was astounded. Apparently Miss Whitaker's interview had won out over Mrs. Wilson's. Soon Laura and Jill became not only coworkers but friends. Laura knew Jill's faith was important to her, and it didn't take Laura long to find out that Jill was LDS. This had intrigued Laura, who had heard of the LDS Church but had never personally known a "Mormon." Laura asked Jill about the Church, and Jill was more than willing to talk about her faith. Eventually, she invited Laura to attend Sunday meetings with her, and after Laura attended for a few weeks, she decided to meet with the missionaries at Jill's apartment.

Laura's mother had been leery at first, telling Laura that she didn't trust the Mormons but not forbidding her to learn about the Church. Eventually, Sarah came to admire her daughters persistence at studying about her newfound religion and commented that Laura seemed more determined about the LDS Church than anything else she had put her mind to. Though her cancer was quite advanced at the time, Sarah even attended Laura's baptism, and at the end of the evening, Sarah had said to Jill, "Well, if it gets Laura out of the house and meeting good people, I suppose it can't be too bad."

* * *

Laura wouldn't let Agnes get to her the way Principal Wilson had gotten to her. She turned from Agnes and squared her shoulders as she started up the stairs, the boards creaking faintly under her feet. Agnes and Roger followed, and Laura wished they would let her explore the mansion alone.

In the upstairs hall, Laura made her way past closed doors. Darkness engulfed the passageway, but dim light seeped from a half-moon-shaped window at the other end. It was almost like being in a cave. The wallpaper—a brown background with a nondescript lighter brown floral design—added to the somberness.

She turned to Agnes. "Did my aunt choose this wallpaper?"

Agnes seemed perplexed. "Why, of course she did. It *is* her house."

Roger cleared his throat. "Well, it's your house now, Laura. If you don't like it, you can change it to whatever you like."

Looking back at Agnes, Laura noted her intense frown.

Laura hesitated. "It's not that I don't like it—it's just that it seems so dark in this hall. I think a light color, a pastel, would be better." She turned and studied the walls. "A light yellow with a floral design or something."

Agnes increased her pace and passed Laura, then paused at a door on the right. "This is the room we thought you would find most comfortable." Agnes opened the door.

Mahogany furniture filled the room, the canopy bed covered in an avocado-green bedspread with a white leaf motif. The bedspread's fringe touched the floor, as did the fringe of the matching drapes. A dark mustard paint covered the walls. Laura didn't like the room, but she smiled and nodded at Agnes then continued down the corridor, passing several closed doors, but abruptly stopping at the next-to-last door. "What's in here?"

"That is a child's room," Agnes said, then cleared her throat, her face suddenly red.

Laura opened the door. The room was filled with delightful antique toys, including a dollhouse that resembled the mansion itself. Laura walked over and sat on the double bed, which was soft and covered with a chenille bedspread with pink lambs and blue trim. A simple light blue plaid wallpaper brightened the room, and it felt pleasant and comfortable.

"Whose room was this?" Laura inquired.

"Many children over the years," Agnes answered with a sigh. "I believe it was your mother's room when she was a young girl."

Laura gaped at Agnes, having momentarily forgotten that her mother had lived here. Of course Sarah Buford was born and raised here. Since Laura had walked into the house, she had felt her aunt's influence. But now she could almost feel her mother's presence.

"I would like to stay in this room," Laura declared.

Agnes seemed startled. "But Laura, it's not suitable."

It was the first time Agnes had spoken her name, and Laura could tell she did so awkwardly. Laura said nothing, and Roger looked from Laura to Agnes.

Agnes sighed. "I'll tell George to bring your bags to this room."

"Thank you," Laura said with a smile.

Back in the hall, Laura pointed to the last door across the hall. "What's in there?"

"Stairs to the attic," Agnes replied. Laura decided to explore the attic later, when Agnes wasn't around.

Laura wandered to the hall's end and glanced out the half-moon window to see a grove of trees covering the landscape in the distance. Suddenly Laura felt again like she was in a cave, but this time claustrophobia and panic gripped her. She turned and looked down the hall, then back at the half-moon window. She was having a full-blown anxiety attack, and the only way out of this place was all the way back downstairs.

She turned toward Roger, gasping. "I have to get outside."

They rushed down the hall, Agnes and Roger hurrying in front with Laura scurrying behind. As they started down the stairs, terror swept over Laura, and she felt a sickening sensation in her stomach. She held to the rail, her body swaying.

Roger glanced behind. "Are you okay, Laura? You're a little pale."

"This house isn't haunted, is it?" she asked rhetorically.

A few steps below, Agnes glared up at her, obviously offended. "Certainly not. I've been here for more than thirty years, and no one has ever suggested such a thing."

Laura descended the stairs, pushed passed Agnes, and stopped at the heavy front door. Her hand closed on the ornate crystal knob, and she twisted it. Locked. She fumbled with the lock until it clicked, then twisted the knob and pushed the door open. Standing at the threshold for a moment, she gazed across the lawn and down to the river, then glanced over her shoulder at the staircase. A sense of foreboding came over her, a strange feeling of dread that reached deep inside her. She rushed out onto the front porch, rapidly sucking in the fresh air, and felt her panic subsiding as quickly as it had come. Unsure what had come over her, Laura told herself there was nothing to fear.

It was a warm September afternoon, and a light breeze caught her hair. Birds sang over the musical sound of the river below. Taking a deep breath and closing her eyes, Laura found the air fresh and clean.

She walked down the porch stairs and onto the lawn. A few red leaves clung to the otherwise green oak trees in the yard, and a faint yellow-green persisted in the dying grass. Iron benches, a gazebo, and two iron statues decorated the front lawn. Laura meandered to the east side of the mansion where voluminous English boxwoods surrounded a cement terrace on the crest of the lawn. Below the terrace, a footpath wandered across the sloping lawn to a misty, wooded grove where Laura could just make out a small cottage.

Looking back at the mansion, Laura recognized the blue curtains in the second floor window. Her new room would provide a nice view. She couldn't see the river from there, but she could watch the changing colors of the oak, elm, and maple trees. Under her window grew pyracantha bushes like the ones at the school where she taught back in St. Louis. She knew that planting thorn bushes under windows was a clever if old-fashioned deterrent to intruders. Two blackbirds sat in the bushes eating bright red berries and nipping at each other as they crossed paths. Nearby, a heavyset old man raked leaves into a pile, and when he saw Laura, he approached her quickly. "Hello," he said in a friendly tone. The sun had given his skin the look of dried leather, and his long white hair fell to his shoulders. Laura guessed him to be in his late sixties or so. He removed his broad-brimmed, crudely-woven straw hat and wiped at his brow with his sleeve. Squinting at Laura, he said, "You must be Miss Laura." He gave her a wide smile. "I'm George Walker."

"Hi," Laura said with a grin. "This is a beautiful yard, but there should be steps here, going down to the path in the lawn."

George scratched his head as he studied the vast boxwoods rising in front of the terrace. "There once were steps there," he declared. "Concrete fell apart, I believe."

"What's that little house there in that grove of trees?" Laura was glad there were obvious questions to be asked so she didn't have to come up with small talk.

George replaced his hat and peered out from under the brim. "That would be the gardener's cottage."

"You mean your house?"

George turned from side to side, glancing over each shoulder. "I'm the only gardener around here, it seems."

Laura smiled. He made her feel right at home, and she was grateful for that.

George grunted. "I suppose Agnes will be looking for me to help out. I'll be back soon. It's good to see you." Then he walked away past the pile of leaves.

Laura turned and looked back at the house, glancing at her bedroom window. The curtains were open, but the glare on the window kept her from seeing into the room. Still, she thought she could almost discern a form standing in the window, watching her. *Probably a reflection—an oak tree, perhaps,* she thought, but a shiver ran down her spine.

She moved quickly around to the mansion's front, which faced south toward the river, and gazed across the vista beyond the water. The rolling green hills were speckled with orange and yellow, and in the far distance, Bufordville's steeples and rooftops pierced through the foliage. She eyed a boat on the river, and she almost wished she were on it, gliding smoothly away from Bufordville.

As she turned back northward to face the house, she decided that Buford's Bluff stood proudly, almost arrogantly, on the hilltop, looking down on everything before it. *King of the hill,* she thought.

To the west, where the driveway curved up from the river to circle back around the mansion, stood the massive stone stables. A mass of trees grew between the stables and the mansion, no doubt protecting the house from both the odor and noise. To the east of the house, the lawn sloped sharply down to the grove of trees that surrounded George's cottage.

Agnes stood on the porch with Roger, both of them looking so worried that Laura wondered what they were thinking. Perhaps they had decided that she was a bit crazy and that they would have to confine her to the mansion to keep an eye on her. Indeed, Laura knew she had problems—the panic attacks and the nightmares were proof of that—but she was quite sure she was sane. Still, she thought the mansion seemed more full of gloom than splendor, and it might as well be an asylum for the way she had felt inside it just now.

She knew her feelings didn't make sense. This was her beautiful new home—or at least it would be in a few years—and living here was a great blessing. Yet somehow she couldn't shake a feeling of foreboding, a sense of mystery that she didn't know if she would ever be able to decipher.

1

After bidding farewell to Roger and telling Agnes not to bother with dinner, Laura called Megan to let her know she had arrived safely. Of course Megan was full of questions, so Laura described the house and the grounds as best she could. Barely able to contain her excitement, Megan made Laura promise to report back later in the week.

Laura relaxed on the front porch until dusk, too exhausted to unpack. Finally unable to put off the task any longer, she went up to the room she had claimed earlier and opened her suitcase. Laura picked up some clothes and moved to the closet to put them away. Suddenly she froze, recognizing the same inexplicable panic that had seized her earlier. She tried to reach for the knob on the closet door, but her trembling hand refused to move. *What's wrong with me?* she thought.

"Laura?" Agnes knocked at the bedroom door, and the panic sensation left as abruptly as it had come.

"Yes?"

"I brought you a little snack."

Laura opened the door. "I'm not really hungry," Laura declared, surprising herself with her testy tone.

Ignoring her objection, Agnes stepped into the room and carried the tray to an empty table by the window. "No matter. If you choose not to eat the food, just leave the tray, and I'll take it when I make your bed tomorrow morning."

"I'm sorry, Agnes. I didn't mean to be sharp. I'm just tired, and it's going to take some time to get used to this place, as nice as it is."

"Well," Agnes began, marching to the door, "I shouldn't be surprised. This room is hardly suitable for a grown woman."

Sighing, Laura wondered if she could learn to accept Agnes's overly direct approach. "Sleep well," Agnes ordered, then closed the door behind her.

Laura walked to the table by the window. Gazing out at the lawn where the crescent moon cast an eerie glow, she could see the lights in George's cottage. Nestled among the trees, the small house appeared snug and warm, and Laura almost wished it was vacant so she could live there instead.

From the corner of her eye, Laura caught a glimpse of a moving shadow. She strained her eyes in an effort to see, but she couldn't distinguish where the shadow disappeared into the hundreds of other shadows on the lawn. It could have been a deer or other large animal—or just her imagination. Or maybe . . . maybe the stalker had followed her to Virginia! She hadn't seen him after their encounter on the street several weeks ago, but that didn't mean he wasn't there. Maybe he was here now, watching from the shadows, hiding behind trees, peering into windows. Laura's room would be one of the few with lights on in the house, so he'd have an easy time figuring out which room she was staying in. She wondered how secure the mansion was; after all, it was an old house, so it might not have any of the latest security features. Did Agnes even bother to lock the doors? Buford's Bluff was several miles from town—practically in the middle of nowhere—so perhaps the housekeeper didn't worry about such things. Shaking her head as if to rid herself of her paranoia, Laura pulled the curtains closed, walked over and locked the bedroom door, then sat on a small chair by the table. Despite her lack of appetite, she ate everything Agnes had brought her.

Laura needed to finish unpacking, and as she turned and looked at the closet door, she couldn't dismiss the eerie feelings she'd had earlier. She didn't believe in ghosts, but she did believe in spirits, and she knew that spirits sometimes appeared to warn people. What if her mother was trying to warn her? But Laura couldn't imagine what her mother would need to warn her about; after all, Aunt Laura wouldn't have lived in the mansion herself if it weren't safe here.

As she walked over to the closet and reached for the doorknob, Laura paused, then grabbed the brass knob and opened the door. The closet was very small, with built-in shelves. Breathing a sigh of relief,

Laura couldn't imagine why she'd felt so fearful earlier. Megan had noticed that Laura's panic attacks were more likely to occur when she was tired or particularly stressed, and Laura had come to recognize the same thing. But she was puzzled about the anxiety the closet had inspired. At the moment, she was exhausted, and it had been a stressful day, yet she hadn't previously experienced panic that felt quite like this.

Laura thought maybe she should just go back to St. Louis, but then realized she couldn't live with herself if she gave up so quickly. Buford's Bluff wouldn't be hers to sell unless she lived here for three years. Throwing away that kind of money—millions of dollars—would be extremely foolish. She would have to serve her time. At the moment the thought of living in this place for three years seemed overwhelming, so she tried to put it out of her mind while she finished unpacking,

By the time she had put everything away, Laura felt so tired she could barely move, so she prepared for bed. She knew she should brush and floss her teeth, but there was no way she was going to unlock her door to walk to the bathroom. Besides, Agnes's room was near that bathroom, and Laura didn't want to wake her. The room Agnes had prepared for Laura had its own bathroom, but there was no way she was going to change rooms now. She could see the smug look on Agnes's face, just hear her haughty *I told you so.*

Once in her nightgown, Laura crawled into bed and turned off the lamp. A sliver of a moonlight cast frightening shadows across the room, and the toys became gigantic, dark creatures on the floor and walls. The dollhouse appeared dark and cold, and Laura imagined the stalker as an action figure sneaking around the dollhouse, looking in the windows. Laura felt anxious to get out of the mansion, but that would have to wait. She'd get a good night's sleep, and tomorrow she'd find a way to get to Bufordville so she could explore the town.

After tossing and turning for an hour, Laura finally fell asleep.

* * *

On Thursday morning, Laura woke around nine. Usually she only slept so late when bad dreams plagued her sleep, but surprisingly, she couldn't recall any nightmares this time. The smell of bacon made her hungry, so she dressed and went to the kitchen, where Agnes stood at the stove, finishing breakfast.

"Are you feeling better this morning?"

"Yes," Laura answered with a tentative smile. "I suppose I was overly tired from the long trip."

"It's to be expected," Agnes remarked. "Your aunt always ate breakfast in the kitchen. I hope that suits you." She walked to the place setting at the table and began pouring coffee into a cup.

"If that's for me, I don't drink coffee," Laura informed her.

"Oh." Agnes yanked the cup away, knocking over the saltshaker. "Oh, dear!" She placed the coffee pot and cup on the stove, then picked up a pinch of salt from the table and threw it over her left shoulder.

"The orange juice is fine, thank you."

"Suit yourself."

"Agnes," Laura began, "I would like to go into Bufordville this morning to do a little shopping. Is there a car I can use?"

"I'll have George drive you in."

"Oh, no. That's not necessary. Maybe I can get a taxi. I prefer to shop alone, and I definitely don't want a man waiting while I decide." Laura thought that Agnes could certainly understand that.

"Suit yourself. I'll get you the keys to your aunt's car."

* * *

Laura didn't enjoy the drive to Bufordville. She had no trouble finding her way, since George had explained things well, but she kept getting stuck behind slow-moving tractors and farm trucks. Besides, Laura found her aunt's big car difficult to maneuver; she decided it was probably similar to driving a tank. When she finally made it to Bufordville, she parked on the street near the drugstore.

"That looks like Laura Buford's car," the old man behind the counter remarked as Laura entered the drugstore.

"It is—or rather was," Laura mumbled awkwardly.

"You work there?"

Laura hesitated. "No, I'm Laura McClain, Laura Buford's niece."

The man eyed her more closely. "You don't say! You must be Sarah Buford's girl."

Laura smiled. "That's right. You knew my mother?"

"Of course I knew your mother—everyone knows the Bufords. Your mother went to school with my boy, Leroy."

"Really?" Laura approached the counter cautiously, then gulped and forced herself to speak. "Did you know my father, John McClain?"

The old man's animated smile faded. "No," he murmured hollowly. An awkward moment followed before the man began placing bottles under the counter.

Laura turned to look at the items on the shelves. The store wasn't as well stocked as the drugstore she frequented in St. Louis, but it had the basics. When Laura selected some lotion and tissues, she realized her hands were trembling. *I can't even go to the drugstore without becoming a nervous wreck,* Laura thought.

She placed the items on the counter, and without looking at her the man began to ring them up on the cash register. Finally unable to stand the silence, Laura remarked, "I suppose you may have attended some of the harvest moon festivals at Buford's Bluff years ago."

The man's head shot up, and though Laura couldn't read his expression, she knew it wasn't good. He didn't seem angry—it was more like fear. But that didn't make sense either. Whatever the case, he apparently saw the shock on Laura's face and attempted to soften his own visage.

"When you get to be my age," he said, "you don't remember much."

Laura paid for the items and walked toward the door. She paused, glanced back, and said, "It's nice to meet you."

"Same," the man responded without even glancing at her.

Outside, the brisk, clean air swept across Laura's face. She loved the scent of fall, and the trees made a beautiful red, orange, and yellow tapestry against the brilliant sky. Across the street, a historic house had been converted to an antique shop, and as her mind started conjuring images of all kinds of exotic bottles, she crossed the street.

The boards on the stairs leading to the wide porch squeaked under her weight. A modern-looking wind chime of glass and metal clinked and clattered in the breeze. The window by the door read

"Julie's Antiques" in curly black-and-gold letters. On the porch stood two rocking chairs and a shelf of fifty-percent-off knickknacks that looked like they'd seen better days.

A cowbell clanged as Laura opened the door. "Good morning," the young woman behind the counter called.

"Good morning," Laura replied, smiling nervously. She told herself she wouldn't buy anything—she'd just look.

"Can I help you with something?" the woman asked.

"Just looking," Laura answered. "I saw your sign and couldn't resist. I love antique shops."

"I can't resist either," admitted the woman. "That's how I got into this. I saw the For Sale sign on the shop, and the rest was history."

Laura laughed at the explanation and took a better look at the shop owner. Tall and thin, the woman was all angles and no curves. Long, red hair surrounded a plain yet pleasant face. She appeared to be in her mid-twenties, possibly younger. Rings covered her fingers, and bracelets decorated her arms.

Laura breathed in the musty, waxy smell of the shop as she walked to a shelf full of curios, running her fingers along tabletops, chair rungs, and a ceramic cat along the way. Momentarily forgetting her promise not to buy anything, she briefly considered purchasing the cat. She glanced over at the shop owner, who wore a hopeful expression. Laura suddenly felt a bit sorry for the woman. While pretending to study another ceramic figurine, Laura managed, "I'm Laura McClain." She thought she sounded about as natural as a salesperson reading from a script.

"Julie Morgan."

"How long have you been in the antique business, Julie?" The question felt forced and awkward, but Laura was determined to make friends in Bufordville.

Julie brightened. "I found this town three years ago while traveling the parkway. It was like something out of a travel brochure. Then I saw this little place for sale and fell in love. I always wanted to own my own shop, but that was pretty unrealistic in New York City."

"That's where you're from?" Laura asked.

"Yeah," Julie replied.

Laura made her way to a display of candles that, according to the sign, had been locally produced. Some of the candles in jars were lit,

and the mix of scents—cinnamon, mint, and something fruity—
smelled quite pleasant. Laura noticed that the price on the candles
had been reduced several times. "So, what did you do before you
came to Bufordville?"

"Well, my dad teaches at Columbia, and I went there for two
years. I was going to major in film, but I found out studying movies
isn't as fun as watching them. What about you? Where're you from?"

"St. Louis."

"Are you on vacation or something?"

"Not exactly. My aunt died recently and left me her property."

"You mean Laura Buford?" Julie's eyebrows shot up.

Approaching the counter, Laura nodded. "Yes. Did you know her?"

Julie flipped her long hair over her shoulder, and Laura noticed that
she had a sprinkle of freckles across her nose and cheeks. "She used to
come in here once in a great while. She liked old dresses, and she had
good taste."

"Really?"

"You sound surprised."

"I didn't know my aunt, but aside from some beautiful antiques,
some of the décor in her house is quite old-fashioned, and not necessarily in a tasteful way." Laura felt her cheeks warm. *I can't believe I just
told a total stranger that I think my aunt had bad taste.*

Julie leaned on the counter. "I've been hoping that they—you—
would have an estate sale. I wouldn't mind getting a peek inside the
place.

"Oh, you'll have to come out and let me show you." Now she was
inviting someone she'd just met to come to her house.

Julie's eye's widened. "Really? I'd love it."

Laura hesitated, then realized she felt at ease around Julie—a rare
thing for Laura unless she knew someone well. "I won't be having an
auction until the estate is settled, but I think there's a lot we could get
rid of."

"Well, that maid must have felt the same way."

Laura placed her hand on the counter. "Maid?"

"You know, that Hayes woman."

"Oh, Agnes."

"Is she still there?"

"Yes."

"Are you going to keep her?"

"Well, I don't know. I mean, I guess so. She's probably worked there forever." *Oh, I said too much again!* Laura thought, mentally kicking herself.

Julie's eyes narrowed. "I'll bet she has. I think the woman's creepy myself. She reminds me of the maid in that movie *Rebecca*—you know, the Hitchcock movie about the new wife haunted by the constant reminders of the dead wife. She thinks her new husband killed his first wife . . . do you know it?"

"Oh, yeah," Laura said. "I've seen that movie. I like suspense."

Julie pushed herself up from the counter. "Really? Me too."

"Do you like Agatha Christie?" Laura asked, wondering even as she said it why she had mentioned Christie out of all the novelists she'd read. She suspected that her mind was probably churning up anything that had to do with suspense so she could prove she was being truthful. *I'm not that desperate for a friend,* she thought. *Then again, maybe I am.*

"I've seen all the movies based on her books."

Laura smiled. "Have you ever seen *Wait until Dark*?"

"At least six times, and every time it's as suspenseful as the first," Julie responded. Then she asked excitedly, "What about *Midnight Lace* with Doris Day?"

"Yes," Laura answered. "I've seen that one, too."

Julie leaned forward on the counter again. "There's an old movie theater in town that's showing old suspense movies through Halloween. It's called the Movie House. *The Spiral Staircase* is playing this week. Would you like to go?"

"I would love to," Laura exclaimed, surprising herself at how quickly she answered.

"Do you want to see that box now?" Julie queried.

"What box?"

"The box of old things the maid sold me after Miss Buford's death. Weren't we talking about it?"

"You didn't mention a box," Laura stated.

"Oh. Well, I thought it." Julie hurried to the back of the store and returned with an old wooden crate.

Laura dredged through the clothes at the top of the box: a well-worn cardigan sweater, a white blouse with a stained lace collar, a polyester dress that had pilled, and several other items. Finally, she remarked, "I didn't really know my aunt, but I don't think she would wear things like this—they look like they should be used for rags."

"That's what I thought," Julie said. "In fact, I thought it strange when the maid showed up with a box of old things after the old wom— I mean your aunt—died. So I looked at the store's old accounting records and found that Agnes Hayes used to come here a lot back before I bought the place. She sold odds and ends—old silver and knick-knacks."

Underneath the clothing lay an old jewelry box, and Laura removed it from the crate and set it on the counter. As she carefully lifted the lid, the rusty hinges creaked and a haunting melody began to play. Laura shut the box and turned it over, noticing a tarnished brass plaque on the bottom. It read *To Laura from Ruby.* A wave of nausea shot through Laura like wind, and she dropped the music box back into the crate.

"What's wrong?" Julie asked. "Is there a spider in there or something?"

"I—I'm sorry," Laura stammered. "I should go. Can I buy that box?"

"Of course," Julie said. "I feel guilty selling it to you since that maid probably swiped it from you."

"Well, we don't know for sure," Laura replied quickly. "How much?"

"Ten dollars?"

"Are you sure? That's not much."

"Ten dollars," Julie repeated.

Laura pulled a ten-dollar bill from her wallet and placed it on the counter, then grabbed the music box and started for the door.

"What about the movie?" Julie asked.

Laura stopped and turned, willing a pleasant smile onto her face. "How about Friday night?"

Julie smiled broadly. "Great. I'll meet you outside the theater just before seven."

The cowbell clanged as Laura pulled the door open and left the store. Stepping onto the sidewalk, she spotted a bench nearby, so she walked over and sat down. She wasn't sure why the music box had upset her so much, but the fresh, cool air calmed her nerves a little.

"Laura! Laura McClain!"

She glanced up to see Hattie O'Donnell wobbling towards her from across the street. Another woman Laura recognized from the bus station struggled to keep up with Hattie.

"Laura McClain, this is my sister, Lettie."

"It's nice to meet you," Laura said, taking the frail woman's hand. Lettie was terribly thin, and she looked almost like she'd blow away with the next big gust of wind. She didn't smile back at Laura, who wondered if the old woman was seriously ill.

Hattie began immediately. "Oh, my. I've been hoping to run into you, Laura. I have so much to tell you!"

Lettie tugged at Hattie's sweater. "Hattie O'Donnell, we must go. I have an appointment with Dr. Preston."

"I know, dear. This will only take a minute." Hattie squeezed Laura's arm. "Laura, dear, I must tell you something about Buford's Bluff."

"Hattie, will you shut your mouth and come with me?" As Lettie pulled on Hattie's arm, Laura decided maybe Lettie wasn't so frail after all.

"Oh, all right, Lettie. Laura, I'll talk to you later."

"But Hattie, what did you want to tell me?" Laura prodded.

"Not now, dear. I have to get Lettie to the doctor. I'm sorry, honey!" Hattie and Lettie walked away, leaving Laura to wonder what on earth Hattie could tell her about Buford's Bluff that Lettie didn't want her to repeat.

Laura glanced at the drugstore window and noticed the old man she'd talked with earlier staring out the window. She looked back at the antique store only to see Julie gazing out the window there. Laura glanced at the music box and then at Hattie and Lettie hobbling down the street. *Bufordville is just as creepy as Buford's Bluff,* she thought.

Laura shook her head and tried to focus on her next task. Opening her purse, she took out a slip of paper. Bishop Miller's handwriting was messy, but she could still make out what he'd written: *Aaron Farr, attorney-at-law, The Law Offices of Leonard Davis and Associates, 45 Birch Street, Bufordville, Virginia.*

"I called the bishop of the Lakeside Ward, near Bufordville," Bishop Miller had informed her. "I wanted to let him know you were coming. His name is Bishop Roberts, and he said they'll take good care of you. When I told him your situation, he mentioned there's a lawyer in the ward." He'd handed her the piece of paper. "You may need someone to look after your legal interests."

The more Laura thought about it, the more sense it made. Roger Ballister was executor of her aunt's estate, but Laura didn't really know him, and while she assumed she could trust him to act in her best interests, there was no way she could be sure. Retaining her own attorney would be the smart thing to do.

8

It took some thirty minutes for Laura to find Birch Street, a side street not far from the courthouse. After walking around the block a few times without locating the law offices, she got back in her car and drove around. Finally, she saw the number 45 on a modest colonial building that sat beneath the oak trees.

The receptionist smiled when Laura entered the law offices. "May I help you?"

Laura glanced at the name plate on the desk: *Emily Smith*. The woman looked about fifty years old and had bleached blond hair. Laura swallowed hard and forced herself to speak. "Yes, Miss Smith, I would like to see Aaron Farr, please." She spoke rapidly, and her mouth felt dry.

"Do you have an appointment?"

"No, but I would just like to see him for a few minutes if that's possible."

"Well, I'm afraid Mr. Farr is in court right now. Would you like to make an appointment with him?"

"Yes, I suppose so," Laura answered, attempting to conceal her disappointment. She had hoped to get this over with.

Miss Smith stood and opened an appointment book. Just then a man walked up behind them and brushed past Laura. Reaching over the desk, he picked up the appointment book. "Emily, what time's my next appointment?"

"Twelve thirty."

"Then I've got time to take a quick lunch."

As he turned to walk away, Miss Smith called after him, "Oh, Mr. Farr, you have a phone message."

He walked back to the desk.

"You're Aaron Farr?" Laura asked in surprise. She had expected someone older; this man appeared to be in his late twenties.

Glancing at her and then back at the message, he replied, "Yes. Do I know you?"

Laura smiled nervously, noticing his high cheekbones and the dimple in his chin. He was quite good looking. His dark brown hair was neatly trimmed, and his obviously expensive suit hung nicely on his tall frame.

"She doesn't have an appointment," Miss Smith interjected, obviously annoyed.

Aaron looked at Laura as if seeing her for the first time. His eyes met hers, and she felt herself blushing as she stared into his clear blue eyes. "I—uh—I'm a new member of the ward. I just moved here from St. Louis, and I need some legal advice." She hoped she didn't sound as pathetic to him as she did to herself.

"Why don't you join me for lunch? It will be quick, but you can tell me the basics of your situation." Listening to him speak with a deep Southern drawl, Laura hardly noticed Miss Smith's scowl.

"Well, I don't want to impose," Laura responded nervously, suddenly wishing she could disappear. She would never make it through lunch with *him*—he was too good looking, and she was too nervous.

He grinned. "Nonsense. I'd love the company, and I bet you're hungry. After all, it's almost noon." There was something in the way he said it, something genuine and kind.

Laura nodded her assent, so Aaron took her arm and escorted her from the law offices. As they walked briskly down the sidewalk, she stole a few glances at him. He had an intelligent look and a confident air, yet he didn't strike her as someone who was too full of himself. Perhaps discussing things with a lawyer wouldn't be as boring as she had imagined.

The small diner was crowded. Taking her elbow again, Aaron pulled Laura through the crowd to an unoccupied table for two. Laura reached out to pull out her chair, but Aaron beat her to it. Then she stepped back onto his foot. "Oh, I'm so sorry."

"Quite all right," he said with a smile that lit up his face.

They had just sat down and picked up their menus when a waitress approached the table. "Dora, I'll have the usual," Aaron declared. "I'm in a bit of a rush."

"I'll have the usual too," Laura added hesitantly. The waitress squinted her eyes and frowned, and Laura felt the blood rising in her face.

"Sure, sugar, the usual." The waitress wore a pink uniform with white trim and a cap, something out of the 1950s. She walked back toward the counter, and Laura noticed that it was crowded with customers sitting on small metal stools attached to the floor. Going behind the counter, Dora pinned the ticket to a wheel and turned it toward the cook. Laura could smell grease frying, and it felt as if she had stepped back in time. *This is a real diner,* she thought.

"What do you do here in Bufordville?" Aaron inquired.

"Well, recently I've inherited my Aunt L—I mean Laura Buford's—estate." She hoped she sounded more intelligent this time, hiding her trembling hands in her lap.

The attorney gave a low whistle. "You're the new owner of Buford's Bluff?"

"Well, I will be, I'm told, when the estate is settled."

He raised his eyebrows and smiled, which deepened the dimple on his chin. "You never know who you'll end up having lunch with. When I woke this morning, I would have never thought I'd be having lunch with the richest woman in Bufordville."

Laura blushed and started to throw her hair over her shoulder but remembered it was tied back in a ponytail. Suddenly she noticed that several nearby customers were staring at them. "Well, like I said, I'm not yet . . . That is to say, I haven't yet . . ."

Aaron leaned forward and whispered, "Got your hands on all those millions?"

Laura's face turned even brighter red, and she wished she could hide under the table. "Mr. Farr—"

"Aaron, please."

"Uh, Aaron, I need legal representation. I need someone to help me understand where I stand with the estate." She tried to sound sophisticated, but she couldn't control the slight tremor in her voice.

"I can recommend some good attorneys," Aaron responded matter-of-factly.

Just then the waitress appeared, placing a plate in front of Aaron and one in front of Laura. As Laura looked down at the plate to see a bowl of tomato soup and a toasted peanut butter sandwich, her face must have given her away, because Aaron grinned at her.

"This is my 'usual.' Maybe I should've warned you."

"It's a bit of an odd combination, but that's okay. I like peanut butter." Laura smiled back at him.

Aaron chuckled. "But do you like tomato soup?"

They ate in silence for a few minutes, then Laura sat up straighter and cleared her throat. "Mr. Farr, I want you to represent my interest—to be my lawyer." Realizing how desperate she sounded, Laura slumped back in her seat.

"Well, my specialty is criminal law, not estates."

"Oh." Laura took a big bite of the peanut-butter sandwich, and the bread stuck to her teeth so she pulled hard on the sandwich. When she put the sandwich down, she knocked over her glass of water. Her mouth was full of peanut butter, and she felt like she might choke.

Aaron jumped up, grabbed some napkins, and tried to contain the large puddle of water. Laura tried to wipe her mouth with a napkin, still trying to get the peanut butter down, then stood and noticed that she was soaked. The waitress arrived and handed Laura a dish towel to wipe her jeans. Several customers at the bar snickered.

Finally, Laura swallowed the dense lump of peanut butter. "I need to go," she managed, looking apologetically at Aaron. Then she bolted from the café and headed up the street toward her car. When she heard footsteps behind her, she didn't turn around but knew Aaron was trying to catch up to her. She didn't want to face him so she ran even faster, wondering how she'd gone from the perfect lunch invitation to this.

When she reached her car, Laura found a yellow ticket on the windshield. She'd forgotten she'd parked in a twenty-minute parking spot. Snapping up the ticket, she rummaged in her purse for her car keys.

"Laura!" Aaron called, running up to her. "Are you okay? Did I upset you? I'm sorry. I'll try to help you until you can find a lawyer more experienced with property and estates."

Laura dug deeper into her purse and didn't look up. "I'll make an appointment."

"Why don't you give me that ticket?" he suggested. "I'll take care of it. I have friends at the police station. I'll explain that you're new in town."

"Thanks." Not feeling up to an argument, Laura handed him the slip of paper and watched as he walked away. Her heart was beating fast from her sprint to her car, and her face still felt warm with embarrassment.

When Laura returned to Buford's Bluff, she went straight to her room and took a long nap. As she awoke, it took her a few moments to remember where she was. Then she remembered the events of the day and wanted to go back to sleep, but instead she combed her hair, pinched her cheeks, and carried the newly acquired jewelry box down to the parlor.

Sitting with the jewelry box on her lap beneath her aunt's portrait, Laura stared at the beautiful woman's image for a long while, then surveyed the huge parlor and tried to imagine her aunt sitting in the room. The heavy mahogany furniture was covered in mauve fabric, and the dark wood floor was covered with a tan area rug with corner sprays of pink, yellow, and blue blooms surrounded by lush greenery. The sofa featured a heavily carved medallion back with fruits and flowers carved on its wood frame, and the same pattern was carved in the chairs' arms and legs. Laura scrutinized the arms of the chair in which she sat, noticing a carved snake slithering through the fruit and flowers.

She lifted the jewelry box's lid and listened to the music. It occurred to her that Aunt Laura had once listened to the same music, perhaps while sitting in this room. There was something eerie and surreal about the melody. Earlier in the week, Laura had sat in the comfort of her own apartment, and as she sat in a room almost as large as her entire apartment, it seemed like a daydream, a fantasy, an episode from a Barbara Michaels novel.

Laura heard a rustling noise and glanced up. Agnes lurked at the door, her face pale, her mouth open. "Where did you get that?"

Laura raised an eyebrow. "At an antique shop in Bufordville."

Agnes stepped closer. "I didn't realize you were shopping for antiques."

"I just saw the shop and went in on a whim," Laura explained.

Agnes frowned and smoothed her apron. "Well, dinner will be ready soon. I hope you don't mind leftovers, but since you failed to appear for lunch I saved it all for dinner."

"The thing I like about the music box," Laura began, her heart starting to pound wildly, "was that it once belonged to someone named Laura."

"You don't say."

"Yes, see?" Laura turned the music box upside-down. Agnes walked closer. "There's an engraving on the bottom that says, 'To Laura from Ruby.'"

"Curious," Agnes remarked.

Laura's palms were sweating, and she had to force herself to speak. "I'm going to try to find out who the box belonged to. I want to know who Ruby and Laura were."

"Well," Agnes surmised, "that's a rather strange occupation, but I suppose a person can engage in any activity she wants to engage in." Her voice trembled a little near the end of the sentence. Agnes was obviously trying to maintain her composure, and Laura almost pitied her.

Agnes walked toward the door, paused, and turned toward Laura, her face stern. "They say curiosity killed the cat, you know." Then she turned and marched away.

A chill ran up Laura's back.

* * *

Laura ran down the dark corridor toward the half-moon window. Rain pounded against the glass, thunder boomed like a cannon, and lightning lit the hall, revealing light yellow wallpaper with a floral design of peach and blue. She tripped and fell but got up and looked behind her, then dashed toward her bedroom door. As she ran into the room and slammed the door, lightning flashed through the window, illuminating the daisy-covered walls. She stumbled over toys and furniture as she made her way to the closet, then climbed in and closed the door. Footsteps thudded through the hallway, and the bedroom door squeaked opened. Someone strode toward the closet. The doorknob rattled as someone turned it from the other side, and Laura screamed.

Laura sat up in bed, her limbs trembling and her face drenched with tears. The moon glowed through the window, and Laura switched on the lamp on the bedside table. She saw her blankets in a heap on the floor.

Another dream, Laura thought. Then she heard the floorboards in the hallway groan and jumped out of bed. She went to the door, squared her shoulders, and pulled it open. Agnes stood in the hall wearing a nightgown.

"What're you doing?" Laura demanded accusatorily.

Agnes held up a hand as if to ward off a blow. "I heard you cry out, miss. I came to see if you needed something."

"I was having a bad dream." Laura breathed, trying to calm down.

"Well, if you need anything, I'm down the hall."

"Thank you," Laura uttered with a sigh. Agnes was less threatening now; in fact, she almost seemed frightened. *I wonder why?* Laura thought as she closed the door.

She went to the closet and opened the door, the image of crouching there in terror still vivid in her mind. The dream had seemed so real! She turned and studied the room's blue wallpaper. *No daisies here, but . . .*

Walking to the door, Laura listened but heard nothing. She opened the door cautiously, hoping the hinges wouldn't squeak. By the moonlight shining through the half-moon window, she could see that the hall was empty. Her heart pounded, but she forced herself to tiptoe past Agnes's room. As Laura reached the landing, the familiar sickening sensation momentarily froze her legs. She closed her eyes. *I'm okay. You're okay. We're all okay.* These weren't the mantras, but they would do for now.

She took a deep breath and opened her eyes. For a moment, she thought someone lurked at the bottom of the staircase. Yet as her eyes adjusted, she saw no one. Grasping the banister, she began walking down the stairs. Each time a board squeaked, her anxiety increased, but she managed to make it to the bottom. Her bare feet touched the cold wood floor, and she stepped into the parlor.

Like a spotlight, a moonbeam illuminated her aunt's portrait. As Laura approached it, it seemed as if her aunt's eyes were moving with her. She shuddered and looked away.

Laura found the light on the table by the couch and turned it on. The ornate lamp featured roses painted on a globe with hanging crystals. Laura walked through the shadowy room to the table that held the family photo albums, then picked up two and carried them to the couch.

Sitting down and holding one album on her lap, Laura turned the pages slowly at first, then more quickly as she realized she didn't recognize anyone in the pictures. Then again she hadn't even known what her aunt Laura looked like before she'd seen the woman's portrait. Laura could see a family resemblance—elements of her mother—in the faces of many of the people, but she had no idea exactly how they were related.

Laura set the album beside her on the couch and opened the other album. The first picture had obviously been taken at a family reunion, with everyone posing together on the porch of the mansion. From the clothing the people wore, Laura estimated that the picture was taken sometime around the turn of the twentieth century. She continued to flip the pages, noticing that the photos appeared to be in chronological order. The styles changed quickly, from flapper fashions to dresses that looked like something from *I Love Lucy*.

The people changed too, but Buford's Bluff seemed indifferent to it all. The same pillars supported the grand porch, and the same furniture graced the rooms, although the fabrics changed from time to time.

Laura turned another page and recognized the little girl in the first picture. It was Laura's mother, smiling beneath her dark curls and wearing a frilly dress with white shoes. Sitting on the floor near the Buford's Bluff dollhouse, Sarah clutched a china doll.

Laura had never seen her mother smile like that, carefree and unfettered by the world's cares. As Laura glanced up at the beautiful woman in the portrait over the fireplace, she wondered, *Why didn't you help her? You had plenty of money. And why did you inherit everything? Where was my mother's inheritance? She practically worked herself to death!* Laura looked back at the photograph and outlined her mother's face with her finger. Her gaze wandered across the picture, taking in the bedroom that had once belonged to her mother. Then she remembered why she'd come down to look at these old albums in the middle of the night. The wallpaper. The walls in the photograph were covered with wallpaper in a daisy pattern. The dream! She had seen this same wallpaper in her dream. *Calm down,* Laura told herself. *There has to be a logical explanation.*

But it was too late for that. The adrenaline had already shot through her body, and she felt her heart pounding like a drum in her temples. Her head ached, pain wracked her chest, and she felt nauseous. *You're okay, you're okay,* she told herself over and over, then closed her eyes and said a silent prayer. She knew she wasn't crazy. There had to be a reason why she dreamed about the room with the vivid wallpaper. Perhaps her mother had shown her a picture of the room and Laura had simply forgotten until now. Maybe when she was a child, her mother had told her about the room, and she just hadn't consciously thought of it for a while.

As she felt the comfort that only the Holy Ghost can bring, Laura decided to put the dream—the whole situation—on the back burner and let it simmer. She would console herself with the knowledge that answers often came when she gave up trying to overanalyze everything.

She put the albums away and walked back up the stairs. As she moved from the stairs into the upstairs hallway, the floorboards in the downstairs foyer creaked, and Laura was sure someone was there. She dashed down the corridor into her room and closed the door, locking it behind her, then stood with her hand on the doorknob. Barely audible footsteps moved down the hall and stopped at her door. Laura held her breath. Then the steps moved away from the door. Perhaps Agnes had gotten up to get a drink of water or something. Laura released a heavy sigh and crawled back into bed, covering her head with the blankets.

9

On Friday morning, Aaron Farr sat in his office, trying to concentrate on the documents before him, but his mind kept wandering to the woman he'd met the day before. She needed help, and for some reason he felt he was the person to help her. He chuckled as he pictured her taking an enormous bite of the peanut butter sandwich.

"What's so funny?"

Aaron looked up to see his boss, Leonard Davis, standing in the doorway. Leonard had silver hair, and his shrewd eyes were set deep under dark brows that matched his mustache. His gaze cut through Aaron, and his frown let Aaron know he wasn't in the mood for humor.

"Uh, just a funny thought," Aaron replied.

Leonard grunted. Aaron hadn't totally figured the man out, even though he'd worked for him for a year. Leonard was judgmental, moralistic, and demanding—sometimes even condescending—making him quite difficult to work for. That said, Aaron appreciated the way his boss patiently hovered over legal papers and never tired of the details. In fact, Leonard's eagle eye was part of what made him such a brilliant attorney.

"Have you ever been married, Leonard?" Aaron wasn't sure why he asked the question now, but he had wondered about the subject for some time.

A long pause followed. "I fell in love with the law over forty years ago, and my life is devoted to seeing justice served. The New Testament says that love is the fulfilling of the law. That devotion leaves little room for anything else in my life."

Once again, Leonard was ready with a handy quote. Though he knew the man had faults, Aaron couldn't help admiring his loyalty to the law. There had to be something good in a man who took a kid like Aaron from Virginia's coal-mining region and gave him a scholarship to law school. To top it off, Leonard had offered Aaron a job after graduation. Of course, Leonard benefited as well—for one thing, Aaron was devoted to him and the firm. How could he not be when the firm had invested so much in him?

"I admire you, Leonard. I hope someday I can be even half the lawyer you are."

Aaron saw a rare smile play around Leonard's lips. The older man replied with obvious pleasure, "Well, you keep up the good work. Keep your nose clean, watch, and learn, and you'll turn out to be a fine lawyer."

Aaron grinned but hesitated momentarily before venturing, "Leonard, do you know of a woman named Laura McClain? She inherited the Buford Place."

Leonard's eyes widened. "Yes, I believe Roger Ballister mentioned something about an heir from out west somewhere. A young lady, is she?"

Aaron smiled. "Yes, and pretty."

Leonard pulled at his mustache.

"What's wrong?" Aaron asked.

Leonard cleared his throat. "Don't let beauty blind you, my boy. The Bufords have always been high and mighty. Be careful." Then Leonard turned and left Aaron's office.

I think Mr. Davis just gave me dating advice! Aaron thought. Grabbing the phonebook, he flipped the pages until he found Laura Buford's number, then dialed. After several rings, a female voice answered with an abrupt, "Buford residence."

"Yes, may I please speak to Laura McClain?"

A long wait followed.

"Hello."

"Hello, Laura? This is Aaron Farr."

"Yes, thank you for getting back with me," Laura responded quietly.

"I feel terrible about lunch yesterday, and I wondered if I could make it up to you."

"Oh, no. I'm the one that needs to apologize," Laura insisted. "The way I ran off—I was just so flustered. I'm not very good at meeting new people, and—"

"Maybe I could pick you up and drive you to church on Sunday," Aaron interrupted smoothly. "The meetinghouse is in Lakeside, and it could be hard to find for someone who's never been there before."

There was a long pause. "That's so nice of you. I mean, yes, that would be wonderful."

"I can pick you up around eight thirty," he added.

"Okay."

They spoke their good-byes, and he hung up the phone. Smiling to himself, Aaron realized he would have never been so bold in college. He hadn't really felt like he fit in back then. Unlike many of the students at the University of Virginia, he hadn't come from a well-educated or wealthy family. In fact, his father could barely read and write. His mother worked at a local diner, but she came home every night, fixed dinner, cleaned up after dinner, and read to the family. They didn't even own a television. Aaron's mother read the family portions of the newspaper, as well as history books and, when they were lucky, a novel. Lucy Farr's love for books was what led to the family joining the LDS Church. Some missionaries had stopped by one night with a Book of Mormon, and Lucy had snatched the free book from their hands. Aaron couldn't explain the family's initial fascination with the book, but each night they listened as Lucy read about the Nephites and Lamanites. Even Peter, his father, stopped Lucy to ask questions. Aaron was the youngest of three brothers. His older brothers, Jacob and Joseph, were intrigued to find their names come up in the early chapters of the book.

Finally, Lucy read Moroni's promise that they would receive a witness of the truth of the Book of Mormon if they prayed about it and sincerely desired to know. They had a family prayer, with Peter saying the prayer. Though he wasn't an educated man, Aaron's father was religiously inclined, having been raised in a strict Baptist home.

Over the next few days, each family member prayed and pondered about the Book of Mormon, and each separately decided to be baptized. The nearest branch was forty miles from their house, but they became active members, and Peter eventually served as a counselor in the branch presidency.

Lucy and Peter encouraged their sons to acquire a college education, and all three complied. Aaron had won a scholarship at the University of Virginia, but he still had to work to pay for college. He majored in political science, and with the aspiration of getting into politics, he applied to several law schools. Then, like a miracle from heaven, Leonard had offered him a scholarship to attend Washington and Lee Law School in Lexington, Virginia.

All through his undergraduate years, Aaron felt a little uncomfortable, a bit like a fish out of water, or at least just a kid from rural Virginia. But by the time he finished law school he'd gained confidence in himself, realizing that intelligence and ambition beat money every time. Here in Bufordville, the locals treated him like royalty. He'd dated the few single girls in the ward who were in their twenties, but he didn't have much in common with them. At any rate, the relationships never lasted longer than a few dates. He wondered if things would be different with Laura McClain.

Get a grip, he told himself. *When did this go from helping a client in need to contemplating a date?* For some reason, he felt like a guy who had seen a girl for the first time after having been marooned on a deserted island—and he hoped it wasn't so obvious to her. After all, he was just offering a new member of the ward a ride to church.

* * *

Laura had spent Friday exploring the house and grounds, discovering that the mansion was really a simple two-story design plus a one-story wing. The bottom floor of the house's central section was made up of four main rooms: two enormous rooms on each side of the twenty-foot wide middle hallway. A door divided the front entrance hall from the back entrance hall, and the front hall was two stories high and dominated by the grand staircase. If visitors failed to be impressed by the two-story columned porch that greeted them upon approaching the house, the elegant entry hall provided a second opportunity.

On either side of the front entry hall was a parlor furnished with beautiful antiques and adorned with original paintings. The east parlor contained a door on the north side that connected it to the library, and the west parlor had a north door to the dining room. The east parlor, which Agnes referred to as the "grand parlor," had a door on the east side that led to the solarium. A door on the west side of the dining room exited to a rose garden. Both the dining room and library had doors to the central hallway.

Besides the library and dining room, the back hallway led to a bathroom, a cleaning closet, and laundry room to the east. To the west, a fairly wide hallway connected the main house to the west wing. Agnes seemed to control the west wing where the kitchen was located, and Laura had only peered into a room or two. They were empty, and she assumed they had once served as living quarters for the hired help. For a moment Laura wondered why Agnes didn't sleep in one of these rooms. Then Laura realized that towards the end of her aunt's life she would have needed someone to keep a close eye on her.

Upstairs were four large bedrooms and two small bedrooms. The four large bedrooms each contained a bathroom, though two of these had been added in recent years. Each bedroom also featured its own fireplace. Agnes occupied one of the smaller bedrooms. Since Laura's room had no bathroom, she used the one between Agnes's room and the next bedroom. Agnes's room was on the same side of the hall as Laura's, but nearer to the staircase. Aunt Laura's room had been directly across the hall from Agnes's. Laura calculated that the house had approximately twenty-five rooms.

The stables seemed almost as impressive as the house, though there were no longer horses. Either her aunt had sold them before she died, or Roger had sold them as part of the estate settlement. Laura decided to ask Roger about that later. On the south side of the stables facing the river, there was a huge reception area complete with kitchen and bathrooms. Trees divided the house from the stables, and Agnes had explained that the house had been off limits during large parties. Outdoor activities took place on the lawn west of the stables where the driveway joined a parking lot, and a person couldn't see the house from the west lawn.

Laura had spent so much time exploring the house and grounds that she almost forgot about her Friday night plans with Julie. When she finally remembered, she rushed to get ready and quickly drove to Bufordville.

Located on the edge of town, the Movie House glittered like a palace from a bygone era. The gleaming interior matched the external dazzle: the elegant décor included French tapestry, European-style plaster, and crystal chandeliers. Awed by the theater's splendor, Laura decided that even the tickets were elegant.

"Movies must be a big deal here," Laura surmised as she and Julie walked away from the ticket booth.

Julie smiled. "When they built this theater, movies were a big deal everywhere. Come on, let's sit on the balcony. I love sitting there." Tiny lights lit their way as they ascended the staircase. Once there, they stepped onto the balcony, the theater lights revealed a grand room below that featured a stage with closed curtains.

Laura and Julie talked about old movies while they waited for the movie to start. Soon the lights dimmed and the movie began. The plot involved a psychotic killer stalking a mute servant girl who worked and lived in an eerie old mansion. Laura's mind kept going back to the stalker in St. Louis—the crevices in his cheeks, the circles under his eyes—and to her mysteriously open closet door and mislaid ribbon. *How will I go back to Buford's Bluff tonight?* she thought nervously.

Not surprisingly, the acting wasn't great, but the fast-moving plot kept Laura's eyes glued to the screen. The final scene was almost too much for Laura to bear, so she closed her eyes, then opened them to glance at Julie, who looked calmly at the screen.

Laura turned back to the screen, where a girl peered through the banister of a stairway. Laura screamed, then sprang from her seat, forcing her way through a row of legs into the aisle. She ran through the balcony exit and hurried down the stairs. *Oh, no—there she is again!* A woman was falling down the stairs ahead. And there she lay at the bottom—dead. Yet when Laura reached the bottom of the stairs, she saw no one. Her mind was playing tricks on her, but she didn't stop at the bottom of the stairs. Instead, she tore from the theater into the street.

"Laura! Please stop!"

Laura heard the words but kept running until a hand grabbed her arm. She stopped and turned to see Julie's eyes searching her face. "Are you okay?"

"I—no, yes—I . . . I . . . feel sick," Laura stuttered.

Julie took Laura's arm more gently now. "Was the movie too much for you?"

"Yes, I think so," Laura said.

"I'm sorry," Julie said. "I thought you liked suspense, but I don't think that was a very good one. Hey, why don't we stop by the café and get something to drink, perhaps some pie? They have the best pie."

Laura knew she should feel silly about what had happened, but she was too perplexed to care. She forced a smile. "I'm sorry, Julie. I don't know what happened in there—I guess it's just moving and all that has me so stressed out."

"Come on," Julie prodded. "Let's get some pie."

* * *

As Julie led her down the street, Laura realized they were headed for the same diner where she'd gone to lunch with Aaron. The small brick building featured green-and-white awnings, and a Coca-Cola sign blinked on and off in one window. Julie and Laura entered the café where couples and small groups huddled at various tables. The place seemed less crowded than it had at lunch, and to Laura it felt cozier and warmer—and more safe.

After the two young women sat down in a corner booth, Laura surprised herself by telling Julie about the dream, including the daisy wallpaper and the half-moon window stairs. She also confided in her new friend about Agnes's reaction to the music box. Julie's face was blank, expressionless. "You must think I'm crazy," Laura sighed.

Julie's eyebrows came together as she wrinkled her nose and then leaned back in her seat and folded her arms. Finally, her eyebrows rose and her eyes widened. Leaning forward conspiratorially, she asked quietly, "Do you believe in ghosts?"

Laura suppressed a smile and answered, "No, not really. At least I don't think so." She didn't want to hurt her new friend's feelings, so she proceeded carefully. "I believe in spirits. But I don't believe that people who die remain behind to haunt their houses."

Julie's eyebrows lowered and she frowned briefly, then grinned again as her eyes lit up. "Do you believe in angels, then?"

"Yes, I believe in angels," Laura answered.

Julie smiled. "What kind of angels?"

"What do you mean? Are there different kinds?"

"Do you believe that people that have died can come back to earth as angels to warn people who're living?" Julie ate a bite of pie, then continued. "I mean, maybe your aunt is trying to tell you something. Maybe she's trying to warn you. Or maybe it's your mother."

"Well, I don't know, but if someone is trying to tell me something, it obviously has to do with the stairs."

Julie leaned closer. "The stairs?" Her fork held the last bite of pie, and she paused with it just a few inches from her mouth.

"Yes, that's where I feel things the most—when I'm on the stairs in the mansion. In the movie, as the girl looked through the banister of those stairs—" She stopped abruptly, not wanting Julie to think she was insane. "Never mind," she muttered with a forced smile. "It sounds so silly, and I'm babbling on."

Julie clutched Laura's arm. "Tell me what you felt in the movie," she said insistently. "I mean, as precisely as you can."

"It's not so much what I felt . . . It's more what I saw."

Julie's eyebrows rose. "What did you see?"

Noticing the concern in Julie's eyes, Laura sighed. "Well, I'm not saying it was a vision or anything, but when I was watching the movie, an image came in my mind. I saw a woman falling down some stairs, and it seemed so real that it scared me. And when I was running down the theater stairs, in my mind's eye I saw the same woman falling down the stairs all over again. Except I didn't see the theater stairs. It was the stairs at Buford's Bluff. It's like I was transported back to the mansion for a moment, and I was watching this young woman fall down the stairs . . . to her death. For years I've had recurring dreams about stairs and someone falling—maybe even me. But this was different—this seemed so real."

Julie gasped. "And you thought it was you falling—like maybe your aunt is trying to warn you about falling down the stairs?"

"No, no," Laura corrected. "It's not like that. I saw someone else falling down the stairs, and when I looked at her I could tell she was dead. She was lying at the foot of the stairs, and it looked like her neck was broken. So there. Now you know."

"Who was she?" Julie wondered excitedly.

The answer came back quickly. "Ruby." Laura said it automatically, without thinking. She shuddered and put her hand over her mouth in horror.

Julie's eyes widened, and she fell back against the booth bench. "Ruby? The name on the music box?"

"Now I know I'm crazy," Laura declared matter-of-factly. "First I imagine feelings, and now I'm having visions. I think this has been coming on for a long time. I need to get out of here—I need to get back to St. Louis."

Julie sat up and grabbed Laura's arm. "I don't think you're crazy. Not at all."

Laura sighed. "Then what are you thinking?"

"Are you sure the girl at the bottom of the stairs was named Ruby?"

"I don't know. I'm not sure why I said that name, but now that you've reminded me of the music box, I'm thinking that's where I came up with it."

Julie placed her elbows on the table. "Okay, listen. Let's look at the facts. You envisioned wallpaper that had once been on the wall but isn't there now. Is there anything else that you remember like that?"

Laura tapped her fingertips on the table, then answered, "Well, not exactly."

"Anything," Julie pled.

"Well, there was one other little thing."

"What?" Julie could barely contain her excitement.

"When I first arrived at Buford's Bluff, I went out on the lawn. George, the gardener, was out raking leaves, and I told him there should be stairs going down the incline to his cottage. He told me there had once been stairs there. Do you think I'm seeing the past?"

"Laura, it makes sense."

Laura rolled her eyes. "No, it doesn't. I don't believe in that stuff."

"What stuff? What do you mean?" Julie asked in frustration.

"Psychics and mental telepathy and that kind of thing," Laura responded with a frown.

Julie grabbed Laura's arm and squeezed it hard. "That's not what I'm talking about, Laura."

Laura pulled her arm away and rubbed it. "What're you talking about, Julie?"

"Memory." And with that, Julie leaned back and nodded proudly.

"Memory?" Laura folded her arms and waited for an explanation.

"Your memory, Laura," Julie started, sitting up again and speaking deliberately and slowly. "You're recovering memories from your past, long-forgotten memories. You're being haunted by your memory, not your aunt."

At that moment, a sense of foreboding came over Laura, a strange feeling of dread that almost knocked her over. Her fingers tightened on her arm and she imagined herself twisting a doorknob. "But I've never been here before," she murmured weakly. "I was born in St. Louis. This is my first trip to the East Coast. Julie, I never met my aunt Laura."

"Are you sure?" Julie implored.

Laura dropped her arm. Julie had almost lured her into believing the ridiculous. "Yes, I'm sure," she replied firmly. "I would have remembered coming here, or someone would've told me. There would be pictures, mementos, stories—you know?"

Julie sat back and crossed her arms. "What's the earliest memory you have?"

Laura hesitated, then answered, "I remember Miss King, my kindergarten teacher in St. Louis. I remember my first day of kindergarten."

"You would've started kindergarten at age five, right? Isn't there anything you recall before that? You're missing five years of your life."

Laura frowned. "Don't be ridiculous. No one remembers when they're a baby."

Julie let out a deep breath. "I'm not talking about babies, Laura. I'm talking toddler age here—three and four years old, even two. Most people have at least a few memories from that far back, unless . . ."

"Unless what?"

"Unless they've experienced some terrible shock." She paused dramatically. "Like seeing someone fall down the stairs and die. Shock victims block out memories—that's probably why you're having those dreams you mentioned. Your brain is trying to bring the subconscious memory into your conscious mind." Then Julie looked Laura in the eye and asked, "Why don't we stop arguing about this and do something about it?"

"Like what?" Laura wondered, biting her lip. This evening had certainly turned out differently than she had expected.

"Find out who Ruby was and how you're connected to her."

"But how?" Laura knew she sounded tired, and she felt it.

"Buford's Bluff is a big house with a lot of closets and drawers," Julie explained. "I'm sure it has a basement and an attic. And there may even be some secret hiding places! There must be some clues somewhere in the mansion. You start there, and I'll start at the local library. If someone died at Buford's Bluff, it would have made the local newspapers."

I can do it, Laura told herself as she nodded at Julie. *I'll just get it over with.* Suddenly all the days of her young childhood appeared in her mind like a long row of locked doors, and she realized that she didn't really want to unlock any of them. Somehow she knew that what she would find behind one of them would be absolutely terrifying.

10

That Friday night, when Laura walked in the back door at Buford's Bluff, she found Agnes making herself some tea. "Can I get you anything to eat?" Agnes asked abruptly.

"No, thank you," Laura muttered.

"Are you ill?" Agnes inquired. "You look a little pale."

"I'm just tired, that's all," Laura replied.

"Are you sure there's nothing I can get you? Perhaps a cookie?" Now Agnes sounded genuinely concerned.

Laura stared at Agnes, thinking of her own mother. Sarah McClain had used almost exactly the same words when Laura was an adolescent. Time and time again, her mother had tried to soothe her daughter's woes with candy, cookies, or other treats. It was a wonder she hadn't been overweight, Laura thought wryly.

Agnes looked at Laura, obviously waiting for a reply. For a brief moment, Laura contemplated asking for some hot cocoa, and she thought of actually sitting down and talking with Agnes. Then her inhibitions—carefully cultivated through the years—kicked in. "No, nothing," Laura said with a quick smile. "I just had some pie, and I think I'll go straight to bed." She hurried from the kitchen and raced up the stairs to avoid further questions.

Her room felt cold, so Laura closed the curtains to avoid a draft. Sitting on the edge of the bed, she took off her shoes, then paused. She felt so confused by recent events. She wished she could talk about this with her mother. She crawled under the blankets with her clothes on, buried her face in the pillow, and cried. Her stomach lurched as if emptying all the pain, pushing it up through her throat in great, heaving sobs. Images flashed through her mind like a fast-moving slide show: her father and mother, the stairs at Buford's Bluff, the woman falling, and her conversation with Julie.

Eventually, sleep came, and with it, dreams. In one, Laura's parents smiled happily and told her how much they loved her. As the dream began evaporating into wakefulness, Laura tried to cling to it, wanting nothing more than to retreat into the warm, sweet bliss of sleep where the joy of the dream and the reality of her life were the same.

Yet wakefulness came, and she lay shivering, her heart pounding and her eyes focused on the ceiling. She waited a long while, listening to nothing. The house was perfectly silent. Laura crawled from bed, pulled open the nightstand drawer, and removed a flashlight she had brought from St. Louis.

She opened the door as carefully as possible, but it still squeaked. As she entered the hall, she stepped cautiously to minimize the creaking of the old floorboards beneath her. Flashing the beam of light down the hall, she saw no one there, so she tiptoed to the attic door. She had felt drawn to the attic since her arrival, but now even the door seemed foreboding. She couldn't believe she was contemplating this little expedition at night. She wasn't sure whether this proved she was crazy or suggested she wasn't. Summoning her courage, Laura grasped the doorknob and turned it, surprised to find it unlocked. Now she had no excuse.

Glancing back down the passageway, she wondered if someone lurked in the darkness near the stairs. Her heart fluttered, and she shined the light toward the stairs. Again, no one was there. She flashed the light up the narrow attic stairs, then carefully climbed up.

Just as she had expected, the attic was cluttered with a bunch of old boxes. Shining the light around, she also saw a couple of old couches, several chairs, a brass bed frame, and some old oil paintings leaning against the wall. She located a bare light bulb in the ceiling with a pull chain, but the wattage was too low to illuminate such a large space. She was glad she had a powerful flashlight. She quickly opened a few boxes and found old clothing, knickknacks, and an old button jar. In the far corner, two old trunks stood alone, so Laura tiptoed in that direction. As she opened the first trunk, and the rusty hinges squeaked loudly, she winced. Inside, she found a wedding dress, the fabric yellowed with age. *Maybe it was my mother's,* she thought to herself.

The second trunk was locked, but as Laura pulled at the lock, she noticed that the nails in the metal clasp were loose. Scanning the room with the flashlight beam, she noticed a fireplace poker against the wall. She grabbed it and forced it under the metal clasp until the clasp broke.

Lifting the lid of the trunk, Laura riffled through stacks of old letters until her hand touched something hard. A large leather book lay at the bottom of the trunk. A photo album. She lifted it from the trunk, set it on the floor, and opened it. She scanned the photographs, old black-and-white photographs of people she thought she didn't know. Soon, however, recognition dawned as she came to the color photographs.

On one page, Aunt Laura and Sarah sat on a porch swing. On the next, Sarah and John McClain waved and smiled in front of Buford's Bluff, appearing quite happy. Laura allowed herself to dream for a moment of what those times must have been like. She imagined her mother roaming Buford's Bluff's grand halls wearing a broad smile, not having to work long hours to support a child. She didn't have to shop at thrift stores, and she didn't have to try so hard to make ends meet. Along with her sister Laura, Sarah was the lady of the manor, with John by her side.

She turned the page and her heart skipped a beat as she saw another picture of her parents taken in front of Buford's Bluff. Her mother held a baby, and Laura recognized herself from old studio photographs she'd seen in her own photo album. She scanned the rest of the photos on the page. In one, she sat in a baby stroller in the rose garden with her mother, in another she cuddled in Aunt Laura's arms, and in another she played on the mansion's south lawn with her father. The last photo showed Laura, still a toddler, dancing at a birthday party.

I did live here! I lived at Buford's Bluff! Laura sighed heavily, realizing that the recognition she had felt when she had first arrived at the plantation was real. The wallpaper and the stairs were actual memories—not messages from spirits or ghosts. Something bad must have happened at Buford's Bluff, something that drove her parents to St. Louis. And it had to have been more than a disagreement with Aunt Laura.

There must be a good reason her parents had misled her concerning her birthplace and past. They were protecting her—she was certain of that. But from what? As she thought back on her childhood, she recalled her mother's overprotectiveness. Even when Laura was in high school, her mother had always called to make sure Laura was at home after school, locked in the apartment, doing her homework or reading. Over the years she rarely allowed Laura to invite friends over, and she never let her go to slumber parties.

The result was a shy, awkward, socially challenged girl, though perhaps Laura was a bit shy and awkward by nature. Laura knew that blaming her parents for her personality flaws was counterproductive. But what motivated them—Fear? Of what?

Laura lived with fear every day, and she couldn't remember when she'd begun regularly looking over her shoulder, feeling that perhaps someone or something was following her, wanting to harm her. She was sure, however, that she had learned this insecurity from her mother. Her mother had lived as if some dark shadow was following her, trying to overtake her.

Suddenly Laura could identify that dark shadow. It was the past! Her parents were running from their pasts, something threatening and foreboding. But what had happened, and how did it involve Laura?

She turned another page in the old photo album, and the now-familiar fear seemed to jump from her stomach into her throat. She swallowed hard. There she sat in the nursery with her nanny. She recognized Ruby now, the beautiful young woman with long blond hair, rosy cheeks, and a sweet smile.

Laura traced Ruby's face with her finger as she remembered. Ruby had cared for her and protected her. She had loved her. It was all coming back.

In her mind's eye, Laura could see Ruby lying at the bottom of the stairs. The image was fleeting, but this time Laura saw someone there with Ruby—a figure in a dark hood, crouching over Ruby. Laura didn't know who the person was, but dread filled her heart. Perhaps she feared death, having witnessed it.

Shaking her head to clear it, Laura turned to the next page in the album and saw a photograph of Buford's Bluff's staff, dressed in formal uniforms and holding silver serving trays. Obviously, the staff was preparing for some event. The gold-and-brown shag carpet looked like a 1970s style. Laura recognized Agnes, and she thought perhaps the tall, handsome man in the back row was George. He had dark hair like her father, but his nose was a bit wider.

Laura studied the faces, suddenly recognizing another. She felt the blood pounding in her ears, and her hands trembled as she held the album and scanned the photograph with her eyes. His face was unforgettable: the crevices etched so deeply in each cheek they looked almost like scars and the shadows surrounding his deep-set eyes. The tall, almost gaunt, man looked like a ghost in this photograph, much less real than the person Laura had confronted in St. Louis. But was he even flesh and blood then? Perhaps he was a hallucination, an image created by her mind.

None of it made sense. This picture was perhaps thirty years old, and the balding man of about fifty in the picture would be in his eighties today. How could he have been in St. Louis looking middle-aged a few weeks ago? *Maybe I do believe in ghosts after all,* Laura thought with a grimace.

Laura closed the book and hesitated. She wanted to take the album to her room—it could be useful as she tried to solve this mystery. But she didn't want to think about the picture of that man. What if he was some kind of ghost?

She smiled at the absurdity of her own thoughts. She didn't believe in ghosts! Clutching the book, she headed down the narrow stairs. In the hall, she thought she heard clothes rustling near the stairs. Laura dashed into the nursery and quickly closed the door behind her.

* * *

Laura's body jerked. Her eyes flew open and she sat up in bed. Outside, the rain poured, and the wind howled in great shuddering gusts against the windowpanes. Lightning illuminated the otherwise dark room, and thunder roared moments later. She imagined a hideous monster trying to get in, wanting to snatch her from her bed.

She jumped out of bed and ran to the closet, then climbed in, closed the door, and crouched on the floor. The last time she'd hidden from the monster at the window, Ruby had laughed and told her it was just tree branches scraping the panes. Laura's whole body trembled, and her teeth chattered loudly. Clenching her teeth to silence them, she heard bumping and footsteps. Voices. People were talking in the distance. From the hall? No. Downstairs in the entrance hall, where the two-story entry created echoes.

Laura thought she heard Ruby's voice. Why wasn't Ruby here with her? Ruby always came when there was a storm, always made her feel safe. Laura stood and opened the closet door cautiously, then waited. She could hear her own breath coming quick and raspy. Finally, lightning lit up her room, and she could see no one there—nothing but her bed and her dollhouse and her toys. She needed Ruby. She took a step and stopped to listen, then took another step. Then, with her bare feet, she felt water on the wood floor.

Laura opened the bedroom door and crept into the hall. Cautiously she made her way toward the light coming from the foyer, the light at the bottom of the stairs. She put her hand on the wall to steady herself, and her fingers trailed over the light yellow wallpaper, across its peach and blue flowers.

People stood on the stairs, their shadows stretching like dark giants across the walls. The shadows moved and talked, and they seemed angry with each other. Laura stopped at the top of the stairs and crouched, looking through the bars of the rail along the landing. Ruby stood on the stairs. She'd come in before the party and shown Laura her shiny pink gown. Laura thought Ruby looked like a princess. Her blond hair was piled on her head with ringlets falling around her face. She'd told Laura she had a secret to tell her later, something about a surprise at the party.

But something was wrong. Ruby had been crying. She was looking up the stairs, and she looked scared. Someone stood on the stairs above Ruby, someone in a big coat with a hood. Laura thought it might be a monster. Suddenly it rushed at Ruby, grabbing her arm. Ruby tried to pull away, but the monster pushed her, and she screamed. Ruby tumbled down the stairs, landing on the floor at the bottom of the staircase. Her head was twisted. Her eyes were open; she looked strange.

Laura screamed and jolted up in bed. It was Saturday morning, and the storm was over. She jumped out of bed and darted to the window, then pulled back the curtains, clinging to them. She gazed across the lawn and realized there had been no storm. It was another dry, autumn morning. The storm in her mind had happened twenty years ago.

She released the drapes and pressed her fingers against her temples. Was that a dream or was it a memory? She needed to call Megan, and she needed to get out of here as soon as possible. What would Megan say to her right now? Probably something like she'd said before: "Pull yourself together, Laura. You're a strong woman. It's time to put the fear behind you. It's time to move forward."

What fear? Laura thought. Then she sighed. Megan was right, and Laura knew it. She had to move forward, to stop hiding within herself. She had to determine what was holding her back, and then she had to face it.

Laura knelt beside her bed and prayed. Pouring her heart out to her Heavenly Father, she told Him she needed His help, that she couldn't do this without Him. She needed guidance—needed to know what to do. She was afraid to face her past, afraid to move on.

After Laura finished praying, she stayed on her knees for some time. As she listened quietly, a feeling of utter peace washed over her, and she knew that Heavenly Father loved her and would guide her. Now she could find out what had happened here at Buford's Bluff, find out what was behind her fear. The Lord would help her to find the courage to do what she needed to do, because He wanted her to be happy.

When Laura finally stood, she knew she didn't need Megan's advice. She would call her friend soon to update her about life in Virginia, but she didn't need to ask Megan for help anymore.

After showering and drying her hair, Laura strode through the corridor to the top of the stairs and looked at the foyer below. Her heart beat a little faster as she forced herself down the stairs, the stairs Ruby had fallen down. She lingered at the bottom of the staircase and looked at the floor. She might be standing on the spot where Ruby landed—at least in her dream. An unexpected tear ran down Laura's cheek. Brushing it away, she made her way to the kitchen.

"Did you have a good night's sleep?" Agnes asked, looking up from the stove as Laura entered the room. "I've made you a good breakfast. I hope you like waffles."

"Yes," Laura croaked, then cleared her throat and said more distinctly, "Yes, I do, thanks." Wondering why Agnes was in such a pleasant mood, Laura decided not to question it.

Laura sat down at the small kitchen table. Agnes placed a glass of orange juice in front of Laura. "Squeezed it myself this morning," she announced proudly.

"Thank you."

"Your aunt couldn't tolerate frozen juice. And waffles were one of her favorites."

"I suppose my aunt and I might have some things in common."

Agnes set a plate of waffles and a bowl of strawberries on the table. "The strawberries were frozen—they're out of season, you know. At first I thought you were quite different from your aunt, but the more I'm around you, the more I think you're very much like her."

Laura lifted a small pitcher server of warm syrup and poured some on her waffles, then bowed her head and said a silent blessing. When she looked up, she noticed Agnes staring at her. "That's one difference right there. You're aunt wasn't much of a churchgoer."

"You don't have to be a churchgoer to pray," Laura remarked.

Agnes paused. "No, I suppose not, but your aunt wasn't much for religion, period."

"What about you?" Laura asked then took a big bite of waffle.

Agnes smiled. "I go to church every Sunday. I get the weekend off, you know."

"I wondered about that," Laura commented. "So why are you working this morning?"

"I always fix breakfast on Saturday mornings, but you're on your own until lunch on Monday morning. Of course, there's plenty of food in the refrigerator and freezer, and it's marked by the meal. Just use the microwave to heat something up."

"Thank you," Laura said between bites. Then she asked, "Where will you be this weekend?"

"I spend every weekend with my sister Esther in Bufordville. Thankfully, I do have a life outside of this place."

Laura was glad to hear it. Agnes didn't seem to have much of a life at Buford's Bluff, and it seemed like a pretty lonely place.

"Do you know how to get to that Mormon church of yours in Lakeside?" Agnes questioned.

Laura took a swallow of juice. "No, I don't." She decided not to tell Agnes that Aaron was going to drive her.

"That's what I thought," Agnes retorted. "That's why I wrote down the address and drew a map for you over by the phone there."

"I really appreciate that." Laura realized too late that she sounded surprised.

"That's my job, isn't it—to take care of you?"

Laura stared at Agnes, wondering if she felt insecure about her job. Maybe Agnes wasn't such a mean old woman after all. Maybe they had just gotten off to a bad start, and maybe Laura had misjudged her. "I suppose it is," Laura admitted with a grin, then asked, "But how did you know I was LDS?"

"Mr. Ballister told me. I think he said something about coffee, too, but I forgot that first morning."

"I wonder how Roger knew. I've never mentioned it to him."

Agnes came closer. "Well now, you're not ashamed of it, are you?"

Laura looked up sharply. "No. I'm not ashamed of it."

"Well, good. A person should stand up for what they believe. They shouldn't go around hiding it."

"I don't hide it," Laura responded a bit too defensively.

"Oh, before I forget," Agnes said. "You had a phone call this morning from Julie Morgan, that silly—I mean, that young lady who owns the antique shop. She said it was urgent, but I told her I couldn't imagine what urgent matter she'd have to discuss with you. Then she made some impertinent remark. I'd watch her if I were you."

That's exactly what she said about you, Agnes, Laura thought.

"Her number is over by the phone. You'll also find other information there I thought might be useful while I'm away."

"Thank you, Agnes. If you don't mind my asking, how do you get to your sister's?"

"I have a car—I park it in the stables."

Somehow it'd never occurred to Laura that Agnes could drive.

II

When Agnes left, Laura finished her breakfast, then put the dishes in the dishwasher. She grabbed the phone and dialed Julie's number. When her friend answered, Laura said quickly, "Julie, this is Laura."

"Well, it's about time! Laura, this is no time to be dillydallying. We have a full-fledged murder mystery on our hands here."

Laura felt her heart begin to race. "Julie, calm down and explain what you're talking about."

"Listen, I'll read it to you right from the *Bufordville Bugle*. Are you sitting down for this?"

"Yep, go ahead," Laura answered, settling into the kitchen chair.

> *"Bufordville Bugle, Monday, September 10. Annual Harvest Moon Festival Ends in Tragedy.*
>
> *"The annual Harvest Moon Festival hosted by Laura Buford at Buford's Bluff ended in tragedy Friday night with the death of one of Miss Buford's servants.*
>
> *"Ruby Davis, 22, who worked as a nanny at the plantation house, fell down the central staircase to her death.*
>
> *"According to witnesses, Miss Davis attended the festival, which took place on the banks of the James River in front of the Bufords' manor house. When she heard an approaching storm, she excused herself, commenting to her brother—local attorney Leonard Davis—that Miss Buford's four-year-old niece, Laura McClain, was terrified of storms.*

"As lightning flashed, thunder boomed, and rain fell on the festivities, the hostess moved her guests to the banquet room located in her famous stables. When Miss Davis failed to return to the party, her fiancé, Edward Smith, went to the manor house. He found her lying at the bottom of the staircase.

"Smith immediately located Dr. Levi Preston, who was attending the party. Dr. Preston ran to the accident scene, where he declared Miss Davis dead from a broken neck.

"Sheriff Jackson Buford, a cousin of Miss Laura Buford, also attended the festival. He said Miss Davis had probably slipped on her way up the stairs to check on Miss McClain.

"According to other servants, Miss Davis had worked for the Buford family since young Laura McClain's birth. Miss Davis planned to quit her job just prior to her upcoming April wedding.

"After being informed of Miss Davis's death, Smith went into a rage. Sheriff Buford said Smith was 'understandably upset.' However, servants say that Smith accused the family of a cover-up and made threats, including threats against young Miss Laura McClain. An altercation between Smith and John McClain ensued, and Sheriff Buford escorted Smith off the premises."

Julie paused then asked, "Are you still there, Laura?"

"Yes," Laura replied, so breathless she could barely get the word out.

"Good. 'Cause I've got more."

"Bufordville Bugle, Monday, September 10. A Cursed Evening, by Marsha Prestwich, Social Columnist.

"The scene was magnificent. Bonfires lit up the river-banks. The fire reflected in the James River as did the beautiful Buford Manor house set back on the hill above the festivities.

"Farmers displayed their produce along the riverbanks, selling to visitors and trading with the other locals.

"*From all indications, it promised to be a pleasant evening. Local attorney Edward Smith announced his engagement to Ruby Davis, sister of prominent attorney Leonard Davis.*

"*Mr. Smith, a newcomer to Bufordville and a recent graduate of Washington and Lee Law School, is Mr. Davis's partner in the firm of Davis and Smith. Leonard Davis stood by the happy couple as they made the announcement.*

"*There were toasts all around for the new couple. Then I overheard the Buford maid, Agnes Hayes, talking about 'the curse.' Agnes is known locally for her superstitious beliefs. Apparently, she was upset that the annual Harvest Moon Festival was not being held on the actual night of the full moon, which was last night. The festival was held on Friday night, assumedly to accommodate partygoers and to allow for a later evening.*

"*First, two servers crashed into each other, spilling hot cocoa all over themselves. Then, a careless worker placed poison ivy-covered brush on one of the bonfires, so a guest standing nearby had to be taken to the bath and washed. Next, a sudden and unexpected thunderstorm pushed the party into the stables. The night's climax was Miss Davis's tragic death. With this turn of events, even those of us who are not superstitious can't help but wonder about Agnes's warning.*"

"*Bufordville Bugle, Tuesday, September 11. Edward Smith Found Dead.*

"*Edward Smith, a local attorney and partner of Leonard Davis, was found dead in his apartment Sunday morning.*

"*Police officer Buddy Baker said that a preliminary investigation indicated Smith might have died of asphyxiation. He indicated that there were no signs of struggle and no obvious foul play.*

"*Police director Joe Lewis said a gas leak from the stove apparently produced deadly fumes that caused the victim to suffocate.*

"Some neighbors have speculated that Smith committed suicide as a result of his fiancée's tragic death Friday night.

"After Ruby Davis's death late Friday, Smith reportedly went into a rage, making threats against the Buford family. Sheriff Buford escorted him off the property.

"Smith returned to the property early Saturday morning when the family was still sleeping. He placed a ladder against the manor's east side, attempting to enter the nursery window.

"The gardener, George Walker, saw Smith and ordered him to come down. Smith did so, and the two men argued.

"The household staff heard the commotion and went outside to investigate. At that point, Smith ran away into a nearby grove of trees. He was later picked up on the road between the plantation and Bufordville by Sheriff Buford, who had been summoned by the family.

"Smith was arrested and retained in the Bufordville County Jail until Saturday afternoon when his employer, Leonard Davis, posted bail.

"After he was released from jail, a family member took Smith to Dr. Levi Preston's home office to be treated for poison ivy. When Smith arrived at Dr. Preston's home, John McClain was already there, also being treated for poison ivy. According to Preston, the two men exchanged strong words and threats. Smith made threats against Laura McClain, John and Sarah McClain's four-year-old daughter.

"According to police department sources, Smith was angry with young Laura McClain because a toy was found on the steps of the mansion. Smith said the toy caused Davis to fall to her death. One police officer stated that Smith believed McClain saw Davis fall but failed to obtain assistance. Sources close to the family say young Laura is in shock and confined to her bed at this time.

"Preston separated McClain and Smith and told McClain to leave, then treated Smith. As Smith was

leaving, he informed Preston he was going home to his apartment to get some rest.

"No one saw Smith again until Sunday morning when Leonard Davis found him dead in his apartment from an apparent suicide. Davis turned the gas off and then called police.

"Workers from the gas company were called to the scene. They found no leak and indicated that someone had purposely turned the gas on.

"Bufordville police confirmed late yesterday that the death is being treated as a possible suicide. The police department would not comment on the possibility of foul play. However, on Sunday night, police questioned John McClain at Buford's Bluff. Sheriff Buford, who has jurisdiction over that area of the county, was also present. According to Dr. Preston, McClain had threatened Smith's life, but McClain denies any involvement in Smith's death.

"An inside source at the police department confirmed that Smith's door had been jimmied open and was unlocked when Davis found the body."

By the time Julie had finished reading the newspaper articles, Laura's muscles were so tight she thought they would explode. She had been virtually speechless with shock as Julie had read. Now the queasy feeling that had started in the pit of her stomach had risen until it lodged in her throat.

"Laura, are you still there?" Julie asked.

"I think so," Laura mumbled.

"Are you okay?"

"I'm not sure. I mean it's all happening so fast. It's like . . . like . . . I don't know."

"Like finding out who you are for the first time?" Julie offered melodramatically.

Maybe it will *be like coming home for the first time,* Laura thought ironically.

"Yes," Laura mused. "I think I'm gaining a little insight into why my parents were the way they were. Agnes was right—there was a curse there that night."

"Well, the reporter obviously didn't have all the facts, Laura. And maybe you're the only one who knows that Ruby was pushed down those stairs."

"Yeah, the only one except the person who pushed her." Laura sighed, then queried, "Julie, what did the paper say about a toy on the stairs?"

"It's hearsay, Laura, and even if it's true, the chances Ruby fell to her death because of a toy seem pretty remote to me."

"I had a dream about Ruby's death last night, Julie."

"A dream or a memory?"

"I'm not sure," Laura admitted, but even as she said it she knew it was more than a dream. Suddenly the terror came flooding back, and a chill started in her back and culminated in a shudder as Ruby's scream echoed in her head. Laura's eyes stung with tears, and she gulped, trying to focus on Julie's question.

"Tell me about it," Julie prodded.

Laura hesitated. If she put the dream into words, it would seem even more real. Yet she knew from the newspaper article that it was something that had in fact happened years ago. *Get on with it, Laura. Push through it.* With the memory of her mother silently urging her on, she described the dream to Julie, even the details like the wallpaper and the shadows. When she finished, she found herself standing, staring out the kitchen window across the fading lawn to the orange-speckled woods in the distance. A choking sob of fear, confusion, and frustration constricted her throat.

"Hold on a minute, Laura. I'm trying to write all this down."

Laura cleared her throat. "Why are you doing that?"

"Why? I'll tell you why. We have a murder investigation on our hands! Someone pushed Ruby Davis down those stairs. I have no doubt about it now." Julie spoke in a higher register now, and Laura realized her friend was serious about solving this mystery.

Laura wasn't so sure. She knew that dreams and memories could merge into a gray unknown. Perhaps her guilt over Ruby's death had caused her mind to assign the blame to some unknown form, the form under the hood. Maybe Laura herself was beneath the hood because the hood represented nothing more than her denial of the whole incident, her unwillingness to face reality.

Sighing, she began in a panicked tone, "Julie, what if my mind is creating the details? I read somewhere that the mind will do almost anything to protect itself from trauma. Maybe the hooded figure is my guilt and denial. Maybe it was really my fault that Ruby died!"

"Laura, do you really believe that? I doubt they even told you about the toy, if there was one on the stairs at all. You couldn't have felt guilty. The newspaper said you were in shock and confined to your bed. I'm sure you would have been upset to hear about Ruby, but to be shocked and confined to your bed would mean that you'd experienced something frightening. Seeing her fall would have been horrible, but I think you saw the person who killed Ruby, and your mind won't allow you to remember because it's too traumatic. You probably knew the person who killed Ruby, but you can't face the truth. Your mind placed a hood on the person so you wouldn't have to face the facts."

Though she wished it were otherwise, Laura felt deep in her heart that the dream was an actual memory. Someone had pushed Ruby down the stairs! The trauma had caused Laura to go into shock and suppress the memories, and with her return to Buford's Bluff, the memories were coming back. Of course, she'd had nightmares for years about someone falling down a staircase, but now vivid details were coming through.

Suddenly Laura thought of something. "Julie, what if I don't *want* to know who killed Ruby Davis? What if the truth is too much for me and sends me over the edge?"

"I thought of that, Laura, but don't you think that *not* knowing is more likely to send you over the edge? Think about how you panicked at the theater last night. It can't be healthy to have this secret stuck in your brain somewhere for twenty years."

Laura sighed. "So where do I go from here? I can't show up at the police station and report a twenty-year-old murder that I think I remember."

Julie laughed. "No, you can't. Besides, you might tip the murderer or murderers off."

Laura's heart jolted. Of course the murderer could still be alive. Staring harder at the orange-speckled woods outside the window, she wondered if someone was out there watching her. A chill passed through her, and she sat back down. "Julie, what do you mean murderers?"

"The person or persons who killed Ruby Davis and Edward Smith—our tragic lovers."

"The newspaper said Smith's death was an accident or suicide."

"Don't forget the jimmied door. Why the police overlooked that crucial piece of evidence is beyond me! The man was murdered—of that I have no doubt."

"They insinuated that my father had something to do with it, but maybe they eventually caught the person who really did it,"

"Not a chance, Laura. I went through several years of newspaper articles, and I carefully checked the indexes. Edward Smith wasn't mentioned in Bufordville papers again."

"That's odd."

"Very odd. You'd think social columnist Marsha Prestwich would have found a way to work him into her nosy little column, wouldn't you?"

"What does it all mean?" Laura wondered, then realized she'd spoken out loud.

"It means you and I are going to start conducting a quiet little investigation of our own, Laura. We have to somehow find out who was at the party that night. We already have a small beginning, thanks to our friend Marsha. Look, can we get together and talk in person?"

"Are you doing anything tonight?" Laura asked.

"You mean besides eating leftovers and talking to my cat?"

Laura smiled. "Good. Agnes is away for the weekend, so why don't you come over here for dinner tonight?"

"Great."

"How about six?"

"I'll be there."

12

Later that evening, Laura busied herself in the kitchen preparing dinner for Julie. It was easy, since Agnes had left enough food to feed an army. Laura heated a casserole and a couple of vegetable dishes and was setting the table when the doorbell rang.

"You're early," she said as she opened the door wide enough for Julie to enter, then locked the door after her.

Julie removed her sweater and threw it on the bench by the door. "I couldn't wait to see this place—it's got to be sensational!"

Laura smiled. "Come on, I'll show you around."

In the west wing hallway to the kitchen, Julie stopped to peruse a china hutch that was full of glassware. "Wonderful," Julie uttered, sounding almost awestruck.

Laura started for the kitchen, but Julie burst out, "Wait, what's in here?"

Across the hall from the hutch was a door Laura had never been through. "I think it's a pantry."

Julie opened the door and reached for the light switch. "Hey," she exclaimed when the light came on, "it's an office." Then she disappeared through the doorframe.

Laura stepped to the door and stuck her head into the spacious office, which smelled as if it had been closed up for a while. The computer and printer were obviously modern, but the oak desk could have been in the room for over a hundred years. Julie stood by the stone fireplace, gazing at several framed photographs that lined the adjacent walls. Laura walked over to get a closer look, noticing that some of the people wore Victorian clothing and that the faces looked a bit arrogant.

Above the marble fireplace mantel hung a painting of a young woman sitting on a swing in a garden. In the distance, behind the woman, lay a house that resembled Buford's Bluff. The woman's head was tilted, and she looked dazed and dreamy. Perhaps the woman was dreaming of her boyfriend or life somewhere away from that garden, a life outside the shadow of that big house.

Other than the photographs and the paintings, the walls were covered with tall shelves filled with books. Laura ran her hand along the book spines, noticing classics mixed in with gardening books.

Julie sat in the big leather chair behind the desk and scribbled something in a small notebook.

"What're you writing in that thing?" Laura asked.

"My impressions. It could help solve a crime."

"I don't think the crime happened in here, Julie."

Julie looked up. "No, but I'll bet it started in here, at the seat of power. This is obviously your aunt's office. I take it the maid didn't bother to show you this room."

"No," Laura admitted. "I thought it was a storeroom or something."

"Odd," Julie murmured and began opening desk drawers.

"Let's finish the tour and then eat before we start digging around," Laura suggested.

Julie stood. "Okay, but I'm so excited I don't know if I can eat anything."

Laura showed Julie the rest of the house, as well as the stables. Not surprisingly, Julie showed interest in the nursery and the staircase, or, as she called it, "the scene of the crime." She scribbled in her notebook as they toured.

Finally, they sat down to eat. "Do you mind if I bless the food?" Laura asked.

Julie shook her head. "No."

Laura said a quick prayer, then Julie began questioning her about the mystery right away.

"Do you remember anything else about the night of the Harvest Moon Festival?"

"I don't think I've thought of anything new since we last talked."

Julie looked disappointed. "Well, between your memories and the corroborating information in the newspaper, I think we might have enough to find out who murdered Ruby Davis."

Laura shivered uncontrollably. To Julie, this was a murder mystery like in the movies, or a game of Clue, perhaps. She was gathering pieces of evidence and would soon be ready to announce that Colonel Mustard did it in the foyer with a push down the stairs. But to Laura, it was real life—a life she'd forgotten existed until now.

"Where do we start, Detective Julie?" Laura asked with a forced smile.

"Well, I thought we should start with Friday, the night of the murder."

"Okay, and how do we do that?"

Julie paused, her brow furrowed. "Well, we already have a good start—we have some details from the newspapers. Now we need to get eyewitness accounts. Let's make a list of people who we know attended the festival and try to contact them as soon as possible."

Laura tried to remember the newspaper articles. "Well, let's see. There was Ruby Davis. But she's dead."

"Yes, we've determined that," Julie said dryly.

"You're serious about this, aren't you?" Laura chuckled.

Though the corners of her mouth turned up slightly, Julie threw a stern glance at Laura. "Yes, and you should be too. This is murder we're talking about!"

Laura straightened her face and cleared her throat in an exaggerated manner. "Okay, let me think. Leonard Davis was there—he's Ruby's brother."

"Yes, I know him," Julie stated. "He has an office on Birch Street."

Laura dropped her fork on her plate with a loud clang. "Oh, my goodness, I completely missed the connection. The offices of Leonard Davis and Associates . . . he's Aaron's boss!"

Julie leaned forward, her eyes wide. "Aaron?"

"You know, the good-looking lawyer I told you about."

Leaning back, Julie waved a hand. "Oh, yeah. This is good, you know. I mean, we have an inside connection to a potential witness. You can get your friend Aaron to set up a time for us to interview Leonard Davis."

"I can't do that."

"Of course you can," Julie urged, stirring her food unconsciously. "What are you scared of? Are you afraid you'll owe him a favor? It may not be such a bad thing, you know."

Laura picked up her fork and poked at her food. "Okay, let's get back to what we were talking about. We have one name so far."

"Okay," Julie said, reaching for her notebook. "There was that Hayes woman—your maid, I mean—and we both know her track record. I wouldn't put anything past a thief like her."

Laura sighed. "Julie, we really don't know that much about Agnes. Maybe she didn't steal the box. We can't judge her without more facts."

Waving her notebook in Laura's face, Julie declared, "I have all the facts I need! I looked into her eyes. You can tell everything about a person by looking into their eyes. And besides, I would never trust a woman over sixty who dyed her hair pitch black."

Laura rolled her eyes. "Write her name in that book of yours, and let's move on."

"Okay, okay."

"If you're going to suspect Agnes," Laura said, "it's only fair that you suspect all the other employees as well, and we have no idea how many there were."

"Is Agnes the only one left?" Julie asked.

"No. The gardener is still here."

"Aha!" Julie exclaimed. "That reminds me of that Don Knotts movie. What was it called?" She began tapping her head with the notebook. "Oh, yeah—*The Ghost and Mr. Chicken*. You remember—the gardener murdered a woman with some pruning shears."

Laura sighed. "Yes, I do remember, but it wasn't the gardener."

"Sure it was," Julie insisted. "I remember the old woman was killed with garden shears."

"Yes, but the gardener was set up. He didn't do it."

Julie frowned. "Really?"

"Yeah. Anyway, our gardener's name is George Walker," Laura indicated, biting her lip. "I guess you'd better write his name in the book with Agnes's. We'll try to compile a list of domestic help and get their stories."

Julie wrote in her notebook, then looked up. "Okay, who else?"

"Well, there's the doctor who examined the body," Laura ventured.

"Dr. Preston," Julie interjected, writing as she spoke. "He's still around, and he runs his office from home. The man must be pushing eighty."

"Do people still go to this Dr. Preston?"

"Oh, yeah. Most folks in Bufordville hate change. Some people have been going to Dr. Preston since the day they were born."

"Well, now we're up to three people who were there that night," Laura said. "Oh, there was the sheriff, Aunt Laura's cousin."

"Yeah, Jackson Buford. I'd never heard of him until I read those newspaper articles. I wonder if he's still living. I'll make a note to check the obituaries at the library."

"And don't forget the fiancé as a suspect, even though we can't question him," Laura said.

"Yes, of course." Julie scribbled in her book once more. "Perhaps Smith and Ruby had a lovers' quarrel, and maybe he threw her down the stairs in a jealous rage. It does happen, and apparently he was acting a little over-the-top after he found Ruby at the bottom of the stairs. It could have been his way of covering up his involvement in her death."

Laura wiped the corners of her mouth with her napkin. "Trying to keep track of all of the potential suspects seems almost impossible. There's my Aunt Laura, my father, and my mother, but they're all dead. If the killer is dead, we may never know who pushed Ruby down the stairs."

"True. But maybe he—or she—is still alive and living right here among us," Julie retorted.

After finishing dinner, they cleared the table, and "retired to the study," as Julie put it. Laura pulled at the top desk drawer. "Locked."

"I'll bet Hayes has the key," Julie muttered with a frown, pulling open one of the side drawers and riffling through some papers. "This place looks sanitized to me."

"What do you mean?" Laura asked.

Julie looked up at Laura incredulously. "Don't you watch spy movies? When the government censors its top-secret documents or covers evidence, they call it sanitizing. Someone has gone over this room with a fine-tooth comb, and they've taken all the important stuff. We're not going to find anything here."

Laura moved to the bookshelves and scanned the titles—Melville, Hawthorne, Dickens. "So how do you know what's important?"

Julie shrugged. "You just know, I guess."

Laura ran her hands across the book spines. "In a library, if you find an empty space you can assume a book that was once there has been removed, but the holes aren't so obvious with desk papers. I mean, a careful person wouldn't leave incriminating evidence around."

Julie stood and walked to the bookshelf. "Criminals aren't perfect, though. Most of them make mistakes."

Laura pulled out a copy of the collected works of Edgar Allen Poe. "We're talking as if my aunt had something to hide, but there's no evidence for that. It seems to me she is the most unlikely suspect. After all, it was her party—she was the hostess. People would have been seeking her out. It's not likely she'd leave the party, go inside, push her niece's nanny down the stairs, and return to the party. Her absence would've been noticed."

Julie pulled out a leather-bound copy of *War and Peace*. Do you think your aunt actually read this stuff, or did she put it here for show? This copy doesn't look like it's ever been read."

"I don't know," Laura replied, replacing the Poe book. "I really didn't know her."

Julie pushed *War and Peace* back into its spot. "That's the problem—we know next to nothing about these people. We especially need to know about Ruby Davis, and she's gone."

Laura sat in the huge leather chair. Of course, Julie was right. Someone had wanted Ruby dead, and if they could figure out why, they could find the killer.

"Julie, what if Ruby stumbled on a burglar or saw something she shouldn't have? Something so happenstance would be impossible to unravel, even if we knew all about Ruby."

"I suppose it's a possibility," Julie admitted. "But even if she stumbled upon a burglar, she probably recognized him or her—otherwise, why kill her?"

"Good point, but stranger things have happened."

"Laura, we need to know who would have had a motive to kill Ruby. It was probably someone within her intimate circle—it usually is."

"I don't know much about the lives of domestic servants, but I don't think they're on intimate terms with their employers. My father or mother wouldn't have pushed Ruby down the stairs, because they probably didn't know her well enough to want her dead. Besides that, I know that neither of them would ever do such a thing."

Julie remained silent.

"What?" Laura asked.

"Nothing," Julie replied. "Just thinking, that's all."

Laura frowned and crossed her arms. "You're quiet, and coming from you that's a very loud response."

Julie shrugged. "Well, it's natural you want to assume your parents are innocent, but I think we need to try to be as objective as possible if we're going to get anywhere. I mean, for all we know, your father was having an affair with your nanny, and your mother found out and threw her down the stairs. Or Ruby threatened to tell your mother, and your father threw Ruby down the stairs. That would explain your trauma."

"I guarantee you that my father wouldn't have had an affair," Laura sighed, shaking her head irritably.

Julie sat on the edge of the desk. "Well, right now you have no reason to suspect your father since we have little or no evidence to go on, but I hope you're willing to keep your mind open and not get offended over all of my speculations."

Laura frowned again. "I'll try not to, but you're asking a lot."

"We'll have to take your natural bias into consideration as we analyze the evidence." Julie stood and wandered across the room to another bookcase, then ran her hands along the spines. "That's odd."

"What?" Laura walked to her side.

Julie pulled a book from the shelf. "This book." She turned it on its side and opened it. "It's hollow—one of those fake books for hiding things." Julie pulled out a plain leather key ring with a single key on it. "This is getting good," she said, then walked over to the desk and tried the key in the top drawer. "Not it."

"Too bad," Laura said with a pout.

Julie looked around the room, and Laura followed her eyes. In the far corner was a built-in cabinet with heavy oak doors. Julie walked over and put the key into the cabinet lock. The door sprung open. "Bingo!"

Laura rushed to her side. On the middle shelf was a series of daybooks with dates labeled on the spines. Reaching in, Laura grabbed one and opened it. "It's a diary," she concluded after a few moments. "Aunt Laura must have used these day calendars to keep track of what she did each day."

Laura scrutinized the book. Aunt Laura was not much of a detail person. Each day contained a sentence or two describing the day's events: "*July 5, I walked along the river today. George has the banks looking beautiful with moss roses and marigolds. July 6, Went to the market. July 7, My dear friend Gloria stopped by for a visit. July 8, Met with Roger on important business matters. Took a walk.*"

Julie selected a volume and began browsing its contents while Laura pulled out several day calendars until she found the year of Ruby's death. She leafed through the book until she came to September 10. *The annual Harvest Moon Festival ended poorly today with the death of Ruby Davis. Little Laurie must have seen something, because she is in shock and confined to her bed. We are all worried about her. I told Roger I would talk with Laurie tomorrow to determine exactly what she saw.*

Laura's heart leapt in her chest as she read the words. Until now the mystery had felt somewhat surreal, having little to do with her reality, but now . . . She turned the page back to September 9. "*Roger Ballister came by for our monthly meeting. We talked about the Ruby Davis problem. He said he would take care of Ruby tomorrow night at the festival.*"

Julie read over Laura's shoulder. "Oh, my, Laura. Do you know what this sounds like? A plan to do away with Ruby!"

"I can't believe it," Laura interjected. "Roger seems like a decent man, for a lawyer at least. And I can't believe Aunt Laura is in any way involved in Ruby's death."

"But you don't even know your aunt."

"I still can't believe it. It's too easy, and besides that, she wouldn't leave something incriminating lying around for anyone to read."

"Well, Laura," Julie remarked, "she didn't exactly leave it lying around. It was in a locked cabinet, after all."

Laura looked through the daybook, going back several months before Ruby's death. But she found nothing except pithy sentences about day-to-day affairs on the plantation. "She doesn't say anything else about Ruby Davis, as far as I can tell. Why didn't she give more details?"

"It looks like she wrote this book for herself. She recorded daily events in case she needed to review something for herself. She penned a few notes to remind her of incidents. I doubt she was trying to provide details for curious nieces." Julie winked at her.

Laura rolled her eyes. "Well, armchair detective, where do you suggest we go from here?"

"The witnesses," Julie responded excitedly. "We've heard from the dead. Now let's concentrate on the living."

13

On Sunday morning, Laura was waiting inside by the back door when Aaron rang the doorbell. She waited a few seconds and opened the door. He greeted her with a big smile, and her heart flip-flopped.

"I appreciate this," Laura said as they walked to Aaron's sporty red car. "I'm a little nervous—a new ward and everything."

Aaron opened the passenger door for her and replied, "Well, I don't think you have anything to be nervous about. The people in Lakeside are friendly. They're always happy to welcome new members."

While Aaron made his way around the car and hopped in, Laura buckled her seat belt. He cleared his throat. "I hope you enjoy the drive. It's beautiful this time of year with the leaves changing."

Laura glanced over at him and was struck yet again by just how handsome he was. *Megan would die if she could see me now,* Laura thought.

As they pulled around the circular driveway, Aaron asked, "So I hear you're from St. Louis?"

"Yes," Laura croaked, her throat suddenly dry.

"Was your father's family from that area?"

"No, he was from Virginia. He and my mother moved to St. Louis when he got a promotion—he was an insurance agent."

"A salesman?"

"Yes," Laura answered.

"My father worked for a coal mine," Aaron revealed, glancing over at her.

"That must have been dangerous."

"Not really," Aaron responded. "He wasn't a coal miner—he was a maintenance man. He didn't get paid as well as the miners. In fact, his salary barely fed our family, but he took pride in his work. He felt that coal production was important to society."

Aaron looked over at Laura again, and she smiled. "Well, he's right. In many ways, coal is vital to the American economy."

"That sounds like something my father would say," Aaron said with a chuckle.

"Where do your parents live?" Laura inquired.

"Well, my dad died a few years ago—his heart finally gave out on him. My mother still lives in the same town I grew up in. It's a little place in southwestern Virginia you've never even heard of."

"I'm so sorry about your father. My father died of a heart attack too."

"Well, I guess that's one thing we have in common," Aaron said with a sigh.

"Sadly, yes," Laura agreed. "I just wish I'd had a chance to get to know my dad better. I was only seven when he died."

"Oh, that's rough," Aaron sympathized, gripping the wheel tighter as he rounded a curve in the road. "What about your mother? Is she still in Missouri?"

"She died last year."

"I'm sorry to hear that. Do you have any brothers and sisters?" he queried.

"No," Laura replied. "I guess I'm all alone in the world."

"Oh." This was followed by silence. Laura stared out the window. "What did you do back in St. Louis?"

"I taught kindergarten."

"You're a teacher?" He sounded pleasantly surprised.

"I was," she corrected.

"Retired?"

She smiled. "Something like that."

"I guess you're a plantation owner now." Aaron laughed. "Oh, by the way, I compiled an attorney list for you. Roger Ballister is probably the best estate lawyer around, but I'm assuming since he represented your aunt you'll want someone different to represent you."

"Yes," Laura said, "but let's not talk about that today."

"I'm sorry," he said, sounding a bit perplexed.

"Oh, no," she stammered. "I didn't mean—I mean I appreciate the information. I just don't want to discuss business on the Sabbath, you know?" Laura blushed, hoping she didn't sound holier-than-thou. Scrambling to redirect the conversation, she added, "And I was just wondering what your father thought about your becoming a lawyer." It sounded lame to her ears, but it just came out.

"Oh, Dad was pretty proud when I got into law school," he admitted. "In fact, it was his idea to have an attorney in the family. It all started years ago with a dispute over Dad's property line. He couldn't afford an attorney and didn't understand the laws, so he lost. Didn't take him long to decide we needed a lawyer in the family."

"And you were the chosen one?"

"I was the only one who had any interest in it. My brother Jacob went into business, and Joseph is a teacher in Pennsylvania."

"Did you go to BYU?"

"No. I got a scholarship to the University of Virginia, and Leonard paid my way through law school at Washington and Lee."

"Is Leonard Davis a relative or something?"

"No. He's just a benefactor to poor law students."

"I would like to meet Mr. Davis. I've heard a lot about him."

Taking his eyes from the road, Aaron glanced at Laura. "Like what?"

"Oh, my friend Julie mentioned him, and I've come across his name in some reading I've been doing." She thought of the mysterious words in her aunt's diary: *He said he would take care of Ruby tomorrow night at the festival.* Before leaving for church, Laura had vowed to avoid talking or thinking about Ruby today, but Aaron's mentioning Leonard Davis's name brought out the detective in her.

"He's well known around these parts as a brilliant attorney," Aaron explained. "He's extremely devoted to his job."

"Is he married?" Laura asked.

Aaron chuckled. "Yes, I guess you could say that. Leonard's married to his work. I can't imagine any woman living with him. He's got a one-track mind—the law is his life. I don't think any woman could meet his standards."

"It sounds like he might be hard to work for."

"Yeah, he's sometimes hard to please."

"Does he have any family around here?"

Aaron looked thoughtful. "I don't think so. He lives alone in a big house on Elmwood Lane, and he hasn't mentioned anyone. But then again, he keeps his private life to himself." Looking over at Laura with a slightly furrowed brow, Aaron asked, "Why the interest in Leonard Davis?"

Laura gazed out her passenger-side window at the thick pine forests blotched with red and orange maples, then looked back at Aaron. He seemed at ease and confident in himself without being arrogant. As he glanced at her and smiled, she decided the dimple in his chin made him look slightly boyish. He was waiting for a reply. She wanted to tell him Ruby's tragic story, but first she needed to find out if she could trust him.

"I'm just trying to learn more about a prominent member of my new community," Laura finally said, then realized that her words sounded contrived.

Timing seemed to be on Laura's side, as just then Aaron pulled the car into the church parking lot. Laura quickly unbuckled her seat belt and climbed out without waiting for Aaron to get her door. The building where the Lakeside Ward met was an older brick model in a modified colonial style. The members welcomed Laura with open arms, just as Aaron had predicted. When they entered the foyer, several people greeted them and asked Laura where she was from, then inquired about her life in St. Louis and her plans in Bufordville. She found it wasn't as difficult to meet new people with Aaron by her side.

Aaron sat with Laura in sacrament meeting and Sunday school, then escorted her to Relief Society and hurried off to priesthood meeting. Laura didn't have a chance to feel out of place, though, as several women immediately welcomed her into the fold. In fact, the sister who sat beside her in Relief Society kept explaining things to her like she was an investigator. Finding the attempt sweet, Laura just smiled and nodded.

After the closing prayer, a plain, freckled, middle-aged woman approached Laura. "Mama wants to talk to you," the woman murmured shyly, pointing to an elderly woman crumpled in a wheelchair in the corner of the room.

A bit surprised, Laura maneuvered through the crowd of exiting sisters and extended her hand to the old woman. "How do you do? I'm Laura McClain."

"Sit," the woman demanded in a hoarse whisper.

Laura sat next to the wheelchair, and the woman took Laura's fingers into her cold, dry hand. "So our little Laurie has come back home."

"Do I know you?" Laura asked.

"No," the woman responded with a croaky chuckle, "but I know you."

Laura felt a flutter in her chest. "How do you know me?"

"A long time ago, when you were a youngster, I worked for your Aunt Laura at Buford's Bluff. Gertrude Lawrence is my name."

"Did you know my parents?"

"Oh, yes. They were fine people. It was a real shame—all that fuss that caused them to leave."

"You mean all that fuss with Edward Smith and Ruby Davis?"

"Yes. I never believed your daddy had anything to do with that man's death."

"I can't believe it either." Laura was gratified to meet someone who had known her parents and who had trusted her father. "Were you there that night—the night that Ruby died?"

"Yes, I was there. I worked the buffet in the stable reception hall. At first we served the food there. People went through the line, got what they wanted, and went back outside to mingle on the lawn. Everything looked beautiful that night. Chairs and tables covered the lawn, and the whole west lawn was lit with lanterns. But an unexpected storm came up. For autumn, it was a strange storm, with a lot of thunder and lightning. Miss Buford had the guests crowd into the reception hall and even into the stables themselves. Of course, a lot of people ran to their cars and went home. Miss Buford was disappointed, since the party was just getting started. Your aunt loved a good party."

"How did the guests react when they found out about Ruby's fall?" Laura asked.

Gertrude cleared her throat. "No one found out that night, because the Bufords kept the whole thing quiet until the guests left. Of course,

Miss Buford told the sheriff and Doc Preston, but most of the staff didn't find out until after the guests were gone. I still remember it. We were all in the reception hall cleaning when one of the fellas yelled, 'A hearse is here!' Then the big, black car from Riley's Mortuary came up the drive and parked in front of the back door. They carried the body out covered in a blanket. That was a sad night." The elderly woman slowly shook her head.

"Gertrude, what can you tell me about Ruby? What was she like?"

"Oh, she was a real beauty. All the boys on the staff chased after that one. Of course her brother would have none of it—he despised the fact that his sister worked for the Bufords. He resented the Bufords because they had things he didn't, and he was embarrassed Ruby worked as their nanny. She liked having her own job and making her own money. But her brother raised her, you know."

"No, I didn't know."

"Oh, yes. Ruby was a lot younger than Leonard, and their parents died in a car accident when Ruby was young. It was left up to Leonard, who was much older, to raise her, and he was strict with her. When she was a teenager, Leonard hardly ever allowed her to leave their house on Elmwood Lane. Leonard forbade her to date or attend socials. It surprised no one when she went a little wild after she graduated from high school. All kinds of stories about her circulated, but most were gossip. She was a good girl who just liked to have fun. They say she always talked about traveling—she used to read about Paris and Rome. She'd plan trips and tell people about how she was saving up to travel the world."

"She didn't have any enemies, did she?" Laura queried, now feeling almost like a journalist or detective conducting a full-fledged interview.

"Well, now, that's an odd question," Gertrude replied, looking askance at Laura.

"I'm just thinking that with someone so pretty and fun, everyone would like her."

"Not everyone," Gertrude responded. "Agnes didn't care for her."

"Agnes?"

"Agnes Hayes. She used to work there."

Laura wanted to correct the woman, to tell her Agnes still worked at Buford's Bluff, but she stopped herself.

Gertrude continued. "Everyone at Buford's Bluff knew Agnes's secret. Well, I guess I should say everyone on the staff. I don't think the family knew."

"What secret?" Laura asked, lowering her voice.

"Well, like I said, it wasn't a secret because everyone knew."

"Knew what?"

"My dear, Agnes Hayes was a sick woman. She couldn't help herself, poor thing. She had what we called the itch."

"The itch?"

"Yes, a compulsion to take things. Not necessarily expensive things, mind you. Sometimes just insignificant little things."

"You mean kleptomania?"

"Yes. Agnes Hayes was a kleptomaniac."

"Do you think she stole things to sell them and make money?" Laura asked, remembering the music box.

"No, I don't think so. Of course, she may have done that too. But this was more an obsession with taking small things—things that might not be noticed."

"So what does this have to do with Ruby Davis?" Laura asked kindly.

"Well, I'm getting to that. Like I said, everyone knew about Agnes. That is, everyone on the cooking and cleaning staff. Ruby was different. She spent her time with little Laurie—I mean you, of course. She was apart from the other servants, if you know what I mean. She was closer to the Buford family. But on the festival day, Ruby helped set up. The Bufords needed every hand possible on festival day.

"While working in the kitchen that day, Ruby saw Agnes slip a silver spoon into her apron pocket. For years, we had all kept our mouths shut, but Ruby Davis immediately confronted Agnes about stealing. Of course, Ruby may have been looking for trouble—she and Agnes never got along. They had a bit of a personality conflict. You should have seen the shock on Agnes's face! She was as white as a ghost, and I thought she was going to drop over dead."

"What happened?"

"Well, Agnes denied the whole thing. In fact, she remained composed and even acted insulted. She left Ruby in the kitchen and went out to the reception hall, where she stayed for the rest of the

day. Of course, we could all see the spoon's outline in her pocket as
she left. Ruby was on to her. Ruby was a bright girl, and she told
Agnes she was going to talk to Miss Buford about the matter after the
party."

"Did she?"

"No. She couldn't, because she was dead."

"Oh, yes. Of course."

Gertrude's daughter stepped forward. "We should go, Mama."

"Oh, all right, Louise. I suppose we've taken enough of this young
lady's time."

Louise grasped the wheelchair handles and turned the chair
around. Then Gertrude put her withered hand on the wheel to stop
the chair. "One more thing, young lady."

Laura leaned close to her. "Yes?"

"Ruby Davis loved you like you were her little sister. You two
were always together. She'd be pleased to know you've come home."

* * *

As they started the drive home, Aaron tried to carry on a conversation, but Laura just stared out the side window. He finally asked her if
something was wrong, so she told him she was just pondering some
things she had learned in Relief Society. This apparently satisfied him,
since he drove the rest of the way in silence. When they reached the
mansion and pulled up near the back door, he jumped out and rushed
around the car, but Laura opened her door before he could. "Thanks
for the ride, Aaron," she offered with a small smile as she climbed out.
"You were right—everyone was friendly." Then she turned and hurried
up the stairs and into the house.

14

The aroma of food reached Laura as soon as she entered the back door. She scurried down the hall and into the kitchen. "Agnes, you're back."

"Yes. I hope you don't mind. Esther's grandchildren were coming for a visit today, and I had a bit of a headache."

Laura looked at the dishes of food, including hot buttered rolls and a Jell-O salad. Her mouth watered, and her stomach rumbled. "You didn't need to cook anything—the refrigerator is still full. But this looks so good!"

"Sunday dinners at Buford's Bluff were always special," Agnes declared, smoothing her apron. "Miss Buford wanted it that way."

"I see," Laura said, wondering how that was the case when Agnes had Sundays off. Then she realized the woman must have been referring to earlier days, when the staff included a whole slew of kitchen help. "Well, can I help you with anything?"

Agnes held her hand up. "Oh, no. I have things under control. Make yourself comfortable in the dining room, and I'll serve you in a moment."

Laura placed her scriptures on the buffet in the dining room and sat at the head of the table, where Agnes had set one place. A few minutes later, Agnes entered the room with a full serving tray.

"Aren't you going to eat with me?" Laura asked. As soon as she'd spoken the words, she realized she must be in a serious mystery-solving mood. Agnes stuck her nose in the air. "Oh, no. I always eat in the kitchen."

"Why don't you make an exception today? I would enjoy the company."

Agnes stared at her suspiciously, then replied, "Well, if you insist." The older woman left the room and returned a moment later with another place setting. Then she finished placing the food on the table and sat in the seat next to Laura.

"I'll say the blessing," Laura said with a smile.

"Thank you," Agnes responded with an unreadable expression.

Bowing her head and closing her eyes, Laura asked a blessing on the food and gave thanks for Agnes's presence as well as her careful preparation. When Laura looked up, Agnes was beaming like a child who had just been praised. Agnes and Laura filled their plates with food, then ate in silence for a few minutes.

Laura wanted to get as much information as possible from Agnes, but she knew she had to broach the subject cautiously so as not to give away her own motives. "Agnes, how long have you worked at Buford's Bluff?"

Agnes finished chewing and swallowed. "I've been here for over thirty years." She sighed mournfully.

"I'll bet you've seen a lot of history."

Agnes took great care to wipe both corners of her mouth. "Oh, my, yes. I've served some important guests here at Buford's Bluff. The governor came here for dinner one year."

Impressed, Laura raised her eyebrows. "Really?"

"Oh, yes," Agnes answered, waving a hand at Laura. Then, leaning in as if giving away a secret, she added, "And there have been senators, too."

Hoping she had sufficiently broken the ice, Laura braced herself to spring the surprise. "Agnes, I must tell you something."

"Yes."

Laura cleared her throat. "Um, since arriving here at Buford's Bluff, I've been recalling memories. My parents told me I was born and raised in St. Louis, but I know I used to live here."

Agnes had started to take a bite, but instead placed her fork on the plate, took her napkin, and wiped her mouth. "Yes, I thought as much."

"You did?"

Agnes placed her napkin back in her lap. "I suspected you were remembering when you mentioned the wallpaper in the upstairs hallway. And I was quite sure you were remembering when you chose to stay in the nursery. George also mentioned that you recalled the old stairs on the east terrace."

"Why didn't you say anything? And why didn't my parents tell me that I lived here?"

Agnes gulped from her water glass and wiped her mouth again. "Mr. Ballister instructed George and me to say nothing to you about your former life here at Buford's Bluff. He said your mother had told your aunt years ago that you remembered nothing about Virginia. Your mother wished you to forget . . . all about it."

"You mean Ruby Davis's death?"

Agnes's jaws tightened and her forehead creased. "You know about Ruby?"

"Yes. I don't really remember everything, but I've been reading about her in old newspapers."

"You must understand, Laura," Agnes implored, "that we had your best interests in mind. You were so small and so fragile. The whole incident shocked you horribly. We didn't want to bring up anything to remind you of that awful night." She clicked her tongue and shook her head.

Laura leaned forward in her chair. "But I want to know all about that night—I'm having nightmares about that night. Actually, I have been for years—though I didn't recognize what they were until yesterday. I think the only way to make them go away is to know what really happened." Observing the startled look in Agnes's eyes, Laura forced herself to breathe more slowly and tried to make her own face calm.

"Where would you like me to begin?" Agnes asked resignedly.

Laura sighed in relief. "Let's start with the last time you saw Ruby that night."

"Well, I served the guests in the reception hall until I heard the thunder," Agnes recited as if she'd told the story a million times. "I knew it was going to be a bad storm. I warned Miss Buford, but she insisted on having the festival on Friday night."

"Why?" Laura asked. "If they forecasted rain, why would she choose to have the festival?"

"Because they forecasted cloudy skies with only a low chance of rain. No one expected rain because no one followed the *Almanac*."

"The *Almanac*?"

"Yes, the *Gardener's Almanac*," Agnes responded. "It made it clear that it would not only rain, but that it would be a banner storm. The rest of the staff laughed at me when I told them."

"So you expected the storm?"

"Yes."

"And that's why you wanted to change the festival date?"

Agnes frowned. "Well, not entirely. The old Bufords—your grand-parents and great-grandparents—they always had the festival on the night of the harvest moon, which is the full moon closest to the equinox. That was the whole purpose—to celebrate the bounteous harvest under the harvest moon. The full moon would be on a Sunday that year, but Miss Buford wanted to have the festival on Friday. Changing the date was bad luck. They didn't believe me, but look at what happened. I was right, and they couldn't deny that after the fact."

"You mean you believe the change in dates caused Ruby's death?"

Agnes shrugged. "All I'm saying is it's bad luck to go against tradi-tion. We don't understand all the reasons why things are done the way they're done, but it's downright foolish to change time-honored cere-monies. Bad luck follows that kind of thing, and that's what happened that night."

Laura pushed her plate forward and put her elbows on the table. "So what happened?"

Agnes frowned, glaring at Laura's elbows. "Well, first Bobby Briggs and Marshall Jones collided right into each other carrying trays of hot chocolate. Some food servers had to clean the floor while George took Bobby and Marshall to his cottage to change. That seemed appropriate since the bathrooms in the reception hall were being used by the guests. We all wore black-and-white uniforms, and thankfully there were extra ones on hand in the reception-hall kitchen."

"Well, that was a simple accident," Laura remarked. "Things like that happen all the time."

Agnes nodded. "Yes, that's what everyone claimed when I told them, but when you take everything together, it's different. Anyway, the thunder and lightning started soon after that, so we directed the guests into the stables. The area became a bit crowded, and some of the guests left."

"And that's when Ruby left the party, right?"

Agnes glared at Laura in amazement. "You already seem to know a lot about that night."

Laura considered telling Agnes about her conversation with Gertrude but decided against it. "Like I said, I've read about it in the old *Bufordville Bugle.*"

"Well," Agnes continued, "the storm started around eight o'clock. I know the time because we were supposed to have the drinks ready at eight o'clock so Miss Buford could give a toast. The storm, however, turned our plans upside down. Anyway, I remember I saw Ruby walking toward the house, and that's the last time I saw her. It was just as the rain started."

"And you're sure that's the last time you saw her?"

"Yes."

"If you were in the reception hall serving guests, how did you see Ruby walking toward the house?"

Agnes's mouth fell open, but she closed it quickly. After a long silence, she finally replied, "Well, that's a good question." She nodded her head toward Laura. "You're quite observant."

"I taught kindergarten. They paid me to be observant," Laura returned with a grin.

Agnes frowned, apparently not seeing the humor in Laura's comment. "Well, I had remembered that earlier in the day, when I'd worked in the kitchen, I'd left a window open. When I heard the thunder, I decided I'd better go check to make sure it was closed. As I walked to the back door, I saw Ruby walking toward the front of the house."

"Did you think it odd that Ruby had left the party?"

"Oh, no, not at all," Agnes answered, shaking her head briskly. "I assumed she was checking on you. The whole staff knew thunderstorms scared you to death. You used to scream and say, 'The sky is yelling at me!' I don't want to speak ill of the dead—it's bad luck—but Ruby spoiled you terribly. If you had a bad dream, she'd sleep in the nursery with you."

"So you were in the house when Ruby fell down the stairs?"

Agnes paused, and her eyes narrowed suspiciously. "I suppose I could have been."

"Didn't you hear anything?"

Biting her lip in concentration, Agnes hesitated. "No," she finally answered. "The kitchen is in the west wing. Ruby fell from the stairs in the front foyer. A tumble down the stairs would hardly be loud enough to hear from the back."

Laura remembered her dreams. Ruby's death involved more than a "tumble." In Laura's dream, Ruby struggled with the mysterious hooded figure, and loud voices echoed through the foyer. "So you're sure you didn't hear anything?"

"Positive," Agnes insisted, pointing her nose higher.

"If there had been voices—a scream for example—would you have heard that from the kitchen?"

"It's likely, yes. But like I said, I heard nothing."

"Was the window open?" Laura asked.

"Window?"

"The open window you were checking on. You know—your reason for going in the house."

Agnes looked like she'd been caught in a lie. "Oh, yes, it was open. I closed it. Good thing I checked."

"What did you do next?"

"I went back to the reception hall."

"When did you find out about Ruby's fall?"

"After the guests left, Mr. Ballister told the staff about Ruby, on Miss Buford's behalf. We were all in a great shock."

"Did Mr. Ballister say how Ruby fell?"

Agnes's brow furrowed. "Well, I'm not sure I remember that."

Laura's eyes widened. "How could you not remember that?"

Agnes squared her jaw, lifted her nose, and sighed disapprovingly. "Very well, if you insist. Mr. Ballister said Miss Davis had tripped on one of your toys as she walked up the stairs to check on you. Ruby had told you repeatedly to remove your toys from the stairs, but, like I said, she did spoil you."

Blood rushed to Laura's face, and she clenched her fists. "Agnes, where did you get the music box you sold in the antique shop in Bufordville?"

Agnes sighed, then muttered, "I wondered when you'd get around to that." Then speaking more clearly, she said, "If I tell you, it might spoil the game you're playing."

"Game?"

"The game of trying to find out whom the box belonged to," Agnes answered smugly.

Laura's nails cut into her palms as she tightened her fists. "I'm not playing games anymore, Agnes."

"I guess I can see that," Agnes replied darkly. A tense silence filled the room, finally broken by Agnes. "The music box belonged to you—Ruby gave it to you as a birthday gift. She used it to put you to sleep at night. A couple weeks ago, Mr. Ballister instructed us to remove anything that might remind you of Ruby Davis, so I did. We were trying to protect you."

"From what?"

Agnes pushed her plate away and threw her napkin on it. "From your past." She sounded upset now. "They found you that night huddled on the closet floor. You were shivering, your teeth were chattering. You refused to speak, and you were in shock. We assume you heard Ruby fall, and when you ran out to the landing, you saw her at the bottom of the stairs, her neck twisted and broken. For months, you were silent and unexpressive." Agnes's eyes grew misty, and she sniffled loudly.

Laura closed her eyes but couldn't stop the scene from replaying in her mind. There was Ruby again, crashing down the stairs, over and over. "I'm not feeling very well right now, Agnes. If you'll excuse me, I think I'd better lie down." Laura stood and rushed out of the dining room.

When she got to her room, Laura curled up on the bed, her mind racing. Finally able to slow her thoughts a bit, she came to the conclusion that she related Ruby's death to loss—all the loss she'd ever suffered. Everyone Laura had loved had left her alone, and she couldn't stand the pain of loss again. That was probably one of the reasons she was afraid to get close to people—why she was something of a loner. But could the loss of a loved one be any more painful than a life of self-imposed loneliness?

Of course she'd loved Ruby. That was obvious from the painful muteness that had followed Ruby's death. Laura had certainly regained her speech, but she'd never regained her security. Love scared her. In her mind, love had entwined itself with death and pain. Perhaps a portion of the fear, anger, and guilt she had felt at her mother's and father's deaths was somehow related to Ruby's death. So maybe she could resolve these feelings by solving Ruby's death! Agnes said that Ruby had tripped on a toy, yet in her dreams—her memories—Laura could see someone pushing her nanny down the stairs.

Laura got off the bed and moved to the window. The trees looked peaceful, and George's cottage sat snugly among the changing leaves. It looked so much more tranquil than the mansion, where mystery and memories seemed to lurk around every corner.

15

Laura knocked on the door of the cottage and waited. Finally, George cracked the door, but when he saw Laura, he opened it wide and smiled. "Miss Laura, what can I do for you?"

Returning the smile, Laura replied, "I thought I would drop by for a Sunday afternoon visit. I hope you don't mind."

"Not at all. I could use the company—it gets pretty lonely here. Come in, come in."

Laura stepped into the humble living room, noting the worn furniture with avocado- and rust-colored upholstery from the seventies. A television with broken knobs and a rabbit-ear antenna stood across from a couch and recliner. George went to the television and turned it off, then made his way to the couch, where he threw the Sunday newspaper on the floor. "Please sit, miss."

As Laura sat on the couch, George eased himself into the recliner. "You have a cozy place here," Laura remarked, trying to quell her nervousness. This was the first time she had stopped by someone's home uninvited and unannounced, at least as far as she could remember. In addition, she knew the old gardener would soon realize that this wasn't actually a social call.

"Well, it's comfortable for a dog-eared old man."

Laura laughed awkwardly and jumped right in. "George, Agnes told me she's spoken to you about my memories. I've remembered some things from my childhood here, but I want to know more."

George's eyes widened. "Well, I told Agnes you remembered. I thought it was a silly idea in the first place to keep it from you." He sighed and shook his head. "Ballister is the one who told us to do it. I never agreed with it, mind you, but who am I to tell a fancy lawyer how to go about his business? I'll be glad to help you in any way I can."

"I appreciate that so much, George. Let's see . . . where to start . . . um . . . Do you remember me? I mean from before."

"Oh, yes, Miss Laura. You were a pretty little thing, always smiling and running around the lawn. All the staff loved having you here."

"And do you remember my nanny, Ruby Davis?"

George's smile faded. "Yes, that was a terrible tragedy."

"What do you remember about that night, the night Ruby Davis fell?"

George tugged at his ear. "Well now, that's a long time ago. I don't remember yesterday too good, much less twenty years ago. Ask me something specific, and maybe it will jog my memory."

"Do you remember that two servers knocked into each other with trays of hot chocolate?"

George laughed. "Oh, yes, I remember that. It was old Bobby Briggs and Marshall Jones. We never let them live that down. Bobby now runs a café up at Mountain Dale Lake—it's kind of a resort up in the mountains south of town. There's a motel up there too. A lot of folks around here go up to the café just to eat a good meal. I eat there every once in a while to catch up on the local talk. Marshall died a few years back."

"Agnes said you brought Bobby and Marshall here to the cottage to change."

"Yes, that's right—I remember now. Miss Buford asked me to let them change here. Bobby and Marshall weren't regular staff. They were temporaries, working just at the festival. We all wore these fancy black-and-white uniforms." A faraway look crossed George's face.

"So you served that night too?"

"Well, my job was to make sure the guests had seats out on the lawn. I also gathered trash and emptied the trash cans."

"George, I know it was a long time ago, but do you remember about what time you brought Bobby and Marshall here to the cottage?"

He rubbed his nose with his finger. "Well, miss, you're really testing my moth-eaten memory now! I don't think—well, wait a doggone second here—I do remember. Let's see. Agnes was fussing about something—I think she wanted us back to help serve drinks. Yes, Miss Buford always gave a festival toast."

Laura prompted, "Agnes said it was at eight o'clock?"

"That's right." George nodded. "I think Miss Buford always gave her toast around eight o'clock."

"So about what time did you leave in relation to the toast?"

"About twenty minutes before, I think. I remember because Agnes was fussing about us being back in twenty minutes for the toast."

"That's great. So we can pinpoint your leaving the party to around seven forty. How long did it take for Bobby and Marshall to change?"

George tugged at his ear again. "Well, all I remember is that they each took a turn changing in my bathroom, and it didn't seem like they were rushing or anything."

"Did you make it back in time for the toast?"

"Well, they didn't end up having a toast at all, because the storm came."

"Oh, that's right. Did you make it back to the party before the storm hit?"

"No. I remember it started raining while we were at the cottage. I remember that because Bobby started complaining that everything was going wrong, and Marshall said something about Agnes Hayes's curse." George laughed. "We used to joke about Agnes and her superstitious ways."

"You're referring to the fall moon thing?"

"Yeah, and all her other strange notions. Of course, Agnes felt vindicated that night, and she pranced around saying, 'I told you so,' all over the place. If ever Agnes Hayes had a night, that was it."

"So you all returned to the party together?"

George scratched at his chin. "Well, no. Bobby and Marshall left first. I stayed behind a minute because, as we were leaving, we realized they had just left their uniforms on my bathroom floor. I had to find a bag to put them in so I could carry them back to the hall. I told them to go ahead so Agnes didn't send someone for us."

"How long did you stay behind?"

"I figured I'd use the facilities myself as long as I was there, so it may've been a good five minutes or so all told. When I left, it was sprinkling."

"Which way did you go back to the reception hall?"

"I went around the front of the house."

"Did you see Ruby when you were returning?"

"No, I didn't see Ruby, but I saw Roger Ballister. He went in the front door of the house."

Laura thought of Roger with his genteel manners and soft voice. He was a real charmer, but she wondered what he hid behind the mask. According to Laura's aunt's diary, he'd agreed to "take care of Ruby," and perhaps he had. "You're sure you saw Roger Ballister going in the house?" she asked George with a frown.

He nodded. "Yes, probably running an errand for Miss Buford. She kept that man hopping."

"And you didn't see Ruby Davis?"

"Not at that time. Of course, I saw her earlier in the evening with her brother when I was gathering up garbage in the reception hall." George was being helpful, but Laura started to get the feeling he wasn't thrilled with her extended interrogation.

"Did you know her brother?"

"Not well, but he seemed like a stuck-up fella. He watched over Ruby like a mother hen over her chicks. Of course, he raised her, so I suppose he felt a certain responsibility, but sometimes he took it too far."

"What do you mean?"

"Well, rumor has it Ruby loved some local fella—I don't recall his name. When her brother found out, he demanded she break it off. He didn't think the locals were good enough for Ruby. She pretended to break it off but kept secretly meeting with her local beau, but her brother found out about it and established her with that lawyer in his office."

"Edward Smith?"

"Yep, that's the one," George confirmed with a heavy sigh. "She got engaged to him even though she didn't love him."

"Why would she do that?" Laura wondered.

"I don't know. Maybe to make her brother happy. Maybe she liked the idea of being married to a lawyer like her brother. Maybe the money. Who knows?"

"I understand you had an encounter with Edward Smith the day after the festival."

George scratched his head and squinted. "Yeah, that's right. Early Saturday morning I heard someone scrounging around in my work shed out here behind the cottage, so I got dressed as fast as I could and ran out. I looked out back and didn't see anything, but the door to the shed was open. I peered up the hill, and there was Smith, climbing on a ladder to the nursery window."

"What did you do?"

"I raced up there and started yelling at him to come down, of course." George's face reddened, and he seemed agitated.

"And then what happened?"

"He started yelling some nonsense and making a big fuss. It drew the staff's attention, and everyone came out. Agnes even swung her amulet at him. He fled. Of course, Agnes claims her amulet scared him away." Then George chuckled and added, "The rest of us on the staff tended to think Agnes herself was enough to scare him away without the amulet."

Ignoring his barb, Laura asked, "So that was the last time you saw Edward Smith?"

"Yep, it was."

"Why do you think he climbed to the nursery?" Laura asked hesitantly.

"Well, I don't want to speculate and upset you, miss."

"George, it was twenty years ago. I'm not a scared little girl." As Laura said the words, she suppressed a shudder.

George sighed in resignation. "Well, I think he wanted to hurt you."

"Why?"

He shook his head. "The man was out of his mind, and he blamed you for Ruby's fall. We all know it was an accident, but he saw things differently. In his mind, the Bufords had hurt him, and he wanted to hurt the Bufords—an eye for an eye."

A chill shot down Laura's back, and she felt goose bumps spring up on her arms. "Well, I've taken enough of your time, George. I'd better go."

"Oh, no, miss. I enjoyed the company. I was about to offer you some tea."

"Oh, thank you, but no. I should get back to the house. It's starting to get dark."

"Well, thanks for stopping by. It does this mangy dog good to have Sunday visitors."

As Laura left the cottage and hiked the narrow dirt path to the mansion, the sky glowed magenta, deepening into purple at the mountaintops and black along the foothills. But Laura barely looked at the sunset as she reviewed the facts in her mind. George had seen Mr. Ballister enter the house about the time the storm started—about the time Ruby fell. What happened in the foyer? Laura knew she needed to talk to Roger Ballister to find out what had happened between Ruby and her employer. She had to find out what her aunt had meant when she told Roger Ballister to take care of Ruby. Until she did this, Laura might continue to suspect her aunt of somehow being involved in Ruby's death.

Laura also needed to talk to Leonard Davis—after all, he had probably known Ruby better than anyone. Maybe he could provide some information about Ruby's mysterious beau. But he might refuse to talk, and Laura wasn't sure how to approach a man about his sister's death, even one that occurred twenty years ago. What if he blamed Laura like Edward Smith did? Maybe Aaron could help her find out what she needed to know from Mr. Davis.

As she thought of Aaron, guilt washed over her. She hadn't been totally forthright with him. He'd asked her why she wanted information about Leonard Davis, and she hadn't told him the truth. He had been kind to her from the moment they'd met, and she felt in her heart that he was a good man. She needed to tell him the truth—she made up her mind to call him right away. When she reached the mansion, she hurried to the study, where she closed the door. She located Aaron's home number in the phone book and dialed.

"Hello," he answered after a few rings.

Relieved to hear his voice, Laura quickly said, "Aaron, it's Laura McClain."

"Hi, Laura. How are you?"

"Well, Aaron, I've called to confess."

"Confess?"

"Yes. I was dishonest with you this afternoon. You asked me why I'm interested in Leonard Davis. Well, I'm interested in him because I saw his sister die twenty years ago here at Buford's Bluff."

Laura waited for a reply but heard only silence. "Aaron?"

"I don't know what to say. I think you'd better tell me the whole story. Start at the beginning, please."

For the next forty minutes, Laura told Aaron everything: about the dream, about the flashbacks—though she hardly knew which were which anymore—and about her and Julie's little investigation into Ruby's death. Occasionally, Aaron asked a question or two, but he mostly just listened.

After Laura had rehearsed the whole matter, Aaron said, "Laura, I'm glad you told me all this. You've obviously been under a lot of stress. I'm sorry you've had to go through this."

"And I'm sorry I wasn't forthright about this," Laura said with a sigh.

"It's no big deal. You had every right to protect your privacy, especially under the circumstances. Look, I'd like to help you somehow."

She imagined him on the other end of the line: his thick chestnut hair, his expressive blue eyes, and his dimpled chin. But Aaron's good looks were clearly more than skin deep. He seemed sincere in his offer of assistance.

"Aaron, do you understand why I need to find out all I can about Ruby Davis?"

"Yes, of course I do," Aaron assured her.

"I need to talk to Leonard Davis. Can you help me?" Silence. "Aaron, are you there?"

"Yeah, I'm here—just thinking. Let's see . . . I've got a meeting with Leonard tomorrow morning at ten o'clock. I'll try to arrange a time for you to speak with him."

"Thank you, Aaron."

A click sounded on the line.

"Laura, are you still there?"

"Yes. I thought maybe you hung up on me."

"No. But it did sound like someone hanging up."

"Oh, maybe Agnes needs to use the phone. I'd better go. I'll see you tomorrow."

Laura hung up the phone, suddenly paranoid. Agnes had obviously been on the other line in the kitchen! Now Laura remembered hearing a click a few minutes into her conversation with Aaron, but it hadn't occurred to her that someone could be listening.

Opening the door, Laura dashed through the hall to the kitchen, but no one was there. Agnes had made her getaway.

16

On Monday morning, Laura sat eating breakfast in the dining room when Agnes announced that Roger Ballister had arrived. As he entered the room, he smiled broadly and asked, "How's our little Laurie this morning?"

Laura swallowed hard. "Hello, Roger. I wasn't expecting you. Would you like something to eat?"

"Thank you. That would be wonderful." He sat down, and Agnes served him breakfast. Laura wondered why he had stopped by without warning, and her palms began to sweat. Then she reminded herself that she wanted to talk to Roger about Ruby, so no matter what he'd come to talk about, she would ask her questions.

They ate without speaking until Agnes left the room. Then Laura couldn't stand the silence any longer. "Well, what brings you here so early?"

"Agnes telephoned me yesterday afternoon. She tells me you're remembering things about Buford's Bluff," he said a little too cheerily, his Southern accent seeming thicker than before.

Laura wiped the corner of her mouth with a cloth napkin. "Roger, why didn't you tell me about Ruby?"

He smiled a broad smile that seemed a bit forced. "That's what I've come to explain. I fear you think the worst of us, but we wanted to protect you, Laura. You must believe that."

Laura clenched her jaw, then spoke slowly and firmly. "I'll decide what I'll believe, Roger." She found speaking her mind—a new practice for her—both liberating and disconcerting.

"Yes, of course. But please allow me to explain," he urged, holding his hands out pleadingly.

Laura placed her napkin in her lap. "That's all I'm asking."

Roger cleared his throat. "Laura, you experienced a great shock here at the mansion. Agnes told me you've been reading about Ruby Davis, so I'm sure you know the details. Apparently you heard Ruby fall that night. You came from the nursery and looked down the stairs and saw Ruby lying at the bottom. You went into shock, Laura. It was terrible. We didn't know if you were ever going to recover."

"But how did you think you were going to keep something like this from me?" The question came out in more of a demanding tone than Laura had planned.

"It was a foolish notion, I'll admit. At first I was confident we could do it. But when I slipped and called you 'Laurie' in the car, I knew it was going to be difficult. Nonetheless, I worked for your aunt, and before her death she insisted I try to keep your past from you."

Laura frowned. "But why?"

"She feared you would have bad feelings about Buford's Bluff and refuse to run the plantation. She also believed your mother would have wanted it that way." His words dripped with a sweetness that almost made Laura cringe.

She took a sip of juice, and as she placed the glass on the table, it clinked against a saucer. She tried to will her hands to stop shaking. "Roger, can you tell me in your own words what happened to Ruby that night?"

"Well, as far as we know, Ruby heard the storm approaching and excused herself to go check on you. You were scared of storms."

"So I've been told." Everyone seemed to have this story down to the last detail, Laura decided, as if they'd all read from the same script before she arrived.

"Apparently, you'd been playing with a toy on the stairs. Ruby stepped on the toy, slipped, and fell to her death." He recited the details as if reading off a grocery list.

"So it's my fault?"

He reached across the table for her hand, but Laura pulled back. "Of course not," he retorted unconvincingly. "It was an accident."

"I'm not sure it was, Roger."

He frowned, wrinkling his forehead. "What do you mean?"

"Did you know my aunt kept a diary?" Laura's voice wavered.

Roger suddenly looked pale, as if all the blood had drained from his face. "No."

"Well, she did. It was sparse, but a diary nonetheless. In one entry, she states that she instructed you to 'take care of Ruby Davis.' On the night Ruby died, someone saw you entering the house just moments after Ruby did. Can you explain this to me?"

He shrugged and shook his head slowly. "Yes, I can explain it all to you, but please don't jump to conclusions before you've heard me out." Taking out a handkerchief, Roger wiped his forehead. "Leonard Davis was close to his sister."

"Yes, yes," Laura interjected impatiently.

"Ruby had been involved with a local boy—" Roger began.

"Who was this local boy?" Laura interrupted again.

"It was Roscoe Buford, the sheriff's son," Roger answered. "Ruby ran off with Roscoe when she was nineteen. Leonard hired a private detective to track his sister and bring her home. Understandably, she was furious with Leonard. When Ruby applied for the nanny job at Buford's Bluff, Leonard was annoyed because he envied the Bufords, their money, and their power in Bufordville. He relented, however, because the job would keep Ruby close to home. After Ruby started work at the plantation, there were all kinds of rumors flying about the girl. Her running off like that gave her a permanent reputation as a jezebel. Leonard suspected she was seeing Roscoe again, and he was determined to make sure she didn't end up with him."

"Isn't that kind of obsessive? I mean, he had no right to tell her whom she could or couldn't see."

"Yes, Leonard's relationship with his sister was obsessive, but Roscoe was also a little obsessive when it came to Ruby."

"What do you mean?"

"Roscoe showed up at the festival drunk. When he heard she was going to marry Edward Smith, he made a scene."

Laura leaned forward. "What kind of scene?"

Roger threw his hands up in frustration. "I don't know—I wasn't there. Roscoe found Ruby and Leonard by the river. Your father escorted Roscoe to his car, asking him to leave and not come back."

"And he left?"

"As far as we know," Roger replied, his voice rising.

"This still doesn't explain your involvement," Laura indicated bluntly.

Roger's fork clanked as he placed it on the china plate with more force than necessary. "I'm getting to that. Edward Smith was young, handsome, successful, and devoted to Leonard. You see, Leonard helped pay Edward's way through school. He offered Edward a partnership and paid him to date Ruby. In fact, he paid Edward to make Ruby forget about her local boyfriend."

"Edward didn't love Ruby?"

"That's where the problem arose," Roger responded with a slight smile. "Edward and Ruby fell in love."

"And Leonard was unhappy about that?"

He shrugged. "Like I said, Leonard had an obsessive relationship with his sister. He didn't want Ruby to marry anyone, because in his mind, no one was good enough for her."

"But he set them up—he got them together."

Roger paused as he wiped his goatee with a napkin. "Yes, but only to distract her. He never planned on Edward and Ruby falling in love. Leonard refused to believe they loved each other, and he insisted that Ruby was marrying Edward to spite her overprotective brother."

"Maybe she was."

"Well, that's what I wondered until she and Edward announced their engagement. Leonard was in shock. He had convinced himself it wouldn't go that far. You see, a few days before the party, he came to your aunt to call in a favor she owed him. Leonard was worried that Ruby and Edward were getting too close, and thought that Laura could help. At the time, your aunt had arranged a European trip for you and your mother. She— uh—thought it best that Sarah get away from Buford's Bluff."

"You mean away from my father."

"Yes, that was the general idea. Though your parents had been married for five years or so, Laura thought that distance would 'bring Sarah to her senses.' Your aunt believed your mother had made a mistake in marrying John McClain. Anyway, Leonard asked your aunt to encourage Ruby to go as your nanny. Ruby had always wanted to go to Europe, so it seemed simple enough. Your aunt told Leonard she would have me make the proposition."

Laura pushed her plate away. "She wanted you to bribe Ruby?"

"In a sense, yes. When I saw Ruby heading toward the mansion on the night of the festival, I recognized an opportunity to talk to her privately, so I followed her into the house. She headed up the stairs, but I called her back down and offered her a significant pay raise and a new wardrobe if she would act as your nanny on an extended trip to Europe."

"What did she do?" Laura wondered.

"Ruby laughed. She said she knew Leonard would try to break them up. And she claimed she was going to stop Leonard from breaking up this relationship as he had done all the others."

"What did you do next?"

"I told her Leonard paid Edward to date her—I thought it would shock her back to reality." Roger let out a long sigh.

"And did it?"

"No. She already knew the whole story. When Edward had developed feelings for her, he'd told her the whole story. Ruby insisted that she loved Edward and that he had proven his love by announcing their engagement. He actually sacrificed his job for Ruby. She said she and Edward planned on moving away and starting a new life, and she said she never wanted to see her brother again."

"What did you do?"

Roger pulled at his goatee before answering. "What could I do? I left. Ruby must have fallen right after that."

"Did you see a toy on the stairs?"

"I don't remember seeing anything on the stairs," Roger replied, sounding sincere.

"Where did you go after you left Ruby?"

Laura stared at Roger's hand that was pulling at his beard, and he quickly stopped.

"I returned to the reception hall, and I ran into Leonard as he came from the bathroom. Some careless worker had placed poison ivy on the bonfire. Leonard had to wash his eyes out. I went to him, shook his hand, and told him I had failed. I told him everything Ruby had said."

"How did he react?"

"Furiously. He marched out into the rainstorm."

"Where did he go?"

"I don't know."

"Roger, if Ruby had such a bad reputation, why did my parents hire her?"

"Ruby was trying to make a clean start. Your mother admired that. She believed that Leonard was the cause of many of Ruby's problems, and she wanted to help her."

For several moments, Laura stared silently into Roger's blue eyes. "Roger, I want to apologize for being rude earlier. This whole thing has upset me quite a bit." She realized she didn't need to tell him that, as he could undoubtedly hear the tremor in her voice.

Roger's face brightened. "Oh, I understand. I wish we had handled things better on our end. We wanted to do the right thing."

Laura stood and walked over to the window, noticing the cloudy sky as well as the thin mist of fog floating across the yard. It seemed secrets were hidden everywhere at Buford's Bluff. Turning and looking at Roger, Laura asked, "Why didn't Aunt Laura help my mother when she was struggling to raise me on her own?"

Roger stood and walked towards her. "She tried, but your mother refused. Your father and aunt had a falling out before your parents left. Unfortunately, harsh words were spoken, and grudges were held. As far as I know, nothing was ever resolved between the three of them."

"What kind of words could have been said that would have lead to a twenty-year grudge?"

Roger cleared his throat. "Your aunt accused your father of killing both Ruby Davis and Edward Smith, and of having an affair with Ruby."

Laura stood speechless, staring at Roger. A lonely, haunting train whistle echoed in the distance, and she recalled that she'd heard the whistle one night after waking from a nightmare. Was she on the verge of waking from another one? This certainly felt like a nightmare.

"What made my aunt suspect my father of having an affair?" Her voice quivered.

"There were rumors among the servants that Ruby was seeing an older man. The day after Ruby's death, one of the servants told your aunt that she'd once seen your father kissing Ruby in the woods near the house. I paid the woman off to keep her quiet, and we arranged for her to find employment elsewhere. But your aunt held on to the uneasy idea that your father may have gone into a rage after Ruby announced her engagement that night. She couldn't let go of the idea that he had been unfaithful to your mother. Of course, she'd never really liked your father, so she was looking at the whole thing from a biased perspective. Maybe she just saw what she wanted to see."

"We don't know whether the woman was telling the truth, right?"

"No, we don't, and as far as I could determine, that was the only reason your aunt suspected your father."

Laura turned her back to Roger and looked out over the lonely countryside. "I don't believe it. I'll never believe it."

Roger stepped closer to her. "Does it matter now, Laura? Not to be harsh, but they're all dead and gone."

Laura turned sharply, and Roger stepped back. "They may be dead, Roger, but they're not gone. I feel them in this house. Their secrets are here in this house, and I won't be able to live here peacefully unless I find out what happened."

"It seems rather pointless," Roger concluded.

"To you. But to me, it means everything." With that, Laura spun on her heel and left Roger standing alone.

17

After Roger left, Aaron called to let Laura know that Leonard Davis would be in his office the rest of the morning. Aaron said that if she got there quickly, he could arrange a meeting between her and Leonard. Laura jumped in her aunt's car and drove toward Bufordville. A heavy fog billowed up from the James River, and Laura could barely see the road. The woods on the sides of the road had disappeared behind a foggy gray wall.

Laura tried to concentrate on maneuvering the car around the sharp curves, but her mind was busy wondering whom she could trust. She knew she had to be careful about jumping to conclusions— she had prejudged Roger Ballister without giving him a chance to explain. She wouldn't make that mistake with Leonard Davis.

As Laura drove into Bufordville, a fine mist of rain dotted the windshield. She turned on the wipers and strained to see her way through the narrow streets, finally finding a two-hour parking spot a few blocks from Aaron's office building.

When she opened the door and got out of the car, the freezing mist hit her face. A cold front had moved into the valley, and the sprinkling rain began turning into fine sleet.

"Laura McClain!"

Laura looked toward the sidewalk and saw no one.

"Laura McClain!"

The voice seemed ethereal and detached, so faint she could barely make out the words. She stepped toward the sidewalk, and a hand grasped her arm. As she jerked her head back, she found herself staring at Hattie O'Donnell.

"Oh, my, Laura! I thought I would never see you again. I'm glad I've run into you without my sister Lettie."

"Hattie, what are you doing out on a day like this?"

"Wasn't so bad when I started out, but I'm fine. Don't worry about me. I'm not as feeble as people like to suppose." The old woman paused. "I've been thinking about you—I even started to telephone you, but Lettie stopped me. She told me to mind my own business— she says I stick my nose in things that are none of my concern. But I feel an obligation to tell you."

"Tell me what?"

For the next few minutes, Hattie rehearsed what Laura already knew: the story of Ruby's death. "Ever since Bobby Briggs told me the story," Hattie said, "I've had an impulse to tell you everything, Laura."

"You know Bobby Briggs?"

"Oh, my, yes. He's married to Lettie's sister-in-law, Ruth."

"Do you think Bobby will talk to me?"

"Why, yes! Bobby will talk to anyone who will listen. But I warn you, once he starts, he never stops."

Before she disappeared into the fog, Hattie explained to Laura how to find Bobby's mountaintop café. Laura quickly pulled some paper and a pen from her purse to jot down the directions, then wished Hattie well and made her way toward Aaron's office.

It was at the intersection a block from the law office that Laura saw him. He stood motionless, staring across the street. It was the same man that had followed her in St. Louis—of that she was sure. How could she forget that face?

Laura's heart seemed to jump and then almost stop, and she nearly stumbled as she walked towards the man. When she followed him into the crosswalk, she could hardly believe she was doing such a crazy thing. Just then, he increased his pace. Did he know someone was following him?

As the man approached an old building, Laura glanced around to see if anyone was nearby. When she looked back to where her stalker should be, all she saw was a door closing. The man was gone. She took several more steps and stopped in front of the old building. The eaves dripped in the gloom, and Laura shivered. She was sure he had entered this building. Looking up at the sign on the brick wall by the door, she read aloud, "Roger Ballister, Attorney-at-Law."

Laura turned and darted back down the sidewalk. Her legs felt weak, and she could barely breathe. Suddenly, she heard footsteps behind her and wondered if she dare turn around. Maybe the stalker was following her now—maybe he hadn't gone into the law offices after all. But if he had, how was Roger Ballister involved with this man? Maybe Roger was after the estate and had sent the man to hurt her. And what about Ruby's death?

With her head down in panicked thought, Laura collided with someone and let out a scream. She thrashed with her fists until she felt soft flesh and heard a grunt. Tearing herself free, she looked up into Aaron's surprised face.

"Laura?"

"Aaron?"

"What's wrong?" Aaron asked.

She collapsed into his arms and managed to mumble, "I thought someone was following me."

"Who?"

"I don't know. Maybe I imagined it, but . . ." Still trying to catch her breath, Laura added, "Actually, I was following—uh . . . I need to sit down."

They stood just a few steps from the building where Aaron worked, so he helped her inside. "Here, Laura, sit right here. I'll get you some water. You know Emily Smith, don't you?"

The receptionist gaped at Laura from behind her desk.

"How—do—you—do—Miss—Smith?" Laura spoke between breaths.

"Miss Emily Smith, this is Laura McClain," Aaron stated as he returned with a cup of water and handed it to Laura. "She inherited the Buford Place."

Emily's mouth fell open. "Oh, I had no idea."

"Yes," Aaron explained, "she's here this morning to talk to Leonard about his sister's death. Did you know Leonard had a sister?"

"Yes, I certainly did," Emily muttered softly.

Just then Leonard Davis stepped out of his office, distinguished looking and tall, with gray hair and a gray mustache. "Leonard," Aaron said, "this is Laura McClain. She'd like to talk with you about your sister, Ruby."

If Leonard was shocked at the mention of his long-departed sister, his expression did not show it. Yet Laura thought his face lost a bit of color.

Laura remained seated, but Leonard stepped forward and grasped her hand. "Miss McClain, it is an honor." His hand was cold and dry.

"Thank you," Laura responded.

* * *

After a few moments of small talk, Leonard escorted Laura into his office. Staring at the closed door, Aaron commented, "Until yesterday, I had no idea Leonard had a sister who died." Then he looked at Emily. "How did you know?"

Emily glared at Aaron and pushed her blond hair back from her eyes. "I knew Ruby. She was engaged to my brother, Edward."

Aaron walked closer to the receptionist's desk. "You're Edward Smith's sister?"

"You sound surprised."

"I had no idea."

Emily gave him a chilly stare. "There's no reason why you should know about Edward. He's been dead for more than twenty years."

"I'm sorry about that. And I understand they never caught his killer?"

"That's right. I don't think they gave it much effort either." She turned away from Aaron's gaze and started shuffling papers.

Aaron sat down on a chair near her desk, positioning it so that she couldn't avoid his eyes so easily. "You believe Laura's father, John McClain, killed your brother?"

Emily's head shot up, her eyes piercing and angry. "That's right."

"But you have no proof, do you?" Aaron questioned.

Emily slammed her fist on the desk. "I don't need proof! I just know. I know in my heart that John McClain killed my brother. It's the only logical explanation."

Aaron leaned back. "Emily, the heart's illogical."

Emily took a deep breath. "I'm not arguing a case. I know what I know. The two fought in Dr. Preston's office, and I heard John McClain threaten Edward with my own ears."

Aaron leaned forward onto the desk and spoke softly. "I heard that Edward threatened the McClains, so it's understandable John would be upset. They caught Edward climbing a ladder to the nursery. Your brother must've been planning to hurt Laura, or worse."

Emily's face tightened, her lips pale. "I don't believe that. Edward wanted to get to the bottom of Ruby's death. And he didn't threaten to physically hurt anyone. He only threatened to expose the family."

Aaron frowned. "What was he exposing?"

"I talked to Edward the afternoon before he died," Emily replied. "Edward believed something funny was going on between Leonard and the Bufords. He didn't tell me much, but he said he needed to put it all together. He thought Ruby's death was suspicious."

"Edward thought someone murdered Ruby?"

"Well, he didn't say it, but he implied it."

"In what way?" Aaron queried.

Emily moved closer to the desk and leaned over it conspiratorially. "Edward said Ruby's body looked like it'd been thrown down the stairs. He said the toy on the steps—a metal horse and buggy—was big and bright. Ruby would have seen it. He insisted it looked like someone had thrown the toy on the stairs to make it *look* like an accident. Edward was a criminal lawyer, and he knew a crime scene when he saw it."

Aaron shrugged. "But why would the Bufords want to hurt Ruby?"

"I don't know. That night, Edward saw Laura Buford and Roger Ballister huddled up whispering to Leonard, and he knew they were up to something."

"But Leonard wouldn't have been involved in hurting his own sister. He obviously loved her."

"Perhaps their plan was to hurt my brother, and something went wrong."

"Why would they want to hurt your brother?"

Emily's face flushed. "Leonard Davis was insanely jealous of my brother. He paid my brother to date his sister, and it didn't turn out the way he'd planned."

"Why would he pay someone to date Ruby? Laura told me her nanny was a beautiful young woman. I hardly think Leonard needed to set her up."

Emily clinched her fists. "Oh, but he did. Ruby had run off with some local yokel in the past. Leonard wanted to make her forget about him, so he asked Edward to make her forget, but Leonard never planned on Edward falling in love with Ruby himself. Leonard was obsessed with her, and he wanted to keep her to himself. He used anyone and everyone who could help him. He used my brother!"

"Why did your brother agree to do it? Did he need the money that badly?"

"It wasn't about money. It was about loyalty to Leonard. Edward idolized Leonard. Edward was a poor kid from the Virginia back-waters before Leonard picked him up, sent him to law school, and gave him a job. Edward would have done anything for Leonard."

Aaron's heart pounded so hard he could almost hear it, and his head throbbed. He understood Edward Smith—he was an earlier version of Aaron himself. Because of Edward's loyalty to Leonard, he had probably magnified Leonard's virtues and shut his eyes to Leonard's flaws. Leonard manipulated his employees and demanded total loyalty. Just as Leonard wanted his employees to center their lives on him, he wanted his sister to be totally loyal to him. Leonard would accept nothing but total loyalty. Aaron hated to admit it, but he suspected that Leonard Davis would put his right-hand man to death if he disobeyed orders.

Aaron fell back in the chair. "How do you know your brother loved Ruby?"

Her eyes became misty. "He was my brother. I just know he loved her."

"Maybe Edward used Ruby to get to Leonard. Maybe Leonard's control over him caused resentment. Maybe he decided to use Ruby as a way of getting something from Leonard."

Emily glared at Aaron. "Mr. Farr, I think you're trying to project your own feelings onto my brother. I assure you that you know nothing about him! He's been dead over twenty years. He was loyal to Leonard, and Leonard used that loyalty. Besides, you have the whole scenario backwards. Ruby feigned love for my brother—she used him."

Aaron frowned and narrowed his eyes. "In what way?"

"I was in the reception hall that night when Edward and Ruby announced their engagement. I saw the joy in my brother's eyes. From the way he looked at Ruby, it was obvious he loved her. But Ruby looked smugly at Leonard, who was in shock. She was gloating—throwing it in her brother's face. Ruby used my brother to get back at Leonard. She was going to ruin my brother's life for her own selfish purposes."

"What did Leonard do after Edward made the announcement?"

"He grabbed Ruby's arm and pulled her to a corner, and I followed them. Leonard told Ruby she was making a foolish mistake, then he let Edward have it for betraying him. I think Leonard could have killed them both at that moment."

"How did Ruby respond?"

"She stood there basking in Leonard's anger, with a wicked little smirk on her face. I could have slapped it right off, and I'm sure Leonard felt the same way. Edward, however, argued with Leonard. I think he realized for the first time the depth of Leonard's obsessiveness. Their argument drew attention to us, and then two waiters collided into each other. While everyone else looked at the mess, we all went out onto the lawn, then walked over to a bonfire by the river. Leonard and Edward continued to argue, and Leonard demanded to speak to Ruby alone. He thought Edward had brainwashed her, but I believe it was the other way around."

"Did you leave Leonard with Ruby?" Aaron asked.

Emily fell silent for a moment, frowning thoughtfully. "Yes. Edward kissed Ruby on the cheek and told her to be firm. Then Edward took me back to the reception hall to introduce me to some people. I was new in town, and Edward had worked it out with Leonard for me to be their receptionist."

"How long were Ruby and Leonard out there alone?"

"Not long. Later I learned that Roscoe Buford also confronted Ruby around that time. I didn't see it, and I never saw Ruby alive again. Leonard came into the reception hall with red eyes. A worker had accidentally placed poison ivy on the fire, and the smoke got in Leonard's eyes. As it turned out, Edward and I both had been exposed to the poison ivy smoke before coming in, but we didn't realize it until the next day."

"What did Leonard do?"

Again, Emily paused to think. "He hurried into the bathroom, and Miss Buford had someone go in there with him to help him wash his eyes. Edward ran to Leonard and asked him about Ruby. He told Edward she'd gone to check on the little McClain girl. It'd started to thunder, and apparently the girl feared thunderstorms. Edward continued introducing me to the local people. A while later, Roger Ballister came into the reception hall. He was a little wet—it was raining by then. Leonard came from the bathroom, and the two huddled in a corner, whispering again."

"What happened then?" Aaron asked urgently.

"Edward and I watched and listened, but we couldn't hear what they were saying. Leonard got angry and stormed out, and Edward went after him. I felt silly standing there alone, so I left the party."

"You drove your own car?"

"Yes. Edward came a little early."

"And you went home?"

Emily clenched her jaw. "Yes, your honor."

Aaron ignored her sarcasm. "When did you hear that Ruby Davis was dead?"

"The next morning. Leonard came over and told me."

"And when did you see your brother again?"

"Saturday afternoon. Leonard got him out of jail, and then Edward and I went together to Dr. Preston's home office because we had both broken out with hives from the poison ivy. We left the doctor's office together, then I dropped Edward off at his apartment. I didn't go in with him. He said he was going to sleep all afternoon. He looked exhausted, and I think he was still in shock from Ruby's death."

"Did you go into the apartment with him?"

"No."

"When did you find out your brother had died?"

Tears now flowed from Emily's eyes, so she grabbed a tissue from the box on her desk and dabbed at them. She sighed. "The next day. Leonard came by and told me after he found him."

"Why did you keep working for Leonard?"

A mock smile formed on Emily's face, and her eyes narrowed. "I have few options, Mr. Farr. When you live in a small town, you take your breaks where you can get them. Leonard offered me a raise. He wanted me to stay."

"How did Ruby's death affect Leonard?"

Emily shrugged. "I don't really know, but to me he seemed unaffected. I think he replaced his obsession with his sister with his compulsion for work. He's been that way ever since."

Aaron studied the receptionist's face, deciding that she seemed sincere in her grief. "Emily, you don't blame Laura McClain for your brother's death, do you?"

She pouted her lips. "Well, I've never been a Buford fan. Now, Mr. Farr, if you will excuse me, I have work to do."

"One more thing, Emily."

"Yes?"

"Your brother found Ruby's body, right?"

"Yes."

18

Laura's first impression of Leonard Davis's office was the smell—a combination of furniture polish and old books. The large room was full of oak and leather furniture against a backdrop of bookshelves and wooden panels with elaborate moldings. The room was dark except for a desk lamp that splashed light on the gold lettering on the backs of the books that lined the shelves. Not waiting for an invitation, Laura sank into a large, slightly worn leather chair in front of the massive desk.

Her heart still raced, and perspiration broke out on her forehead, so she took a tissue from her purse and wiped her brow. Attempting to calm herself, she took a deep breath and released it slowly.

Leonard Davis sat in a large, leather desk chair with wheels. "Well, Miss McClain, what is it you would like to know about Ruby? She's been gone a long time, and just between you and me, my memory is not what it used to be."

Laura cleared her throat. "Mr. Davis, I want to say how sorry I am about what happened. If I could go back in time and change it, I would."

Leonard pulled at his grizzled mustache, then lifted his hand and waved it casually. "No need to apologize. That was twenty-odd years ago. It was an accident, and Ruby was careless. The universe has its own way of meting out justice—we must accept what is. As they say, time heals all wounds."

In her heart, Laura agreed with Leonard Davis, realizing that perhaps she too was paying for her own mistakes. At least now she knew she had to face the pain she had tried to block out for twenty years. Her mother used to always say if you couldn't go around it or over it or under it, you had to go through it—but Laura had always tried to avoid going through it. She could see a pattern in her life—a pattern that had started more than twenty years ago when she had turned off her memories of Ruby Davis. She had avoided facing the pain, and she'd done that ever since in every aspect of her life.

"Mr. Davis, I know you were close to your sister. I know those wounds were deep."

He frowned. "Yes, well, none of us can make it through life without some battle scars, now can we, Miss McClain?" His voice sounded professional, almost cold.

"I suppose not. Mr. Davis, I find I'm still healing from my own wounds caused by Ruby's death."

"You've reminded me of a George Elliott quote," he quipped suddenly, almost interrupting her. "'With memory set smarting like a reopened wound, a man's past is not simply a dead history, an outworn preparation of the present: it is not a repented error shaken loose from the life: it is a still quivering part of himself, bringing shudders and bitter flavors and the tinglings of a merited shame.'"

"Oh," Laura managed, unsure how to respond.

A slight smile appeared on Davis's face so briefly that it might have been no more than a muscle spasm. "My dear girl, Ruby loved you very much. It was the first time I ever saw her care about someone besides herself. I was unhappy with Ruby working as a nanny, but I must admit it did the girl some good. She learned a certain amount of responsibility."

"I'm sure I loved her too, Mr. Davis. I just wish I could remember her better." Laura tried to adjust herself in the chair, but its timeworn contours were too deep to allow it. Then, realizing her time with Leonard might be short, she shifted into interview mode. "I'm hoping you can tell me more about the Harvest Moon Festival. What do you remember about that night?"

Mr. Davis leaned forward on his desk, his forehead wrinkled. "Well, it's all a blur to me now. I remember Edward announced his engagement to Ruby. We disagreed on the matter, and we had a few sharp words."

"Why did you differ on the matter?"

He sighed. "Ruby had always jumped into situations without thinking. When she was nineteen, she ran off with a local rowdy."

"You're talking about my cousin, Roscoe Buford?"

"Uh, yes. No offense, I hope."

"None taken. I don't even know the man."

"Well, Miss McClain, he was trouble. Ruby had difficulty making decisions—she always jumped into things with both eyes closed. She needed guidance and direction, and being the only authority figure in her life, I tried to give it to her that night, as I always had. We walked out on the lawn by the river. It was nippy, so we huddled near a bonfire. Edward and his sister, Emily, went back to the reception hall, leaving Ruby and me alone to talk."

Laura held up her hand, stopping him. "Your receptionist is Edward's sister? I had no idea."

"Yes, and a faithful employee, too. Anyway, Roscoe showed up, and he was quite drunk. Someone told him about the engagement, and he made a scene, begging Ruby to marry him instead. When she told him to go away, he threatened her."

"Did he mean it?"

He shrugged. "I don't know. Like I said, he was drunk. Your father came and escorted him off the property. Around that time, I heard thunder, and Ruby said she had to go check on you because thunderstorms scared you. I think it was an excuse to get away from me."

"What happened next?"

The creases in his forehead deepened. "Well, I stood there contemplating for a few minutes, and then my eyes started to burn like crazy. A worker who was putting wood on the fire yelled for water. He said he'd accidentally thrown some logs on the fire that were laced with poison ivy. A waiter helped me to the reception hall, and Laura Buford had him take me into the restroom to wash out my eyes."

"Did you manage to get the poison out of your eyes?"

"Yes, with quite a bit of effort."

"Did the smoke affect anyone else?"

"Yes. I understand that Dr. Preston treated several people the next day for poison ivy. They were exposed without realizing it, I guess, because the rash can take a while to appear when a person is exposed only to the smoke. I suppose Ruby was also exposed but unaware of it. She stood there with me by the fire, and Edward and Emily stood near the fire also. When the wind shifted and blew the smoke in my face, my eyes started burning. The worker feeding the fire also had to wash out his eyes—I understand he was in great pain."

Once again Laura tried to situate herself more comfortably in the big chair. "What did you do after you washed your eyes out?"

"When I came out of the restroom, I ran into Roger Ballister, your aunt Laura's attorney. He'd agreed to talk with Ruby for me. When he told me Ruby had her mind made up about Edward, I left the party to go think."

"You were angry?"

"I was furious," Leonard admitted.

"Where did you go when you left the party?"

"I went to my car, but Edward followed me and confronted me. It was raining hard by then, so I told Edward I was cold and wanted to go home. He just stomped off in the rain."

Finally, Laura managed to sit up taller and move to the edge of the chair. "Was he going toward the house?"

"Yes, as a matter of fact, he was."

"What did you do after he left?"

Leonard pulled at his dark mustache. "I got in the car and drove in the rain for hours, then, finally, I went home and fell asleep."

"When did you find out about Ruby's death?"

"Edward pounded on my door sometime after midnight. He acted like he'd been drinking, and he said crazy things about Ruby being killed. I had to call the sheriff's office to find out what had happened, and then I sent Edward away."

"Did you go to the Buford mansion when you found out?"

"No. I knew there was nothing that could be done. She was gone." Leonard sighed.

"I understand they arrested Edward the next day for trying to break into the mansion."

Leonard raised his eyebrows. "That's right. He was out of his mind, and I realized he really had loved Ruby."

"You posted his bail?"

"Yes."

"Why?"

He shrugged. "I knew he didn't have the money, and I could sympathize with his pain. Plus, I thought his being in jail would make matters worse."

"You took him home?" Laura continued.

Davis shook his head. "No. Emily took him to Dr. Preston's home office, because both Edward and Emily had broken out with a rash caused by the poison ivy smoke. After that, she took him to his apartment."

"So Miss Smith was the last person to see Edward alive?"

"That's right."

"And you found the body the next morning?"

He frowned. "Yes. I went by on Sunday morning to see how Edward was doing. I knocked and knocked at his apartment, and when he didn't answer, I tried the door. It was unlocked, and as soon as I went in I could smell gas. I ran in and found Edward lying on the bed, and I called the police."

"They declared it a suicide."

"Yes."

"Do you think Edward killed himself?"

"It's the logical conclusion."

"But didn't some evidence contradict that theory?"

"Yes, or so the police thought. They found scratches and some broken wood on the doorframe as if his door had been jimmied open. However, based on the events of the past few days, suicide seemed the most logical explanation. Edward may have locked himself out on Friday night, and in his state of mind, he probably did what it took to get his apartment door open."

"There was nothing else that suggested foul play?"

"Nothing whatsoever."

* * *

Aaron paced the floor outside Leonard's office. Eventually he'd memorized the patterns in the ornate carpet on the floor and the nicks and cracks in the old, wood-paneled walls. As he passed the paintings on the walls, he stopped in front of the most intriguing of the group: the four horsemen of the Apocalypse, their swords drawn as they savagely struck down the wicked of the earth. This was

Leonard's favorite painting, Aaron recalled. Maybe that explained a lot about the man.

Aaron looked at Emily, who avoided looking at him as she quietly filed documents. He could tell he'd upset her, and he realized how little he knew about the people he worked with.

Then he thought of Laura. He was developing feelings for her, and yet he barely knew her either.

The door to Leonard's office finally opened, and Leonard and Laura walked into the reception area. "Thank you so much, Mr. Davis," Laura said.

"My pleasure, Miss McClain," Davis purred, shaking Laura's hand. "And remember, the universe has its own way of working things out. Don't worry too much about the past. I try to remember a quote by Ralph Waldo Emerson that says, 'Finish every day and be done with it. You have done what you could. Some blunders and absurdities no doubt have crept in; forget them as soon as you can. Tomorrow is a new day; you shall begin it serenely and with too high a spirit to be encumbered with your old nonsense.'"

"That's very wise," Laura responded, smiling at him. "Thank you."

Gently taking Laura's arm, Aaron said to her, "I'll walk you out." He shot a smile in Leonard's direction. Once outside the building, he released Laura's arm. "How did it go in there?"

"Well, I don't know. He's a hard man to read—he sort of wears a mask. He looks polite, and he acts polite." Laura paused thoughtfully. "He was helpful to a certain extent. But he also seems a bit insincere, like he's hiding something."

"Well, based on the way you two parted, you must not have accused him of anything."

"No, I tried to act professional. I wanted to get as much information from him as I could, and being rude wouldn't have helped. Besides, he's your boss—you set the meeting up, and I certainly don't want to jeopardize your job. I've done enough to mess up people's lives."

Aaron put his hand on her shoulder, stopping her. "Don't be ridiculous. You haven't messed up anyone's life. Have lunch with me this afternoon, and I'll fill you in on the Emily Smith angle."

"Mr. Davis said she was Edward's sister," Laura stated.

"Yes, and a very bitter woman."

"Oh, Aaron, I would love to have lunch, but I have things I need to get done."

"I'll tell you what," Aaron began. "Here's an offer that will be hard to refuse. Spend family home evening with me tonight. You can't have things planned for tonight—it's family night." He winked and gave her an impish grin.

Laura smiled. "Okay. I accept. So what's the activity?"

"Dinner at the best restaurant in town."

"Wait a minute. That doesn't sounds like a family home evening activity."

"Why not?" Aaron innocently queried with another smile.

"Okay, what time are you picking me up?"

"Seven o'clock."

"Perfect."

Aaron walked her to the car. The fog lingered, though not as dense now. "Wait, a minute," Aaron said. "When you were running down the street earlier, who did you think was following you?"

Laura sighed. "It's a long story, and I'm not even sure if I saw what I thought I saw. It was pretty foggy, and maybe my mind was playing tricks on me. And actually, he wasn't following me—I was following him." At the stunned look on Aaron's face, Laura got in her car and added, "I'll tell you about it tonight."

19

Laura parked on the street in front of Julie's shop, then stepped out of the car and onto the street. Stopping for a moment and listening to the silence of the town, she decided there was something unnatural about the near-quiet. There was almost no traffic, and only a handful of people strolled down the sidewalks.

As the faint sounds of Bufordville came to her on the rain-cleaned air, Laura smiled—she did love that scent. A bird sang in a bare tree nearby, and though Laura couldn't identify the bird by its call, the sound was melodic and haunting. Then wind swept across Laura's face, and as the branches swayed overhead, the bird fluttered away.

She walked around her car and stepped onto the sidewalk, then hurried through the door of the shop, causing the cowbell to clang loudly. Julie stood behind the counter helping a customer, and she looked up at Laura and smiled. Laura nodded and walked over to peruse a nearby table covered with odds and ends. As she looked at the bottles, vases, and figurines, she wondered who'd once owned them—and what secrets those families were keeping.

When the cowbell clanked to announce the departure of Julie's customer, Julie came quickly from behind the counter. "What's going on?"

Going into great detail, Laura filled Julie in on her conversations with George Walker, Roger Ballister, and Leonard Davis. As she listened, Julie leaned on the counter, seemingly mesmerized.

When Laura finally finished, Julie burst out, "Well, I've been doing some snooping too, I found the apartment address where Smith was killed, and guess what?"

Laura raised her eyebrows. "What?"

"It's the Colonial Manor Apartments," Julie declared as if this bit of information had great meaning.

"So?" Laura responded, not recognizing the name.

"That's where I live!"

"You're kidding."

Julie leaned closer and lowered her voice, though the two young women were alone in the store. "No. And Mrs. Reed, the building manager, lived in the apartments when Smith died."

"Did you talk to her?" Laura asked.

"Yes, but she doesn't remember much. She lived on the first floor, and Smith lived on the third floor. She didn't really know him."

Laura frowned. "So it's a dead end?"

"Not exactly. Mrs. Reed said Lucille Gordon lived across the hall from Smith, and Lucille still lives in the same apartment she did twenty years ago."

"What did Lucille have to say?"

"Nothing, at least to me. I haven't had a chance to talk to her."

"Why don't you give me her address? I'll stop by when I get a chance."

"Oh, I wish I had time to get more involved," Julie complained. "It's just that I have so much going on right now."

As Julie wrote Lucille Gordon's address on a sheet of notepaper, the cowbell on the door sounded. A tall, thin man entered the shop, followed by a young man and woman.

"Oh, yes, this would make a lovely gift shop," the young woman stated.

The tall man directed the couple to a large window. "Isn't this window charming? It's a true period piece."

"When did you say the property would be available?" the young man asked.

The tall man threw a snide glance in Julie's direction. "Soon."

Julie slammed her pen on the counter. "Okay, Heaps, get these people out before I call the police and have you all thrown out."

The tall man stood even taller and held his nose high. "This is a public shop. We have as much right to browse as that lady there does."

Julie moved from the counter. "Actually, this is private property, and I'm the owner. And I expect my customers to browse for antiques, Heaps, not for antique shops."

"Well, this shop won't belong to you much longer," Heaps declared. "It's a matter of weeks before the bank forecloses. Your business is a failure."

Julie grabbed a broom. "That does it, Heaps. Get out before I call the police and have you thrown out!"

Heaps backed away. "Come along, Mr. and Mrs. Morris. I'll show you the unique architectural features of the building's exterior."

The three marched out, throwing condescending glances at Julie as they left. Julie turned and looked at Laura, who asked with concern, "Julie, is the bank really foreclosing on your shop?"

Julie sighed. "Not yet, but I suppose it's only a matter of time."

"Why didn't you tell me?"

"I figured you had enough on your mind. You didn't need me to add to it."

Laura's heart sank, and she realized she'd been so self-absorbed in her own drama that Julie probably hadn't felt comfortable confiding in her. "What are you going to do?"

"I don't know. Life has its own way of working things out. It's not always what I would like, but it's usually best."

That sounds just like what Leonard said, Laura thought. "Is there anything I can do?" she inquired.

Julie smiled. "Thanks, but I'll be okay."

"Maybe we can figure something out," Laura sympathized with a sigh. "I wish I had access to my full inheritance, but that won't happen for three years. My current stipend is generous, but not enough to buy a business with. If I had all the money now, maybe I could've bought out half of the shop and we could've run the store together."

"To tell you the truth," Julie answered with a half smile, "I don't think antiques really work in this area. I thought about changing or expanding into something else, but it takes money and know-how, and I'm a little short on both right now."

"I do have a little bit of money in savings. Maybe I could loan you enough to make the back payments so you won't lose the store," Laura offered.

Julie smiled. "I really appreciate the offer, but I already owe so many people that I don't know that it would be a good idea to get further into debt. Plus, accepting a loan from a friend isn't always the best thing for keeping the friendship intact. Anyway, I should probably just sell the shop and pay off what debts I can."

"Then what?" Laura asked.

"I don't know," Julie replied. "I don't like thinking that far ahead. Let's change the subject."

Laura watched as Julie placed the broom against the wall. She could tell that her questions had made Julie uncomfortable. "What would you like to talk about?" Laura asked, knowing they would both keep thinking about Julie's plight even while they talked of something entirely different.

"Let's talk about our investigation," Julie responded with a dramatic smirk. "I haven't told you about Sheriff Buford yet."

"What about him?"

"He's in the Buford County Nursing Home on Village Hill Road," Julie replied, obviously pleased with herself.

"Great. I'll check him out tomorrow. See, Julie? You've helped a lot. I should pay you for all your hard work."

"You better not! This is fun, and if you pay me it will be more like a job. Anyway, back to the investigation . . . you're going to be very busy." Julie smiled longingly.

"Honestly, as of right now I feel like I'm spinning my wheels."

Julie shrugged and grinned. "Well, maybe you need to make something happen."

"Like what?"

Julie stepped closer and leaned in, then spoke softly. "Like making the killer expose himself."

Laura furrowed her brow. "What? How on earth can I do that?"

"Well, at first I thought we should keep our investigation under wraps, but the more I think about it, the more I think we need to push things along. Let me tell you something I learned one summer at my grandparents' house in upstate New York. You see, they had an extensive lawn," Julie explained, "and they had problems with groundhogs tunneling through it."

Laura released a heavy breath and grinned. "I can't wait to find out how this connects to my problem."

Julie crossed her arms and leaned against the wall behind the counter. "Before my grandfather could catch the groundhogs, he had to smoke them out. He would light a torch and stick it in one of the groundhogs' tunnels. The smoke channeled through the tunnels and forced all the groundhogs out."

Laura wrinkled her forehead. "I need to light a fire in the hole?"

"Yeah."

Laura turned her palms up and shrugged. "And how do I do that?"

Julie paused, then her eyes sparkled. "Well, I once saw this old movie—"

"Not another movie scenario," Laura groaned, rolling her eyes.

Julie held up her hands. "Well, just listen before you judge!"

Laura bit her lip and placed her hands on the counter. "Okay. Go ahead."

"Well, in this movie, this man wants to catch his brother's killer, so he makes everyone think he knows who the killer is. Then the killer has to make a move."

"What are you suggesting?" Laura queried, leaning forward.

"As far as anyone knows, you could have seen the face of Ruby's killer all those years ago. If we could make the killer think you remember that night—that you know who pushed Ruby down the stairs—he or she may try to make a move."

Laura stood up straight and put her hands on her hips. "Make a move? You mean try to kill me? I don't have a death wish, you know!"

Walking around from behind the counter, Julie put her hand on Laura's shoulder. "If we plan it carefully, we can pull it off. First we have to somehow spread the word you're regaining your memory of that night. Let's have a Harvest Moon Festival."

Laura stood up straight. "What? When?"

"This week. Isn't it time for it?"

Laura threw up her arms. "I don't know—I never even thought about it."

Julie went behind the counter and pulled out a calendar. "The full moon is September eighteenth. That's Sunday."

"We can't have it on the Sabbath," Laura said.

"Let's have it Friday night then," Julie suggested. "This Friday. It was held on a Friday when Ruby was killed, so it will add to the mystique. We'll have the festival, and we'll spread the word through the local gossips that you're having a gala to help regain your memory of that night twenty years ago."

"Julie, we don't have time to prepare a festival by this weekend. It's a crazy idea."

"Well, it doesn't have to be a full-scale festival. It can be more of an open house—you know, a way for you to meet everyone in Bufordville. It's worth a try." Julie looked at her seriously. "You do want to get to the truth, don't you?"

Laura did want to know the truth, and since the chances were remote that the killer was still alive and living in Bufordville, she decided it couldn't hurt to have the festival. Besides, as nervous as the thought made her, Laura really did want to get to know the local people, and this would be a perfect opportunity. "Okay, Julie, but we don't have much time."

Julie beamed. "I'll make some flyers about the festival and post them around town."

"Let's call it a Harvest Moon Open House," Laura directed her. "I don't want people's expectations too high."

"That's a good idea. I'll work on the advertising angle, Laura, and you work on the food."

Laura sighed. "Agnes will love this. She already resents me."

Julie smiled. "Well, make it something simple like vegetable trays and mixed nuts and desserts—stuff like that."

"Explain to me again, Julie, how this is going to help us catch Ruby's killer."

"Well, it's like I was saying. We'll set the killer up. We'll make sure everyone knows you're starting to remember the past. Then we'll have you go to your room with a headache or something. The entire party will take place in the stable's reception hall, just like it did on the night Ruby died. That place has a kitchen and bathrooms, so it's perfect. And the mansion itself will be off limits. I'll watch the door to see if anyone follows you into the house."

"Julie, there's more than one door to the mansion."

"Trust me, Laura. I won't let anything happen to you. You're the only friend I've got right now. We'll get your buddy Aaron to watch the front of the house, and I'll watch the back. That way we have all our angles covered."

"You and Aaron are going to take care of a killer all by yourselves?" Laura demanded.

Julie's forehead creased. "Well, Aaron's a hotshot lawyer, so maybe he can get the police to help us."

"They'll think we're crazy," Laura responded.

"Maybe he could tell them you've been threatened or something."

Laura put her hands on her hips. "You mean lie?"

"Okay, let's just ask Aaron, and maybe he can come up with something to get the police to watch the place during the party."

"I still don't see how all of this is going to prove who killed Ruby. Even if someone follows me into the house and the police nab him—or her—what does that prove?"

"It exposes our prime suspect, and the police can start asking this person some serious questions. You know—lean on them. If this person believes that you remember them, they will probably end up confessing. We all know the police have ways to get people to confess. Don't you ever watch detective shows on TV? The alternative is that a murderer out there can continue going about his life—or her life. It could even be someone you interact with on a daily basis, and you could be in danger."

"I know, Julie, but there's one thing you're forgetting in all this."

Julie scowled. "What's that?"

"The person who pushed Ruby down the stairs may be dead or may have moved away from Bufordville by now."

Julie threw back her long red hair. "That's true, but we still have to try—for your sake. And who knows, maybe just having the festival will cause you to remember more from your early days at the plantation. I think it's worth a try, Laura."

Laura nodded resignedly, knowing Julie was right. They had to do more than ask questions. Laura just prayed no one would get hurt if she and Julie carried out their plan.

20

"This is it," Aaron declared as he held the car door open for Laura. "The best restaurant in town."

Laura stepped out of the car, taking in the large, two-story Randolph Tavern, which featured a wide porch filled with ornate wicker furniture. As Aaron opened the tavern's front door, it squeaked loudly, adding to the old-time feel of the place. Inside, the flickering flames of a blazing fire sent reflections from the silver chandeliers across the hardwood floors and oak-paneled walls.

"Two?" the hostess asked as Laura and Aaron approached her raised desk.

"Yes," Aaron answered with a smile.

"Right this way." The young woman led them to a cozy corner table.

Aaron pulled out a chair for Laura and she sat, continuing to take in the tavern's warm, pleasant atmosphere. Aaron sat down across from her. "Do you like the tavern?"

Laura smiled. "Yes, very much. It's like going back in time to the eighteenth century."

A waiter, wearing a red vest, a ruffled white shirt, and black slacks, approached their table. "Good evening. My name is James, and I'll be your server tonight. Have you visited our establishment before?"

"No," Laura responded.

"She's new in the area," Aaron explained, winking at Laura.

The waiter handed them each a menu then turned to Laura. "The Randolph specializes in traditional Southern food. I hope you will find something to your liking, ma'am."

"Thank you. I'm sure I will."

The waiter walked away, and Laura perused the menu. She had discovered that many Southern dishes were fried, and she wanted to order something fairly healthy.

"See anything you like?" Aaron inquired.

"I think I'll try the baked quail with squash and potatoes," Laura answered.

"Sounds good to me. Looks like we're ordering exactly the same thing again."

They both chuckled, and Laura cringed as she remembered how she'd almost choked on a peanut butter sandwich the day they met.

When the waiter returned with two glasses of water, Aaron declared, "We'll both have the quail, please."

James nodded. "An excellent selection. All of our main dishes are served with two sides. What would you like as your sides?"

"We'll both have the squash and the potatoes."

"Great. Would you care to see the wine list?"

"No," Aaron replied. "Water will be fine."

"Very well," the waiter said, collecting the menus.

As the waiter scurried away, Laura gazed across the table into Aaron's blue eyes. She realized she was beaming. "Thank you for dinner."

Aaron returned her smile. "Maybe you should wait until you've tried the quail before you thank me."

"I don't need to wait on the food. I love this place—it's so peaceful."

Aaron smiled. "Quite a contrast to your life these past few days, I guess. I wish I could help you somehow."

"You already have. I think it really helped me to talk to Leonard, and you made that happen."

"Is he still on your suspect list?"

Laura shrugged. "Well, he was obsessed with his sister, and he was unhappy about her engagement. He had motive and opportunity. In fact, he claims he was driving around by himself when his sister was killed, so there's no way to confirm his alibi. That said, the motive is pretty weak. I mean, he loved his sister so much that he did everything he could to protect her, so it makes no sense that he would kill her."

"I'm not sure of that," Aaron ventured. "Leonard demands total loyalty. Anything less is unacceptable. Perhaps Leonard was an insecure tyrant. When tyrants feel threatened, they annihilate the thing that causes their insecurity." Aaron frowned and shook his head.

"That doesn't sound like the Leonard Davis you described to me yesterday."

"Well, I've been thinking since I talked with Emily this morning. Everything she said made sense. I've been so loyal to Leonard that I emphasized his virtues and pushed his vices to the back of my mind. I owe Leonard a lot—he did so much for me—and I want to think the best of him. But I realized today that Leonard really plays on the loyalty of the people around him, and sometimes that can be downright wicked."

"Do you think Leonard pushed Ruby down the stairs?" Laura inquired, lowering her voice slightly.

Aaron shook his head. "I didn't say that. Remember, I'm a criminal lawyer, so I rule nothing out. I look at the evidence and let it speak for itself."

The waiter returned with a basket of bread. "Would you like anything else before your dinner arrives?"

"No, thank you," Aaron answered, and the waiter walked away.

Laura took a sip of water. "What are the facts telling you now?"

Aaron looked down. "That Emily is a more likely suspect than Leonard."

The ice in Laura's glass tinkled as she set it down a little too hard. "Miss Smith? Why?"

Aaron looked up, and Laura wondered how she could continue to think straight if she kept looking into his eyes. "She loved her brother and felt Ruby Davis used him to get back at Leonard. And she was scared that Ruby would ruin Edward's life, so she definitely had motive. She also had opportunity. She says she left the festival about the same time as Leonard and Edward, and she doesn't have a solid alibi, either."

"Well," Laura remarked as she began buttering a slice of delicious-looking bread, "if we're talking motive and opportunity, no one had it better than Agnes Hayes."

"The maid? Isn't that cliché?"

"No. The butler's cliché," Laura returned with a smile and then a giggle as Aaron laughed heartily. "Usually the maid is above suspicion."

"Why's that?" he questioned with a grin.

"Because maids are loyal—they don't keep a job for long if they're not. Everyone knows that."

"Oh. But Agnes is an exception?" Aaron asked, lifting his water glass.

"Yes," Laura affirmed, "because she had a run-in with Ruby Davis on the festival day. Ruby caught Agnes stealing and threatened to expose her to my aunt."

Aaron put his glass down and raised his eyebrows. "Agnes is—or was—a thief?"

"Worse. Agnes is a kleptomaniac. And she had opportunity—she admitted she was in the house at the same time as Ruby. But she claims she heard nothing."

Aaron shrugged. "Maybe she didn't."

"Well, if my memory of that night is correct, the voices were loud—loud enough that anyone on the first floor would have heard them for sure. And I don't believe her story about going in to close an open window."

The waiter returned with a tray and carefully placed their entrées on the table. Then he deftly cut the meat from the bones on each of their plates. "Anything else?" he queried. Laura shook her head and watched him absentmindedly as he walked away.

"But what about Mr. Ballister?" Aaron asked, regaining her attention. "I thought he was your prime suspect. Wasn't he seen going into the mansion right after Ruby Davis did?"

About to take her first bite of quail, Laura stopped with her fork in the air. "Yes, but he came by to see me this morning. He says Leonard asked my aunt to ship Ruby off to Europe with my mother and me to get her away from Edward. He even offered Ruby a higher salary and a new wardrobe if she would go."

"Well, that would convince me to break off my wedding engagement," Aaron teased. "Who could resist a new wardrobe?"

Laura laughed. "I know what you mean. But Leonard didn't believe Ruby loved Edward, so he naturally thought she'd be more interested in material things than in marrying him."

Aaron's knife clinked as he placed it on the edge of his plate. "Leonard and Emily agree about Ruby's motives. They both thought she was trying to spite Leonard. She'd have to be a very coldhearted person to do that."

"I don't believe Ruby was coldhearted at all. In fact, I think she loved Edward. After all, Roger said she rejected his offer."

"And you believe Ballister's story?"

"Yes. Why not?"

Aaron smiled. "Because murderers are usually good liars."

Laura took a bite of potatoes and thought about Roger for a moment. "Well, I'm not sure what I think about Roger yet, and I am a little leery of him after what happened this morning."

Aaron leaned forward. "What happened?"

Laura paused for several seconds, then spoke. "I don't know if I want to tell you."

He smiled. "Keeping secrets again?"

"Not exactly. I just don't want you to think I'm crazy." Aaron shrugged and grinned. "Okay," she sighed, "I guess we're beyond that, aren't we?" Taking a deep breath, she looked around to make sure no one was listening, then spoke softly. "Back in St. Louis a man was following me around. I think he may have broken into my house, but I can't prove that. I saw him several times, and he had a—how should I put this—a memorable face. And I saw him again this morning, here in Bufordville."

"Has he threatened you?"

Laura pondered the question. "Yes and no. I mean, he never came at me with a knife or anything, but stalking someone is threatening."

"It's also illegal," Aaron declared. "Did you call the police?"

"No, I was scared they'd think I was loony."

Aaron lifted his water glass. "Where did you see this man this morning?"

"I followed him down the street to Roger Ballister's office."

Aaron nearly choked on his water. "You followed him?"

Laura shrugged. "I know. Crazy, huh? I can't explain it."

"So Ballister's having you followed?"

Laura wiped her mouth with the cloth napkin. "I don't know, and I'm not absolutely sure he went into Roger's office. Maybe he was hiding around there or something, or maybe I was imagining the whole thing. It was pretty foggy, you know."

"It wasn't that foggy," Aaron clarified. "But you were pretty shaken up by the time I—uh—ran into you. And if you say you saw this man, I believe you did."

"Thank you . . . you have no idea how reassuring that sounds," Laura murmured.

"So Ballister is still on your list of suspects?"

"I guess everyone is still on my list for now," Laura responded dejectedly. "I don't seem to be getting anywhere."

"Who are your other suspects?" Aaron wondered.

"Well, there's Roscoe Buford, the sheriff's son. He loved Ruby, and he got drunk at the party and made a big scene. I don't know if he has a verifiable alibi because I haven't talked to him yet, but I think it's possible he pushed Ruby down the stairs."

"Maybe he's your prime suspect in Smith's death, too."

"Maybe."

"Emily believes your father killed Edward," Aaron declared, then took a bite of quail.

Laura placed her fork on the pewter plate. "She told you that?"

Aaron swallowed and took a sip of water. "Yes. She was intent on the idea. She disliked the Bufords for some reason."

"Well, it doesn't surprise me. I'm sure the whole town thinks my father killed Edward Smith."

"Well, I don't think your father murdered anyone. In fact, I think Leonard is still a strong suspect in Edward's death," Aaron said.

"Yes," Laura responded in relief. "He got him out of jail, and he found the body on Sunday morning."

"Of course, we can't omit the possibility that Edward killed himself," Aaron added.

"No, I suppose not."

"You don't believe it was suicide, do you?" Aaron asked.

"No."

"Neither does Emily," Aaron pointed out. "She claimed Edward's door had been jimmied open and that he was lying on the bed as if he'd been sleeping. The gas was in the kitchen. If you turned on the gas to kill yourself, why not just stay there by the source, to get it over with, so to speak? Why go into the bedroom?"

Laura nodded. "Good point. We know that my father argued with Edward at Dr. Preston's that afternoon, but I still can't believe he killed him. I can see my father hitting him in a rage or something, but he wouldn't commit cold, calculated murder. I can't see him sneaking in and turning on the gas. If he wanted to protect me, he would have hired a bodyguard or something."

"Solving a twenty-year-old murder—two murders—isn't easy, is it? Is there anything I can do to help?"

She looked into his kind blue eyes. "Well, there is one thing."

"Name it."

"You know my friend, Julie?"

"The antique dealer?"

"Yes—antique dealer and amateur sleuth. She came up with an idea for catching the killer."

Aaron frowned. "What kind of idea? Do I dare ask?"

"We've planned an open-house reception at Buford's Bluff for Friday night, the anniversary of Ruby's death." She said it quickly, then raised her shoulders and furrowed her forehead, waiting for Aaron's reaction.

"Don't tell me—a memorial service," he mused.

"Well, in a way, yes. The general idea is that we make the killer think I remember seeing him or her push Ruby down the stairs. Then he or she will have to make a move to make sure I keep quiet."

Aaron's water glass thudded on the table, and water spilled on the tablecloth. "Tell me you're joking."

"I'm not. I'm completely serious," Laura stated firmly.

"Laura, it's a ridiculous idea."

"I thought so at first when Julie suggested it. But the more I think about it, the more I think it might work. And as a bonus, maybe it will help me get to know people in the community—and maybe it will help me remember some things."

"And maybe it will get you killed," Aaron stated brusquely.

"Well, if I really thought I'd be in mortal danger, I wouldn't hold the open house. I'm beginning to think that the person who pushed Ruby down the stairs is already dead. Even if the murderer is still alive, what are the chances they'd come after me at a party with hundreds of people there? But just in case, I'm asking you to help watch the house. Julie wondered if you might have friends that work for the police department that could help with security. We could pay them, of course." Aaron's face grew stern, but Laura pressed on. "You see, I'm going to develop a headache and go to my room. Julie will announce to everyone that I've remembered something dreadful and need to lie down."

Still looking at her skeptically, Aaron sighed. "Is there any way I can talk you out of this crazy scheme?"

"No," she replied, "but if I can remember what happened to Ruby before Friday night, I'll call off the plan."

"Okay, I want you to close your eyes." Aaron suddenly moved his chair beside her and grasped her shoulders.

"What?"

"Close your eyes. I'm going to help you remember." He released his grip on her, and Laura closed her eyes, thinking, *Whatever it is you're doing, Aaron, it will never work.*

"Now, I want you to concentrate on that night at the Harvest Moon Festival twenty years ago. I want you to tell me what you were doing."

Laura opened her eyes. "This is silly, Aaron. Are you trying to hypnotize me or something?"

"It's not silly. I use this with my clients all the time. It's a concentration method that allows people to recall vivid details."

"Oh, all right, but this stuff never works on me."

"Don't be so pessimistic," he retorted.

Laura closed her eyes. She imagined the nursery, complete with daisy wallpaper, the big dollhouse, and plenty of toys.

"What are you doing?" Aaron asked.

"I'm playing with my dollhouse in the nursery."

"What does the nursery look like?"

"It's got daisy wallpaper and a lot of toys—mainly dolls, but there's a rocking horse, too. Did you ever have a rocking horse?"

"Concentrate!" Aaron commanded sternly.

"Okay."

Aaron cleared his throat. "Now what are you doing?"

"I'm getting into bed and turning out the light. Ruby had taught me how to turn the lamp off by myself."

"Are you alone?"

"Yes. Now I hear something. I'm sitting up in bed looking at the window. The wind is blowing little tree branches against the window—the rain is hitting the window too. There's lightning, and I hear thunder."

"How do you feel?"

"I'm scared. I'm really scared."

"What're you doing?"

"I'm jumping from bed and running into the closet. I get in the closet and crouch down, then close the door. Voices are echoing in the hall."

Aaron leaned forward. "Whose voices?"

"I can't tell."

"Man or woman?"

"I can't tell."

"What are you doing now, Laura?"

"I'm opening the closet door. I go out into the hall, and the floor is cold and wet on my feet. I see lights coming from the foyer . . . and shadows."

"Shadows of people?"

"Yes. I can hear them arguing, so I walk to the banister and kneel down to watch."

"Who do you see?"

"Ruby and someone in a hood. They're standing on the stairs."

"Who's in the hood?"

"I can't tell."

"Is the hooded person's back to you?" Aaron asked.

"Yes."

"And Ruby is facing up the stairs?"

"Yes."

"And you don't recognize the hooded person's voice?"

"No. Now the person is pushing Ruby down the stairs! No!"

"What are you doing?"

"I'm running! I run to the nursery and hide in the closet again. Then footsteps come through my bedroom door and over to the closet. I'm terrified because I just know it's a monster. Then someone opens the closet door, and a voice calls my name."

"Do you recognize the voice?"

"I don't know. I don't think so."

"Is it a man or a woman?"

"A woman—I think."

"What do you hear now?"

"A creaking sound, like the hinge on a trunk or chest."

"Do you know what's being opened or closed?"

"Would you like some dessert?"

Laura opened her eyes and briefly frowned at the waiter. "No, thank you," she answered, pasting on a grin, fearing for a moment that she was unintentionally mimicking his smile.

The waiter looked at Aaron. "I'm full, thank you," Aaron mumbled.

After the waiter strode away, Laura shook her head and said, "He probably thinks I'm crazy too."

"Laura, no one thinks you're crazy," Aaron said with a sigh. "Now, do you want to keep trying?"

"No, I have a headache. I think I want to go home."

The drive home was quiet. Aaron parked the car by the back door, and Laura allowed him to open the car door for her this time. "Well, at least you know more than you did before," Aaron commented as he waited for her to exit the car, then closed the door.

"Like what?" Laura asked, stepping to the back door.

"As you walked down the hall, the floor was wet, which means that Ruby and her killer probably came down the hall as far as the nursery. It was raining, remember? This could change the whole time frame. Maybe Ruby didn't fall coming up the stairs to check on you. Maybe she checked on you and then fell on her way back down the stairs."

"That's true. I didn't think of that," Laura admitted quietly.

"And you heard a woman's voice."

"Yes, but none of it helps me understand what happened to Ruby."

"It will come in time," Aaron assured her, moving closer. "Good night," he said, taking her hands in his and gently squeezing them. His hands felt warm and comforting, and a tingle shot up her arm.

"Good night, and thank you for dinner," she said breathlessly, pulling her hands away. Then she hurried up the stairs and into the house.

21

On Tuesday morning, Laura woke late, dressed quickly, and hurried down to the kitchen. While she gulped down some bacon and eggs, she told Agnes about the open house she planned to hold Friday night.

"It's bad luck," Agnes exclaimed, frowning and shaking her head. "The full moon is Sunday night, and you must have the festival at the full moon. You're making the same mistake your aunt made!"

Laura sighed, then got up from the table, murmured a quick thanks, and dashed out to her aunt's car. As she drove away, she glanced in the rearview mirror and saw Agnes standing at the back door, twisting her apron in her hands.

As Laura drove into Bufordville, she noticed an orange flyer taped to an electrical pole, so she stopped to appraise Julie's work. The flyer read, *Harvest Moon Open House at Buford's Bluff. Come meet your new neighbor, Miss Laura McClain, niece of the late Laura Buford. Friday Night, 6:00 PM. Light refreshments and music.*

Laura wasn't sure that CDs and a DJ would cut it for such an occasion, and she wondered where they would find decent musicians at such short notice. Her stomach churned as she realized that the stress of hosting the open house was already getting to her, and she'd done next to nothing. *Hopefully,* she thought, *I'll be able to find out who killed Ruby Davis and Edward Smith before Friday night, and then I'll just cancel the open house.*

Sighing, Laura pulled out Julie's map and directions to the Colonial Manor Apartments. At least the fog had lifted this morning and the sun was shining.

As Laura drove past the drugstore, she saw Hattie and her sister standing on the sidewalk talking to the druggist. Next, Laura passed Julie's shop, noticing her friend washing the windows as if nothing were wrong, as if she weren't losing the shop in a matter of days.

Turning the car onto Birch Street, Laura passed Aaron's office building and the courthouse. She thought she caught a glimpse of Aaron filing into the courthouse behind a policeman. As she turned onto Elm Avenue, she noticed a Victorian mansion with a sign out front that read DR. LEVI PRESTON'S HOME OFFICE. Laura passed the house and turned left onto a narrow lane that suddenly curved downward. To the right was a charming jumble of brightly colored rooftops. The rooftops—slate, asphalt, and tin—blended with the fading yellow and red leaves to form what looked like a bold patchwork quilt.

Laura carefully maneuvered the large sedan down the hill. As she descended, the houses themselves became visible through a haze of vanishing leaves. She drove through tree-lined streets past brightly painted old homes. At the end of the street stood a massive redbrick building that was as plain as the surrounding houses were ornate. A brick wall surrounded the building, and Laura parked by the wrought-iron gate out front.

Getting out of the car, she walked to the gate and observed the sign overhead: *Colonial Manor Apartments.* Laura opened the gate and made her way along a narrow, stone walk through a flowering wilderness that had obviously once been a garden.

Wild rosebushes nearly covered the rails along the front porch, and a thorn scratched Laura's arm as she made her way up the rickety stairs. Paint was peeling from the frame around the doors. Laura briefly looked back over her shoulder before scanning the surrounding porch for a sign or instructions. Seeing nothing, she grasped the doorknob and pushed the old door open. The rusty hinges squeaked loudly, and Laura cringed as she entered and shut the door.

The entry hall was much lighter than she'd expected, mainly because of a back door that stood open and led to a parking lot in the rear. A gray kitten appeared at the back doorway, stretched as if it'd been sleeping, then meowed and darted for Laura's leg. She could hear it purring as it rubbed against her navy slacks.

"Go away, kitty. You're cute, but you're getting hair all over me."

On the left side of the hall was a narrow staircase, and on the right was a row of battered mailboxes. Gently pushing the cat away with her foot, Laura inspected the mailboxes until she saw the name she was looking for: Lucille V. Gordon—Apartment 3C.

The boards creaked as Laura made her way up the stairs, the cat mewing persistently as it followed her. Stains streaked the carpet in the third-floor hallway, and the walls looked filthy. Laura guessed they hadn't been cleaned—or repainted—in decades. Laura located apartment 3C and paused. Sighing, she knocked on the door, and after about a minute, it finally cracked open as far as the chain lock would allow.

"Yes?"

"Lucille Gordon?" Laura asked, feeling bad for disturbing her.

"Who wants to know?" the elderly woman asked with a shaky voice.

"My name is Laura McClain. My aunt was the late Laura Buford, and my mother and father were John and Sarah McClain. I live out at Buford's Bluff. I've come to ask you a few questions about your former neighbor, Edward Smith."

The door closed and the chain rattled. Then the door opened to expose a frail skeleton of a woman. Her thin hair fell over her head, disclosing her near baldness. A broad smile deepened the network of wrinkles across her face.

"You're the little girl all grown up, are you?" Her voice trembled, but she seemed pleased to have company.

"Yes. May I come in for a moment?"

Lucille stood aside and beckoned Laura in with a wave of her arm. Laura stepped into the gloomy apartment, and the cat followed. Lucille shut the door and opened the curtains, allowing light to stream into the room. Laura walked to a couch so old that the stuffing pushed through the frayed cover, then she sat on a pillow that covered a hole in a seat worn to the wood. Lucille sat opposite her in an armchair stained with age.

"What did you want to know about Mr. Smith?" Lucille asked.

Laura cleared her throat and tried to ignore the stench in the apartment. "Well, I understand you lived here twenty years ago when Edward Smith died."

"That's right. He lived in apartment 3B, right across the hall."

"You have a good memory." Laura gazed across the room's clutter, searching for family photographs, for some sign that there was more to Lucille's life than a dingy apartment and several stray cats.

"It's not every day your neighbor dies of gas poisoning," Lucille said with a wry smile.

"I suppose not. Did you see Mr. Smith on the day he died?"

"Oh, yes. I saw him, all right. He woke me around four o'clock Saturday morning. He was as drunk as a skunk, and he could hardly stand. He pounded on his door for someone to let him in, so I opened my door and told him to pipe down before I called the cops."

"What did he do?" Laura asked.

Lucille's smile faded and formed itself into an awkward frown. "He started crying. He said someone had killed his girlfriend. He said he was going to find out who killed her and then kill the murderer. I told him to go in and go to bed, but he staggered through the hall."

"Where did he go?"

Lucille shrugged. "I don't know. I went back to bed, and I didn't see him again until that afternoon when he was going into his apartment."

"Did he have a key?"

"I don't know. I suppose."

The little gray cat popped its head from under the couch and chewed the cuff of Laura's pants. She tried to ignore it. "Did you know Edward's sister, Emily Smith?"

"I met her a few times."

"Was she with him that Saturday when he went in his apartment?"

"No. He was alone."

"Did you see him again that day?"

"No, not really. I was napping in front of the television later that afternoon when I heard him arguing with someone, so I got up and peeked out the door. A woman came out of the apartment and slammed the door. I didn't see Edward, but it must have been him arguing with her."

Laura winced as she felt needlelike claws grab her ankle. She shook her leg and attempted to shoo the cat away, but it jumped up on the couch. "So you didn't know the woman?"

Lucille leaned forward. "Oh, yes, I did."

"Who was it?"

"Your mother, Sarah McClain."

Suddenly the room seemed to sway. Laura felt sick to her stomach, but she managed to ask, "Are you sure it was my mother?"

Lucille smiled. "Oh, yes. Everyone knew your aunt and your mother. They were the queens of Bufordville society."

Relieved that the lightheadedness had passed, Laura asked her next question. "Did you see anyone else visit Mr. Smith that day?"

"No. I didn't see anyone visit him until the next morning."

"And who visited him then?"

"That lawyer-partner of his."

"Leonard Davis?" Laura asked.

"That's the one," Lucille affirmed.

Laura let her hand fall on the sofa cushion. Startled, the cat jumped back onto the floor.

"Did you see him talk to Mr. Smith?"

"Oh, no. Smith was dead by then. I heard the lawyer knocking on Smith's door. He called Smith's name for a long time, then came pounding on my door. He wanted to use the phone to call the police. He said Smith was dead."

Laura glanced down at the cat that was now licking Lucille's leg. "Why did he use your phone?"

"He claimed Smith's apartment was full of gas fumes, so he was afraid to stay in there. I told him to call the fire department, because I didn't want the whole building to blow up."

"Lucille, do you remember hearing anything like wood cracking or metal clanking on Saturday afternoon?"

Lucille reached down and prodded the cat, which darted under the couch. "No. The police asked me the same thing. They thought maybe someone had broken into the apartment and turned on the gas. It you asked me, the drunk killed himself. He turned on the gas, walked in the bedroom, and went to sleep—forever."

A few minutes later, Laura gratefully inhaled the fresh air as she walked out of the somber apartment building and into the sunlight. She jumped in her car and drove to Dr. Preston's house. After parking on the street, she trudged through the mush of fallen leaves to the front door. A sign read, *WE'RE OPEN—COME ON IN!*

The door buzzed loudly as Laura pushed it open. The Victorian reception hall gave only one clue that it served as the entry to both a house and an office: a large sign by the stairs with an arrow and the words *PATIENT WAITING ROOM.* No doubt Dr. Preston liked things big.

Although the waiting room was empty, voices resounded from somewhere in the office. Laura decided that the waiting room was really just an old-fashioned parlor. Tiffany-style lamps sat on marble-top tables, and medallion sofas and shield-backed chairs sat on oriental rugs. A lyre-based pedestal held a large, open book, and over it a notice read: *PLEASE SIGN REGISTER AND BE SEATED. GOOD THINGS COME TO THOSE WHO WAIT.*

Laura grinned at the notice, then sat down in a chair and shuffled through a magazine stack on a nearby table. The magazines were several years old. Suddenly, the door to the back room opened, and a stooped old woman plodded out, followed by a gangly man with wild silver hair. With a crooked Roman nose over a bushy mustache, the man reminded Laura of pictures she had seen of Albert Einstein. His white jacket covered his clothing from the waist up, except for a black bowtie.

"Now, Mrs. Howard," the man said. "I want you to go home and stay off that bunion. Soak your feet in warm water like I showed you. If it's not better by next week, give me a call."

"Thank you, Dr. Preston," the old woman gushed. "I don't know what I'd do without you."

Dr. Preston helped the woman out the door and turned to Laura. "Now, how may I help you, young lady?"

Laura stood and extended her hand. "I'm Laura McClain, the late Laura Buford's niece. I hoped I could ask you a few questions." Having interviewed several people now, Laura figured she could at least remember the right questions.

The elderly doctor grasped Laura's hand, and his hand felt warm and soft. "Why certainly, my dear. Your aunt was my patient, so I know her health like the back of my hand. I'll try to tell you what I can."

Laura cleared her throat. "It's not my aunt's health I've come to inquire about, Dr. Preston. It's about the death of Ruby Davis, my nanny, twenty years ago."

He frowned and shook his head sadly. "Oh, yes. That was a terrible tragedy for our town—a terrible tragedy. But why are you inquiring after such a thing now? I don't know if I can remember much that far back."

"Well, I only recently found out about Ruby's death. I started to remember things."

Dr. Preston pulled at his mustache. "Oh, yes, indeed. I do recall your case. You went into shock after Ruby died. You remained mute for months, and you buried what happened that night somewhere in your head. I do remember your condition, because it was quite rare. Nowadays we would diagnose you with an acute form of post-traumatic stress disorder, but we didn't have a name for it twenty years ago." Dr. Preston looked away thoughtfully, then back at Laura. "So you still don't remember everything, do you?"

"Not entirely—at least not yet."

The doctor waved Laura toward the medallion-backed couch as if suddenly solicitous of her health. "Oh, my, and it has plagued you all these years. Well, I'll do what I can to help. I'm surprised you haven't sought professional help before now."

Laura sat on the sofa. "Thank you. I hope you *can* help me."

"Oh, I'll do my best," he said, sitting in a chair next to the sofa.

"What do you remember about the night Ruby Davis died, Dr. Preston?"

He leaned back in the chair and looked up at the ceiling. "It's been so long . . . Well, let's see now. I was talking to someone when Edward Smith came into the party yelling that someone had fallen. The Bufords escorted Edward from the reception hall. We all ran into the foyer."

Laura sat up taller. "Who's *we*?"

Dr. Preston seemed surprised at the question. "Well, let's see now. There was your aunt Laura, your father, and Edward Smith. And your mother—she ran upstairs to check on you. I checked Ruby's pulse, but she was dead. Her neck was broken. Ed Smith went moon-eyed, accusing your family of killing Ruby. He started pushing your father around. Your aunt tried to break them up. Ed was out of his mind with grief. He said it wasn't an accident. But I have no idea how he presumed to know that."

"How do you think Ruby fell?" Laura queried.

"Well, I believe someone found a toy on the stairs. It was a nasty fall—those stairs are steep and high."

At the mention of the fall, Laura felt her heart jolt and the blood rush to her cheeks. She steadied herself by gripping the couch with one hand. "What happened next?"

"Your father went for the sheriff, and your mother called for me to come check on you. She said you were sick. So we ran upstairs and found you huddled in your closet. You were cold and your teeth were chattering, so I carried you to the bed and your mother wrapped you in blankets. You were in shock, and I stayed with you for several hours until your body returned to normal. You still refused to talk. You did eventually drink a little warm milk, but that's it."

"What happened to Edward Smith?"

Dr. Preston looked at the ceiling and paused again. "I understand he became so violent the sheriff escorted him off the property. Some of my patients saw him in various taverns all over town that night. He was stone drunk."

"I understand his sister brought him to your office the next day."

Nodding, the doctor answered, "That's right. I remember that. He'd been in jail for causing more trouble out at Buford's Bluff. I understand Leonard Davis posted bail for him. Edward was one of my poison-ivy patients. I had a lot of them that day."

"Really?"

"Oh, yes," he affirmed. "A bonfire polluted the air with particles of poison ivy."

"Who else came to see you about poison ivy that day?"

"Oh, my! Maybe you should ask who *didn't* come to see me. Let's see." The doctor sighed heavily. "Ed and his sister Emily came by—they each had a bad case on the arms and hands, so I covered them in calamine lotion. Your father came by. In fact, he was here when Ed came in, and they had a run-in right here in my office. I don't recall the exact words. It was mostly just general threats. I thought I was going to have to call the police, but John left on his own. Anyway, who else . . . Roscoe Buford came by—he had the rash on his face and neck, and I had to bandage him to keep him from scratching himself to death. Agnes Hayes and George Walker came in together. They both had it on their hands."

"You have a remarkable memory, doctor."

He smiled. "Why, thank you. I have always prided myself on remembering my patients and their illnesses. Of course, it was rather remarkable circumstances, having smoke from a fire cause such a terrible poison-ivy rash."

"Did anyone else come in for treatments?" Laura asked.

"As a matter of fact, your aunt Laura came by. She had the rash on her arms and hands. Leonard Davis had it on his neck and face, and his eyes were affected too. Roger Ballister also stopped in to see me."

"Did my mother come by? Did she have the poison-ivy rash?"

"Sarah? No, I don't believe she did. Why?"

Laura leaned back on the sofa. "I was just curious. I know poison ivy and poison oak can be nasty. One day I took my kindergarten students on an outing in the park, and we ate near a wooded area that turned out to be full of poison oak. The next day, half my class had a rash from the poison oak. Boy, did I have a lot of angry parents."

"Parents are often defensive with their children," Dr. Preston stated with a nod. "However, you can't keep children in glass houses. You have to let them experience life with all its imperfections."

Laura stood. "Dr. Preston, thank you for talking with me."

The old man stood quickly, obviously accustomed to rising when a lady did. "It has been my pleasure, Miss McClain, but I don't think I've been very helpful."

"Oh, but you have. Every detail is important."

The two shook hands, and Laura left the doctor's office. As she walked quickly to her car, she smiled in amazement. Maybe she could solve this mystery by Friday after all.

22

On Tuesday afternoon, the cowbell rang as Laura entered Julie's shop. "Hello?"

"Back here," Julie called.

Laura walked to the back storage room and found Julie on her knees unpacking and sorting a box of secondhand clothes. The room, which had obviously once served as a kitchen, contained an old porcelain sink, a row of wall-mounted cupboards, and a disconnected gas stove. Above Julie's head, a single light bulb barely lit the room.

"What're you up to in here?" Laura asked.

Julie swiped the back of her hand across her forehead and looked at Laura. "I've had a decent offer on this place. I'm going to unpack all this stuff and have a going-out-of-business sale. I might as well get what I can for it."

Laura didn't know what to say as she watched Julie sort the old clothing into piles. In the dim light, Laura could see the weariness and disappointment in Julie's face. Gazing around the room, Laura noticed several large boxes covered in a layer of dust.

Julie used a knuckle to wipe at what must have been a tear. "Well, my father will be pleased. He loves to say, 'I told you so. Julie flubbed up again.'"

Laura sneezed. "Perhaps you can take the money you get out of this place and start another business."

Julie shoved her palms hard against the box as if to push the pain away. Turning her face to Laura, she forced a smile. "I'll be lucky if I come out even. I've missed several payments, so I have to work with a lawyer to avoid foreclosure, then sell the shop and pay off the missed payments."

"Oh." Laura's heart sank. "Well, I think you need a break. Why don't you let me take you to lunch, and then I'll come back and help you with all this?"

Julie frowned. "I appreciate what you're trying to do, Laura, but I'll be fine." She wiped her hands on her jeans. "Besides, you have a lot going on right now. You don't have time to be digging through boxes of junk."

Putting her hands on her hips, Laura stepped closer. "Sure I do, Julie, and I really want to help. In fact, I think it would be kind of fun to go through these old boxes with you. Plus, I need a break from my investigation."

A faint smile appeared on Julie's face. "Really?"

Laura smiled. "Yeah, really. But before we start, I really would like to get something to eat because I'm starving."

Soon, the two friends sat in a corner booth in the café. Laura filled Julie in on all the latest details of the investigation. The shop and its smells and dust seemed far away as they discussed conspiracy and murder over club sandwiches.

"Why do you think your mother went to see Edward Smith?" Julie asked before taking a bite of her sandwich.

Laura sighed. "I don't know." She couldn't imagine her mother or father being involved in anyone's murder, yet she didn't want to think about the reasons her mother might have visited Edward Smith. For a moment, Laura thought longingly of her apartment back in St. Louis. She didn't need to close her eyes to envision the place where she'd spent most of her life. Compared to the mansion, her apartment seemed like an intimate, invitingly cozy refuge, and she briefly wished she could go back. But then she remembered that the stalker had invaded her sanctuary; at least, she assumed it was the stalker who had snooped around in her apartment. Plus, in a strange way the old apartment had become a prison to Laura, and she'd sometimes felt trapped there, like a figurine in one of her bottled gardens. Now that she thought of it, her whole life had been a prison of sorts. Somehow she'd deceived herself into believing that she was escaping her life by coming to Virginia, but she was finally realizing she'd simply brought her problems here with her. The difference was that now she was facing her problems and fears. A scripture from the Book of Mormon came to mind: *If ye have faith ye can do all things.*

Julie was staring at her, and Laura let her arm drop loudly onto the table. "What?" Laura asked.

Julie chuckled softly, folding her arms. "We're a sorry sight—the two of us sitting here wallowing in our sorrows. I've been talking to you for a couple of minutes, and you're looking off into space as if you haven't heard a word I've said."

"I'm sorry. And you're right—we need to figure out a plan. I mean, what're you going to do when you sell the shop?"

Julie looked down. "I don't know," she muttered. "I guess I'll go back to New York—maybe ask my father for help again."

"Is that what you really want?"

"No," Julie responded defensively. "Of course not, but what else can I do?"

"See, that's exactly what I mean. We've got to learn to think outside the bottle, Julie."

Julie laughed. "Don't you mean *box?*"

Laura waved her hand. "Whatever. The point is we're stuck in a rut—always relying on the familiar to get us through, but the familiar doesn't seem to be working for either of us."

Julie looked down at Laura's food. "What did they put in that sandwich of yours?"

"Very funny."

Julie took a sip of water. "Okay, so let's see if I get this right. If I really thought outside the box—or the bottle—I would refuse to go running back to my father. I would stay here where I like it, and I would find another job."

Laura pointed at her. "Good, good. That's a start."

"But—"

"Ah-ah-ah," Laura interrupted, shaking her head. "Don't fall back on the familiar."

"Well, there aren't any jobs in Bufordville," Julie complained, then picked up her sandwich.

Laura smiled. "But you do happen to know the biggest employer in Bufordville."

"Who?" Julie asked with a furrowed brow.

"Me," Laura answered proudly.

"You? That's true, Laura, but I don't know anything about tobacco, and I don't want to work on a tobacco plantation anyway. I think smoking stinks."

Laura laughed. "So do I—literally. And tobacco ruins people's lives. That's why I don't plan on staying in the tobacco business."

"You're going to sell out, huh?"

"Nope. I'm going to diversify and get rid of tobacco altogether."

Julie leaned on the table. "How are you going to do that?"

"I don't know. That's why I need a smart assistant with a lot of imagination."

Julie sat back and held up one hand. "Wait a minute. You don't need to feel sorry for me. I'm not exactly a charity case—yet."

Laura leaned forward. "This isn't about pity, Julie. This is about my needing help. I'm going to hire an executive assistant, and I'm offering you the job. If you don't want it, I'll be forced to run an ad in the *Bufordville Bugle*."

Julie laughed. "I can only imagine the people an ad like that would bring out of the woodwork. Okay, let's say I'm interested in your proposition. How much does it pay?"

"I'm sure we can work out a fair arrangement. I'll ask Aaron Farr what the going rate for executive assistants is around here."

"But wait," Julie began, suddenly crestfallen. "Don't you have to live at the mansion for three years before you inherit the mansion and the money that comes with it? I really don't think you can afford to hire anyone."

"Yes, I do have to live there for three years first," Laura responded. "But I receive a monthly allowance until then, and I was told I have access to additional funds for business expenses if I choose to get involved. There will be plenty in the account for me to hire an assistant."

"Wow. Okay. When do I start?" Julie asked excitedly.

"Right now," Laura answered.

"What?"

Laura hit the table with her palm. "That's right—today. We'll start by getting that storeroom of yours cleaned out so you can liquidate your business. We don't want any conflict of interest."

"But shouldn't I be paying you for that? Don't you have this whole thing backwards?"

"No," Laura insisted. "The sooner you can start, the faster you can help me."

"What exactly am I going to be doing for you?"

Laura smiled. "You're going to start by helping me find out who killed Ruby Davis."

* * *

By the time Laura arrived back at Buford's Bluff, the muscles in her arms and legs were sore. She'd spent all afternoon helping Julie clean out the storage room, and they still had a great deal of work to do. Unfortunately, they'd ended up throwing a lot of Julie's so-called treasures in the garbage. They couldn't fit them all in the store itself for the going-out-of-business sale, and there was just no way to keep them all unless Julie rented a storage unit. Laura convinced Julie that once she put them away, they would never see the light of day again anyway.

As usual, when Laura returned to the mansion, Agnes had dinner waiting. Laura invited her to eat dinner with her in the dining room so they could discuss the plans for Friday night's open house. They sat down, and Laura said a quick blessing on the food, then they each served themselves from the bowls of food on the table.

Trying to ignore the careful manner in which Agnes chewed every bite of food, Laura apologetically said, "Agnes, I know the open house is a terrible inconvenience and such short notice, but it's important to me."

Agnes grimaced. "Miss McClain, you're talking to a professional. I have thrown together bigger parties in much less time than this one. I do disagree with the date of your open house, but since you have already advertised it, we must forge onward. So please don't worry yourself about it. The most important thing is that you get to know the good people of Bufordville."

Laura carefully wiped her mouth with a napkin. "Thank you for being so understanding."

"Well, I'll make sure George surrounds the place with hazelnuts. They ward off evil and bring good fortune."

Stifling a chuckle, Laura smiled. "Thank you, Agnes. Why don't we get started on the menu?"

The older woman grunted in assent, then looked away and tapped her fingertips on the table. "Now, we'll need to have peach punch. It was your aunt's favorite, and Buford's Bluff is famous for its peach punch."

"Well then, by all means, we must have peach punch." Laura placed her water glass on the table.

Agnes nodded. "George and I will bring out your aunt's silver punch bowls for the occasion. We will also use silver bowls for the mints and mixed nuts. I'll call the Bufordville Bakery tomorrow about cakes and cookies. And Edna Brewster runs a little catering service. We'll need about a half dozen of their employees to help out on Friday night."

"Wow, I'm impressed. I can see our open house is in good hands."

Agnes tried to suppress a smile. "Like I said, I'm a professional."

"There's something unrelated I would like to ask you," Laura ventured, wondering if this was the right time to bring up the topic.

"Yes?"

"Did my mother and Ruby Davis get along?"

Agnes dabbed her mouth with a napkin. "Why do you ask?"

"Oh, I was curious about how nannies and mothers work together. Being a teacher, I know how defensive parents can be with their children."

"Well, now that you mention it, your mother was a little jealous of Ruby."

"In what way?"

"Your mother and your aunt were active socially. They had so many brunches and charity meetings that your mother had little time to spend with you. Ruby became like a second mother to you, and no one could separate you two. Ruby was very devoted to you, and I think your mother was jealous of that devotion. In fact, I think your mother felt guilty for not spending more time with you herself."

"Did Ruby and my mother ever disagree?" Laura wondered.

"Oh, my, yes. All the time. Your mother thought Ruby smothered you, and she accused Ruby of spoiling you."

"I see."

"Agnes, did you know my mother went to see Edward Smith the day after Ruby died?"

"Yes, I did."

Laura's eyes widened. "You did?"

"Yes. Your father had gone to Dr. Preston's about his poison ivy. When he didn't return in a timely manner, your mother worried he'd gone looking for more trouble with Edward Smith. She went into town, and Dr. Preston told her that Mr. Smith and your father had argued in his office, so she hurried over to Mr. Smith's apartment. She was afraid that your father might've gone there. Mr. Smith let her in and started verbally attacking the Bufords. Of course your mother begged him to leave her family alone. Then she came home and cried on your aunt's shoulder for over an hour. Your father got home later that afternoon, and he and your mother had a big fight."

"Where had my father been all afternoon?"

Agnes shrugged. "I don't know."

"Agnes, I understand that you and George also went to Dr. Preston's."

"That's right. We both had the poison-ivy rash. I could have taken care of the matter myself with some herbal remedies, but Miss Buford insisted we go to Dr. Preston. It was my afternoon off, and George was driving me into town to meet my sister anyway."

"You stayed with your sister that night?"

"Yes, that's where I always spend my Saturdays, you know."

23

Tuesday night, nightmares invaded Laura's sleep, and she woke on Wednesday morning with a headache. Exhaustion slowed her all morning as she tried to help Agnes and George with the open house arrangements. Noticing Laura's multiple yawns, Agnes finally suggested that Laura take a nap, so she carried her groggy self to her room where she collapsed on the bed.

Falling asleep quickly, Laura dreamed again. In one nightmare, she, Aaron, and Julie ran from a hooded monster dripping with water. It chased them to the top of a great staircase and pushed them down the stairs. They tumbled endlessly until Laura woke and stopped their fall.

When she realized that restful sleep was unlikely, Laura grabbed the notepaper that contained Jackson Buford's and Bobby Briggs's addresses. The time had come to meet her cousin, Sheriff Buford, and if she had time afterward, she would stop by Bobby Briggs's restaurant. After telling Agnes and George she would be back before dark, Laura got in the car and drove toward Bufordville.

Julie's roughly drawn map directed Laura through town and out the other side. Leaving town, she followed side roads and then a rutted and graveled lane just wide enough for her large sedan. At times she thought the bottom of the car would fall out as she scraped along the road—or that she would at least damage the oil pan. Finally, she saw a building partially hidden behind obviously untended hedges, and she stopped in the crude, gravel parking lot.

She got out of the car and looked at the jumble of small cottages sprinkled throughout a grove of large oak and maples trees. A sign at the edge of the parking lot read *Buford County Nursing Home,* and assuming the arrow on the sign would direct her to the office, Laura started down the indicated path.

The dirt path was bordered by thickets of lifeless thorn bushes, which Laura supposed could be a safety feature to discourage people from going either in or out. As she walked along the pathway, Laura inhaled the earthy smell of damp soil and rotting leaves. But as the chilly air nipped at her face, Laura thought she could smell a wintry scent as well. Because she loved autumn, she usually dreaded the onset of winter, but perhaps it would be different here in Virginia.

Laura rounded a curve in the path, and a cluster of sparrows fluttered away, startling her and making her heart jolt. She approached the central cottage, noticing that the front door was marked *Buford County Nursing Home.* As she opened the door and entered the office, the pungent smell of disinfectant assailed her nostrils. A nurse whose skin almost matched her crisp white uniform greeted Laura with a scowl. "May I help you?"

Laura stepped to the desk. "Yes, I'm looking for Jackson Buford."

"Are you a family member?" the nurse asked abruptly, staring at Laura over the tops of her narrow, gold-framed reading glasses.

"Yes. I'm his cousin."

She frowned and took off her glasses. "A cousin?" There was doubt in her tone.

"Yes," Laura replied a bit defensively. "I'm Laura McClain. My aunt was Laura Buford."

The nurse frowned again but finally muttered, "Very well."

Laura followed the nurse through the corridor and around the corner to a side door. As they stepped outside the cottage, the nurse pointed down a slight decline.

"You'll find the sheriff down the hill there in cottage 6."

"Do people still call him the sheriff?"

With a thick Southern drawl the nurse answered, "Darlin', if you want to get along with the old buzzard, just call him Sheriff Buford. He gets offended if you call him Jackson."

Laura thanked the nurse and began walking down the muddy hill. She noticed that a utility road came around the side of the compound and then curved behind it. *Ah. That explains how they get the elderly residents in and out of this place,* Laura thought. Quickening her pace, Laura approached the cabin with a faded number 6 on the front door. The cottage had small windows and a dipping roof, and the boards of the small porch squeaked under her weight. Laura knocked on the door.

"What?" a deep male voice growled.

"A visitor," Laura called, wishing she sounded more confident.

"Well, come in then."

As she opened the door, Laura saw a large man slouched in a wheelchair. There were four beds in the cottage, one of which was occupied by a man whose face Laura couldn't see. To the right, a man sat knitting in a chair next to a bed. The large man's wheelchair was parked next to the bed closest to the door, and the fourth bed was empty.

"Sheriff Buford?" Laura ventured shyly.

"Who wants to know?" Jackson Buford sounded hoarse and tired.

"I'm your cousin, Laura McClain—Sarah's daughter."

The sheriff wore a ranger-type hat, and he had pinned a badge on his robe's lapel. After studying Laura for a moment, he said, "Little Laurie?"

"Yes."

He smiled, revealing gaps where teeth had once been. "You ain't little no more."

Laura made her way over to a chair by the sheriff and sat down. "No, I'm all grown."

"How's your mama doing?" he asked.

"Well," Laura said, "she passed away a year ago."

He shook his head. "I'm real sorry about that," the sheriff responded, shaking his head. "How's your Aunt Laura?"

"Um, she passed away a couple months ago."

The old man looked down for several seconds. "Oh. I think Roscoe told me 'bout that."

Laura looked around the room. A wooden table in the middle of the room was still covered with the remains of lunch: an assortment of plates smeared with ketchup, a half-eaten meatloaf, and several bottles of water. "How long have you lived here?"

The sheriff scratched his head. "Don't rightly remember."

Laura asked him several questions about his career and about the Buford family. In turn, he asked Laura about the condition of Buford's

Bluff and about the happenings in Bufordville. Apparently, he wanted to hear the latest gossip, but being a newcomer, Laura considered her answers inadequate at best. The sheriff, however, seemed happy to get what little information Laura could give him.

Finally, Laura knew she had to get down to business. "Sheriff, I've actually come to talk with you about an old case of yours."

He face lit up. "A case? Why didn't you say so in the first place? What case are we talking about here?"

The chair, hard and cold, creaked as Laura adjusted herself in it. "The case of Ruby Davis."

The sheriff lifted himself taller in his chair in an apparent attempt to look more professional. "That was a nasty thing, wasn't it?"

"Do you remember that night?"

He nodded slowly. "Nasty night. There was rain, thunder, lightning."

He's amazingly astute for a senile old man, Laura thought.

"Do you remember what happened to Ruby?"

"She fell down those stairs. I told them the carpet was worn and too slippery."

"You don't think she tripped on a toy?"

"Maybe. Nothing conclusive." As he looked at her, Laura could see the stirrings of memory in his eyes.

"It looked like an accident to you?"

The sheriff grunted. "Her boyfriend talked some about murder, but it was just talk. He was moonstruck, if you ask me. That talk came from a cracked brain."

A squeal that could have been laughter came from the man sitting across the room. He slapped his knee loudly. "Cracked. All cracked."

Turning back to Jackson Buford, Laura asked, "You don't think anyone would have wanted to kill Ruby Davis?"

The sheriff paused thoughtfully. "Well, now, I didn't say that. I could have killed her myself sometimes. She treated my boy Roscoe real bad. She used him and threw him away, and it hurt him somethin' terrible. Her brother was awful smug. The arrogant fool thought nobody was good enough for his sister. That boyfriend of hers had a high opinion of himself too. Roscoe didn't help matters none—he made a fool of himself, showing up drunk at the festival. When he heard about Ruby's engagement, he begged her to call it off, to take him back, but she laughed in his face. She humiliated the Buford family in front of the whole town."

The man sleeping in the far bed stirred. He rolled over and yelled, "What? I didn't hear that."

The sitting man slapped his knee again and shouted, "Visitor! Sheriff's got a visitor! Be quiet so they can talk." The voice was louder than Laura had expected could come from the frail fellow.

Laura turned back to the sheriff. "So Roscoe could've killed her too?"

The sheriff narrowed his eyes as he studied Laura's face. "I can't say I would have blamed him if he'd killed her."

Jackson's stare sent chills through Laura, and she crossed her arms unconsciously. "But as far as you're concerned, Ruby's death wasn't suspicious?"

He lifted his hat and scratched his balding head. "Well, some things were hard to explain, but for the most part, I was satisfied she fell accidentally."

Laura leaned forward. "What sorts of things were hard to explain?"

The sheriff's eyes narrowed and he spoke softly. "There were the stains."

"Stains?"

The sheriff shifted his weight in the chair. "Yeah, I checked her body to see if she'd been wounded other than breaking her neck. There were red spots on the carpet near the body, and also on the carpet on the stairs. Looked like blood to me."

Laura stared at him for an explanation, but his eyes now looked blank. "She cut herself or perhaps wounded her head in the fall?"

The sheriff hesitated, and suddenly he seemed coherent again. "No. Ruby wasn't bleeding, so I knew it wasn't her blood. Don't know what it was, but there were drops of something red on the carpet."

"And you didn't have the stains analyzed?" After she asked the question, Laura realized it sounded accusatory, but luckily the sheriff took no offense.

"For what?" he asked. "Once we determined there was no foul play in the death—that it was just an accident—we closed the case."

Laura wasn't sure how far to take this line of conversation, but she found herself continuing. "Edward Smith thought you closed the case too fast."

Suddenly looking exhausted, the sheriff sighed. "Like I said, Smith was crazed after Miss Davis died. I wouldn't take anything he said seriously."

"The red spots were the only clues left at the scene?" Laura asked.

The sheriff scratched at his head again. "Well, like I said, it wasn't a crime scene. It was an accident scene. The only other clue at the scene was a rabbit foot."

Laura tensed again. "A rabbit foot?"

"You know," he answered with a grin, "the kind people carry around on a chain for good luck."

"Did you identify whom the rabbit foot belonged to?"

He shook his head. "Nope. Don't know that it mattered."

The sheriff said it with finality, and Laura decided it was time to change her tactics. She glanced over at the man in the bed, who was now sitting up straight with his feet on the floor. He stared at Laura with what looked like curiosity, and she met his eyes squarely and smiled, but he didn't budge. She looked back at the sheriff. "What about Edward Smith's death?" The sheriff shifted his weight and let out a long breath. "What about it?" His tone held a touch of agitation.

"Do you think he committed suicide?"

He pursed his lips. "I've got absolutely no idea. He died in the Bufordville jurisdiction. I had jurisdiction over the outlying areas of the county, so I wasn't involved with the case."

Laura decided to forge ahead. "Your son Roscoe was in Edward Smith's neighborhood the afternoon that Smith died. Did you know that?"

Jackson Buford crossed one ankle over the other and back again, then lifted his hat and scratched at his head. "Nope. I don't know anything about it. You'll have to ask Roscoe about that."

Laura forced a smile. "I would love to talk with cousin Roscoe. Can you give me his address?"

He grunted and stared at her without saying anything for several moments. Finally, he shrugged. "He lives in the trailer court on Little Pine Lane. Can't miss the place. Just ask anyone you see to point you to his trailer."

24

It didn't take Laura long to figure out that Little Pine Lane was part of Bufordville's underside, a slum of old warehouses with boarded-up windows and doors and walls defaced with graffiti. Laura's car quaked across the railroad tracks, and she locked her doors when she saw a group of rough-looking kids sitting on an old truck without wheels.

The trailer court itself consisted of ten or twelve shabby trailers surrounded by lawns glutted with old car parts, rusted-out refrigerators, and what appeared to be bags of garbage. Laura maneuvered the car through the meandering trailer court, stopping at each mailbox to read the name. Near the end of the alley, she found the name she was looking for—Roscoe T. Buford.

Laura pulled the car to the side of the lane and parked. Guardedly scanning the proximity, she got out and slammed the car door. She walked carefully to a dilapidated porch where an angry pit bull bolted toward her, his wet lips curling to reveal large fangs. Just before he could reach Laura, his chain snapped tight, jerking him back with terrific force. He landed on his side with a thud and a yelp.

The trailer door sprang open and a muscular, middle-aged man with a bald head stepped out. "Get out of here, Hit Man." The dog scrambled to its feet and retreated to a corner of the porch. "We ain't gonna buy nothin', lady, so git on back in your fancy car an' head on outa here."

Laura's legs shook so badly she had to steady herself by clutching the porch rail. She assessed the man with his low, heavy jaws and furrowed forehead, deciding he looked a bit like his pit bull. And probably even more dangerous. "I—I'm not selling anything. I'm Laura McClain, your cousin."

"My cousin? Lady, I know all my cousins, an' you ain't no cousin of mine."

"Your father told me where to find you. I'm Sarah Buford's daughter."

He paused. Stepping out on the porch, he studied her with a frown. "Little Laurie?"

"That's right," she responded, hearing the unsteadiness of her own voice.

He snorted. "Well, one of the high an' mighty Bufords has come to call on the poor trailer-trash part of the family. Ellen! Ellen! Get out here, woman. You gotta see this."

A haggard woman stuck her frizzy blond head out the door, and Laura could see she had a beer can in her hand. "Who is it?"

Roscoe waved his hand toward Laura. "It's my cousin, Laurie, all come down from her mansion on high."

The woman giggled. "You ain't told me you had a cousin with a mansion."

Roscoe laughed hoarsely.

Laura forced herself to stand tall. "I've come to talk to you, Cousin Roscoe, about Ruby Davis and Edward Smith."

The laughter stopped abruptly, and the creases in Roscoe's forehead deepened, causing Laura's heart to hammer. Roscoe moved close to Laura and pushed his face close to hers. "I don't talk none 'bout Ruby. She's dead an' gone. An' I don't talk 'bout Smith. He was a no-good scamp who got what was comin' to him."

Laura's chest grew tight, and she thought of running away, of jumping back in her car and never looking back. But she needed to know what had happened all those long years ago, to know why she had locked herself in that bottle and was so afraid to come out. Suddenly, she heard her voice as if it were someone else's, speaking firmly and confidently. "Maybe you don't talk about them because you don't want people to find out."

He backed away a few steps, as if thrown off guard, then snorted. "What're you talkin' about, lady?"

"Roscoe, honey, what is she talking about?" the fluffy blond asked from the doorway.

Laura took a step toward him. "Everyone knows you and Ruby saw each other secretly until her brother found out. You thought she loved you until she announced her engagement to Edward. You got angry and killed them both."

Roscoe chuckled and shifted his weight uneasily. "You're crazy, woman! You don't know what you're talkin' 'bout. I was drunk the night Ruby died—I was outa-my-mind drunk. I heard about the engagement an' decided to give Ruby a hard time. Ruby an' me hadn't been together since she started work at Buford's Bluff, an' we wasn't seein' each other secretly or otherwise. She dropped me flat. She coulda married the king of England for all I cared."

Laura glanced at the blond's perplexed expression and then back at Roscoe. "You're telling me your relationship with Ruby ended long before the night she died?"

"Well, if that's a fancy way of sayin' Ruby an' I broke up—then yeah."

"And you were no longer in love with Ruby?"

Roscoe moved closer to Laura again. "Cousin, I was real broke up about the way Ruby did me wrong and all. I mean, I was angry for a while, sure. But I got over it. I just like to drink a little now and then, and sometimes it makes me do crazy things. I feel a little bad about breakin' up that party, but when you're drunk you really can't take no responsibility for your actions, if you know what I mean."

I know exactly what you mean, cousin, Laura thought. *You're irresponsible and immature, and I want to get as far away from you as possible.*

Looking toward her car, Laura could see that the shouting had drawn a small crowd. "I'm sorry I bothered you, Roscoe." She looked at the woman in the door. "Sorry to have bothered you, too."

The woman giggled, and Roscoe grabbed Laura's arm. "Don't go running off, Cousin Laura. We're just getting acquainted."

"Thanks, but I really must go. It's starting to get dark. I don't drive well in the dark."

Laura forced her arm from Roscoe's grip and hurried to her car. A teenage gang came by on bicycles and surrounded the car as Laura fumbled for her key. When she dropped it in the dirt, Roscoe chuckled and Ellen giggled. Laura nabbed the key and forced it, dirt and all, into the keyhole. The door click unlocked and she pulled it open. Just then, a husky teenage boy rode by on his bike and kicked the car's rear door on the driver's side. Laura jumped in the car, started it, and pushed hard on the horn. The teenagers still sat on their bikes in front of the car, laughing, so Laura put the car in gear and stepped lightly on the accelerator, forcing the car forward slowly. The teenagers scattered in all directions, and Laura switched on the headlights and headed out of the trailer park.

A few minutes later, as she turned from Little Pine Lane onto a safer-looking street, Laura sighed and began to breathe normally again. In the downtown area, she noticed a light on in Julie's shop, so she pulled over and parked nearby. She stepped out of the car and hurried up the street, then peered in the shop window, where she could see Julie packing boxes and crying. Laura tried to turn the doorknob, but it was locked, so she knocked gently on the door, not wanting to startle her friend. When Julie glanced up, Laura could see her wiping her eyes with a tissue. Julie came to the door, opened it, and asked tearfully, "Laura, what're you doing here?"

"I could ask you the same question," Laura remarked, stepping into the shop.

"I'm working. I thought I'd better keep going at it," Julie replied, closing the door behind Laura.

Laura caught the quiver in Julie's voice. "You're going to miss it, aren't you?"

Julie sniffed. "Yeah, well, it was a good experience. Now I'll go on to something else. How are things going in the investigation, anyway?"

Shaking her head, Laura sighed, then told Julie about her day's adventures. "I think I can even add Sheriff Buford to the list of suspects. He seemed very angry about Ruby dumping Roscoe—in fact, old Jackson said he could have killed her himself sometimes!"

"Oh, yeah," Julie said. "I read a book once about the Southern code of honor. You could get killed if you insulted a family name. I mean, that was a really long time ago, but still—"

A knock at the shop door startled them both, and they looked to see Aaron's face in the window.

"It's Aaron!" Laura exclaimed.

Julie opened the door. "Well, hello," she greeted Aaron, motioning for him to come in.

"Julie, this is Aaron Farr," Laura stated. "Aaron, this is Julie Morgan."

Julie and Aaron shook hands as Aaron stepped through the door. "I was driving by and saw your car and the light on," Aaron explained. "I thought I would check to make sure everything was okay."

"Everything's fine, but thanks for checking," Laura responded with a smile. "I was on my way home when I saw Julie's light, so I stopped in to say hi. I really should be getting back to the house—I told Agnes and George I'd be home before dark, and it's pretty much dark now. They'll probably call the sheriff if I don't show up soon."

Aaron looked toward the windows. "It gets dark pretty fast this time of year. Maybe I should walk you to the car."

Julie raised her eyebrows. "That's very chivalrous of you, Mr. Farr. I know Laura won't turn down such a kind proposal."

Laura frowned at Julie, who ignored her. Then Julie walked to the door and opened it. "You two have a good night. I'm going to finish up here and head home myself."

Aaron stepped outside, but Laura paused at the door and took Julie's hand. "Don't stay here too late. I'll call you tomorrow."

Julie closed the door behind Laura, who said to Aaron, "I'm just up the street, but I guess you know that." Aaron quickly reached for her hand, and they began walking down the sidewalk. A tingle went from her hand up through her arm, just like when he'd held her hands at the back door Monday night. She smiled.

"What's happened?" Aaron asked softly.

"What do you mean?" Laura asked in surprise.

"You seem a little shaky tonight. I don't know—has something happened?"

They arrived at Laura's car, and she stopped and turned toward him. He still held her hand, and he grasped it tighter as if to keep her from pulling away. "A lot's happened," she mused, looking down. When she glanced back up at him, he was staring at her quizzically. How could she explain the changes that had taken place in her since arriving in Virginia? How could she explain that although she was genuinely afraid at times, she was also more confident than she'd ever been? It was the first time she'd felt this way, and it felt amazing.

A group of teenage girls walked past on the sidewalk, talking loudly to each other but looking at Laura and Aaron with undisguised curiosity. Laura moved a step closer to Aaron to give the girls room to pass. The girls laughed and moved on. Still holding her hand, Aaron pulled her closer.

Just then a car with a bad muffler rumbled down the street. Laura stood still, enjoying the closeness yet feeling an urge to pull away. Aaron raised his free hand and caressed her face with the back of it. In spite of herself, she closed her eyes and took a step forward.

She felt his lips on hers only for a moment before someone walking by coughed loudly, breaking the trance. Laura opened her eyes to look into Aaron's, only vaguely aware of people walking on the sidewalk behind her.

Aaron stepped back, looking embarrassed, and Laura blushed, warmth coursing through her despite the chilly air. She breathed out slowly, then said quietly, "I should get home."

He nodded. "I know."

They walked to the driver's side of the car, where Aaron released her hand and opened her door. "Drive carefully."

She smiled and climbed into the car, then turned the ignition as Aaron smiled and shut the door. As she drove away, she looked in her rearview mirror to see him standing there, watching her.

25

On Thursday morning, Laura got an early start. She had another witness to interview—Bobby Briggs. The road to Mountain Dale Lake wound up and around the low mountains that looked like they were covered in green felt. As Laura drove higher, the road switched back in ever tighter loops and curves. Laura decided the poorly maintained road, which contained countless deep potholes, was downright dangerous.

When the road forked, Laura followed the road bearing right. Driving down a narrow lane covered with a canopy of trees, she felt like she was traveling through a golden cave. To her right, she caught glimpses of the sun peering through the gaps in the forest canopy as it reflected off the waters of Mountain Dale Lake. The trees along the roadside grew in swampland, and in many places the edges of the lane had actually disintegrated into the swamp. Carefully Laura maneuvered her car around the curves, avoiding the potholes where possible. Finally coming out into the open beside the lake, she noticed that the wind was creating white-capped waves on the water.

When she reached Bobby's Café, Laura noticed that the parking lot was jammed with pickup trucks and jeeps, so she parked on the narrow shoulder of the road. Built from logs, the café looked like an old lodge, and Laura thought the building had a good deal of character.

A bell jingled as Laura opened the door. The room became silent, and all the old men in the place looked up at Laura like a bunch of goats whose dinner had been interrupted. Feeling very much like an outsider in a private club, Laura thought the place seemed more like a male convalescent home than a public café. Laura proceeded to the counter, where a waitress dressed in a brown uniform stood with a pot of coffee in hand. "Are you lost, sugar?"

"I'm looking for Bobby Briggs."

"Oh, well, Bobby's in his office in the back there. Go on back."

"Thank you."

Laura felt every eye in the place following her as she walked to the back room. As she made her way through a narrow passage cluttered with crates and boxes, she nearly slipped on the greasy floor several times. When she finally made it to the open office door, she knocked on the doorframe and peered in to see an elderly man sitting behind a desk.

"Who's there?"

"Laura McClain. I'm a friend of George Walker and Hattie O'Donnell."

"Well, come on in here where I can get a gander at you." The old man waved Laura in with a lanky arm, so she sat in a chair in front of the desk.

"What did you say your name was?" he asked, cupping his ear with his hand as if hard of hearing.

"Laura McClain. My mother was Sarah McClain, Laura Buford's sister."

He slapped his knee, obviously thrilled at Laura's declaration. "Well, for cryin' out loud! I knew you when you were just a little thing. "Hattie told me she met you on the bus. Don't tell Hattie anything you don't want the whole state to know. The woman has a mouth on her the size of a volcano, and it spews forth just as much hot air." He laughed heartily at his own joke, then suddenly become serious. "What can I do for you?"

Laura studied his face and the hollowness around his eyes. Even as an old man, he somehow looked childlike. "I wanted to ask you a few questions about a Harvest Moon Festival you worked at."

He scratched his head. "Well, now, that would be a long time ago. I don't even remember how long ago."

Laura cleared her throat. "It was over twenty years ago—the night Ruby Davis fell down the stairs and died."

Bobby's smile faded, and his face paled as he narrowed his eyes into two dark slits. "Well, now, that's a night easily remembered. I think we all remember the night Ruby fell. In a town where everyone knows everyone, an event like that is noteworthy."

Laura leaned forward. "Mr. Briggs—"

He held up his hand. "Oh, no. Call me Bobby. I don't like that 'Mister' stuff."

"Bobby, do you remember having an accident that night with hot chocolate?"

Bobby chuckled. "Oh, yeah—the hot chocolate. How could I forget? It was actually pretty hot, and it didn't feel so good on my legs. Is that what you've come to talk to me about? Did George tell you to come in here and give me a hard time about that?"

"No, I didn't come to talk about that. I'm trying to find out more about Ruby Davis."

"Oh, why's that?" he asked, leaning back in his chair and eyeing her suspiciously.

"She and I were once close, and I need to know all I can about her."

He breathed in and exhaled slowly. "Well, I didn't know her well. I can't say I knew her at all."

"Do you remember going to the cottage to get a clean uniform that night?"

He scratched his head. "Yeah, we were actually a bit glad for the break, although I did have a bit of a burn on one leg. Agnes Hayes was running us all ragged, as I recall."

"When you left the cottage and came back to the party, did you walk around the front side of the house?"

He nodded. "Yeah, I did, since that was the closest way to go."

"Do you remember seeing anyone near the front of the house? Did you see Ruby Davis?"

Bobby sat silent for so long that Laura wondered if he'd heard her, but she bit her lip and remained quiet. "No, I didn't see her," he finally responded, "but I saw that lawyer guy that worked for the Bufords."

"Roger Ballister?"

"Yeah."

Laura shifted in her chair. "What was he doing?"

"Going toward the house. I passed him as I was going to the reception hall—I went right back to work, you know. Miss Buford was fretting about her guests because of the storm. People left the party, and I don't think she was happy about that."

"Did you see Roger Ballister when he returned to the party?"

"Yeah."

"Did he seem upset or anything?"

"I don't remember that well. I don't think I paid much attention," Bobby replied with a frown.

"Do you remember if he was wet?"

The old man stared at Laura. His thoughts seemed to be far away from the café, fixed upon something long ago. Suddenly he seemed to realize that he'd been lost in time, and his face turned bright red. "I think he might've been a little wet. It was raining, but I don't recall how hard. I don't remember anything much, other than the accident, and I'm not even sure I remember that. I've heard about it so many times I'm unsure what's memory and what's folklore."

Laura sighed. "That's okay. Thank you for your time, Bobby."

As Laura walked back into the café's main dining area, the room went silent as nearly every man in the café ogled her again. She smiled and hurried out the door, finding the cool air a welcome relief from the hot, stuffy café. Yet the sky had become gray, and the smell of rain hung in the air. Laura's car was now sandwiched tightly between two old trucks, and she thought she might be blocked in.

Laura got in her car and with difficulty worked her way out of the parallel parking space. After turning around in a muddy spot the locals obviously used as a roundabout, she headed back toward town.

Fog floated in off the lake, and the car's headlights cast fiery, dancing images on the black water. Along the café's drive, the tunnel of foliage and the mist made it almost as dark as night. She drove out of the swampland and onto the winding mountain road. Outside, the wind howled, and it began to rain, so Laura turned on the windshield wipers. The swishing sound harmonized with the sound of the motor, and Laura instantly felt drowsy.

As she rounded the first major bend in the mountain road, she realized she was going too fast, so she pressed down on the brake pedal. When the car didn't slow down at all, she pressed harder on the brake. Nothing happened. She pulled back the parking brake. Nothing. Laura realized with a quiver of fear that her brakes were completely gone.

Her heart pounded as the terror began hitting her in waves, and she steered the speeding car with sweaty palms, hardly able to keep it under control. The wheels hit one pothole after another, jolting Laura painfully but slowing the car a little. She knew if she couldn't keep the vehicle on the road, she would probably crash into a tree.

Frantic, Laura tried to direct the swerving car around a crook in the road. As she cleared the corner, Laura found herself heading right toward a pickup truck. Screaming, she veered to the right and ran off the road into a deep gully.

* * *

Aaron Farr received the phone call from the county sheriff's department around noon. Laura was in the county hospital with cuts on her head and arm, a concussion, and a lot of bruises. She'd asked a deputy to call Aaron, and at Laura's request, the deputy asked Aaron to tell no one about the accident. But Aaron knew Bufordville well enough to know that the news of Laura's accident was all over town by now.

As Aaron drove to the hospital, he noted that the cloud covering had cast a shadow across the countryside, making everything look gray. The surroundings mirrored Aaron's mood, though the deputy had assured him Laura would be all right. The thought of something bad happening to Laura caused him an almost physical pain, and he realized that his feelings for her were stronger than he would have expected for knowing her such a short time.

When the nurse showed Aaron to the hospital room, he found Laura lying quietly, her arm and head bandaged. Her face looked pale and her eyes hollow, and she barely glanced at Aaron when he entered the room.

"They say someone tampered with my brakes," she finally mumbled, her voice so faint he could hear her only with the greatest of effort.

"Laura." He sat in a chair by her bed.

"Why didn't I leave it alone?" she murmured. "Why didn't I?"

"I wish you had," he said, feeling his heart quicken as he took her hand. "But it's too late now, Laura. More than ever, we have to find out who's behind Ruby's death."

Laura pulled her hand back. "I don't know if I can go through with it."

Aaron grasped her hand again and squeezed it. "Don't worry, Laura. I won't let anything happen to you. I promise."

Suddenly, the door burst open and Julie ran to Laura's bedside, exclaiming, "Laura, I can't believe this happened! Everyone in town's talking about it."

Aaron stood. "Julie, it's nice to see you again."

Her dangly earrings tinkled as she moved animatedly. "I rushed here the minute I heard. I can't believe someone tried to kill you!" she said with a grave expression. "It's all over town. A deputy at the sheriff's office told Betty Jo McGraw who told Slim Jim Johnson who told Joe Webster, the pharmacist, who told me someone rigged your brakes. Laura, we're going to have to call the open house off. We can't put you in danger like this—it's crazy. I don't know what I was thinking anyway. This isn't a mystery movie, you know. This is the real thing."

"Oh, Julie, I feel better already just having you around," Laura smiled weakly.

"Well, good. You just concentrate on resting, and I'll handle canceling the open house," Julie said with a grin. Then she stepped closer to the bed to peer at Laura's wounds like a doctor making her rounds.

Laura spoke quietly but firmly. "We're having the open house. We're going ahead with your plan."

Julie threw her arms up. "No way, Laura. I know it was my idea in the first place, but I won't have your life on my conscience. This is too dangerous. I'm calling it off."

Aaron decided to throw in his two cents' worth. "Girls, if I may—"

"Look," Julie demanded, pointing her finger sharply at Aaron, "you like her. Tell her what a ridiculous idea this is! Tell her how crazy it is." She crossed her arms and nodded, obviously waiting for a supporting argument.

Aaron cleared his throat. "I agree with everything you just said, Julie, but I'm afraid the plan has already been set in motion. When you pick a road, you choose the place it leads to. We can't do anything now except go along for the ride and hope we don't crash."

"I've already crashed, remember?" Laura quipped.

"That's not funny, Laura," Julie barked, then paced the floor with her arms folded rigidly. "I can't believe this. I can't believe this! I always mess everything up."

"I think that's my line," Laura muttered.

"Look," Aaron stated. "I'm going to go out in the hall and talk to the nurse and the deputy I saw out there. You two get our plans for tomorrow night settled, okay?"

* * *

By early evening, Laura was released from the hospital. Julie had agreed to leave only after Laura convinced her to go home and call Agnes and George to let them know what had happened. Laura didn't want them to go into shock when they saw her bandages. Later, Laura would call Hattie O'Donnell to let her know she was okay.

Aaron had questioned the sheriff's deputy, who told him someone had "fiddled" with the brakes on Laura's car. The sheriff was on the case, but he had no leads.

Staring out the window of Aaron's car as he drove her home, Laura sat quietly, unsure of what to say. The sun dropped low across the fields of dry corn stalks, and the tall woods across the James River loomed blackly in silhouette. Laura looked over at Aaron, whose mind was obviously fastened on other matters.

Since the accident that morning, a cold sense of bewilderment and disaster had weighed Laura down, but now she pushed it into the background of her mind. Instead, she focused on the pleasant feelings she'd had when Aaron kissed her. Laura knew she was definitely smitten with him. She told herself she hadn't known him long enough to care so deeply for him, but nothing else could explain the way she felt in his presence. She smiled.

Aaron reached over and touched her bandaged arm. "Are you okay?"

"I'm fine."

Aaron smiled, the tiny wrinkles beneath his eyes creasing. His blue eyes came to life again, and he looked back at the road.

Laura turned her head to look out the window again, her gaze following the scenery as they drove down the hill and across the bridge, then mounted the hill to Buford's Bluff. They passed a county cruiser parked in the driveway near the stables, and the deputy sitting in the car tipped his hat as they passed by.

"Do you suppose he's here to watch out for any more brake tampering? Maybe the guy will turn into a serial brake vandal. I suppose there's always Agnes's car, or George's." Laura tried to laugh at her own joke but suddenly felt like crying instead.

"I hope you don't mind," Aaron said, glancing over at her. "I actually called the sheriff's department and asked them to keep an eye on your place for a few days. So whenever they have a spare deputy, they're going to send him up here. Maybe I should have confirmed it with you or Agnes first."

"No, it's fine," Laura murmured. "Thank you for thinking to do that."

Aaron parked close to the back door, then hurried around to help Laura out of the car. Putting an arm around her, he guided her toward the door, but they stopped at the foot of the stairs and turned toward each other.

"Laura, I have something I want to tell you."

"Yes?"

"But first—"

He moved close to her and gently kissed her lips, and she felt the ground sway beneath her feet. He took a step backward, his hand caressing her face, and they stood quietly facing each other in the near darkness. Laura could hear Aaron's steady breathing, and her own quick breaths seemed magnified in the silence. Because she could think of nothing to say, she turned and walked up the stairs and into the house, leaving him alone. It was only after she shut the door behind herself that she realized Aaron had wanted to tell her something.

26

After Aaron brought her home from the hospital Thursday evening—and kissed her good night—Laura felt much less troubled, and she almost skipped to her room. She fell asleep quickly, and for once she dreamed wonderful dreams. But when she awoke on Friday morning, the reality of the situation closed in on her again, and she wanted nothing more than to retreat back into that uniquely pleasant dream world. Instead, she sat at the nursery window, gazing out on the changing trees. *Life is like those trees, always changing,* she thought. Yet she knew that the trees changed in a predictable way, that nature was much more constant than human behavior. Human nature could be unpredictable. And dangerous.

As Laura reflected on Thursday's events, a chill shot through her. She knew she hadn't yet digested what had happened. Initially, she had felt the shock of disbelief that someone would try to kill her. Her disbelief was followed by outrage, emptiness, and a surge of melancholy nearly strong enough to be called despair. Knowing that despair was a tool of the adversary, she had finally settled on apathy and numbness. She knelt for her morning prayer and soon felt gratitude for being alive, along with a small measure of courage to face the day that lay ahead.

Rising from her prayer and looking around the nursery—the room where she had lived as a toddler, the room where her mother had lived as a child—her gaze lit on the old photo album from the attic. Hesitantly, she walked over and picked it up. Sitting down in a chair, she opened the book on her lap, then flipped through it until she came to the photograph. It was of the man—the one who kept following her—the one with deep-set eyes and heavy lines on his face.

A knock at the door startled her. "Yes, come in."

Agnes stepped into the room. "George and I have a lot of questions for you," the older woman stated. "We're not exactly sure how you want to do things at the party tonight."

Momentarily ignoring Agnes's demands, Laura lifted the album toward her. "Do you know who this is?" Laura asked, pointing to the man with deep lines on his face.

Agnes raised an eyebrow. "Frightening, isn't he? That's Paul Skinner—he used to work here."

"Where is he now?" Laura questioned, her heart suddenly racing.

"Dead. Died years ago."

Laura had known this man couldn't be her stalker, given his age, yet at this news, relief washed over her, and she felt her heartbeat return to normal. She must have simply seen a man who looked a lot like Mr. Skinner. While that wasn't entirely reassuring—she still had a man following her, after all—at least her stalker didn't have anything to do with Buford's Bluff or Laura's family.

Agnes walked to the door. "Are you coming down soon?"

"Yes," Laura said as she shut the album.

Agnes hesitated. "I saw Paul's son, Todd, a few weeks ago. He looks a lot like his father—same awful stare."

Laura felt the adrenaline pulsing through her again. "His son still lives in Bufordville?"

"Yes. He works for Roger Ballister."

* * *

On Friday afternoon as Laura pulled Agnes's old car to a stop in front of Roger Ballister's office building, she peered nervously out the window at its dark façade. It was an odd building: three stories, shades pulled down on all the upper-floor windows, granite walls. Apparently Roger's law firm was the only occupant, and Laura wondered what the structure had originally been built for—perhaps a school or even a hospital or clinic. It could never have been a house, she thought, but then again, some old Victorian houses were as large as public buildings. Yet the style wasn't exactly Victorian, but more a combination of styles.

At least there's no fog, Laura thought as she stepped out of the car onto the street. Walking around the car and standing on the sidewalk in front of the immense double doors, she noticed that their beveled and leaded glass panes were framed in oak so weathered that it was almost as gray as the sidewalk. As she eyed the doors, wondering just how heavy they were and if she'd be able to get one of them open, she suddenly felt she was being watched. The dark building loomed above her, and as she gazed up, she thought she saw a shadow of movement from the shades in a second-floor window.

She looked back at the door. Could the person she'd feared for so long—at least since her mother's death—be here? Knowing she couldn't keep running, she resisted the urge to hurry to the car, drive home, and stay locked in the mansion forever so she didn't have to worry about anything ever again. She squared her shoulders. Like her mother always said, she had to go *through* it. Today she would find out if the man stalking her worked for Roger Ballister. Her heart began to race, but she took a deep breath, grasped the huge door handle, pulled the door open, and walked in.

As soon as the door closed behind her, Laura could sense the tension in the air. A desk stood in the middle of the cavernous entry room, which was perfectly in keeping with the exterior of the building. The woman behind the desk had short gray hair with bangs falling above her sunken eyes, where Laura could read a bit of hostility, even anger. Yes, Laura was certain she could feel the woman's angry eyes boring into her, and the set of the woman's jaw warned Laura to keep her distance. Then Laura realized that the woman was simply mirroring her. Without her conscious knowledge, Laura's fright had turned to anger, and her own forehead was furrowed and her jaw set even more tightly than the woman's. Laura tried to empty her face of emotion and force a smile.

"I'm Laura McClain. I'm here to see Roger Ballister." The words came out in a weak whisper.

"Just a moment," the woman said, sounding nervous herself. She stood and walked backwards, as if fearing to turn her back on Laura, then slipped behind a large oak door.

Laura released a long breath and looked around the room of oak-paneled walls hung with gilt-framed oil paintings. The landscapes and still lifes were darkened with age, and the paneling was lusterless.

Against one wall stood a large aquarium, a saltwater tank, with only one fish in it. Laura walked closer to the aquarium and bent over to get a closer look. The sole occupant was dingy brown with fleshy spines all along its body.

"Sad, isn't it?"

Turning, Laura saw the receptionist, her head cocked to one side and a frown around the corners of her mouth. "A client died and left it to Mr. Ballister."

"Couldn't he buy some more fish to put in with it, to at least keep it company?" Laura asked, glancing back at the fish.

"It's a lion fish," the woman answered. "It has poisonous spines to protect it, and it will kill any other fish you put in there."

Laura turned back toward the tank. "That's some defense system. He must feel very safe."

The woman snorted. "Safe, maybe, but sad and lonely for sure."

The door behind the desk opened, and Roger Ballister appeared in the doorway.

"Laura, what a pleasant surprise." He smiled, but Laura thought he looked nervous. "Please, come into my office." He glanced down at her bandaged arm, and his smile faded. "I was going to call you today. I was so sorry to hear about your accident."

As Laura followed Roger down a long hallway, she could almost imagine that someone was walking just behind her, watching her. The sensation was so strong that she suddenly looked back over her shoulder. For just an instant, she thought she saw a glimmer of movement, but then the hall appeared to be empty again, so she quickened her step to catch up with Roger.

Finally, Roger stopped and swung open a door, and they stepped into an office. The shades were pulled down, but several lamps lit the room, making it slightly more cheerful than the dim hall. Laura decided that Roger's office looked more like an elegant study than a business office. Bookshelves lined the walls, and Tiffany lamps stood on tables at either end of a large sofa that faced a fireplace and was flanked by a pair of blue leather wing chairs. At the other end of the room sat a large desk with comfortable-looking chairs on either side. Roger motioned for Laura to sit in one of the blue chairs by the fireplace, and, after she sat, he took the other.

"I see you have a festivity planned for tonight," Roger remarked, loosening his tie as if speaking the words had made his neck larger.

"Yes, I hope you'll come," Laura said.

He smiled briefly. "Wouldn't miss it."

Laura took in the thick white hair, the neat goatee, the twinkle in the eye, the slight smile—was it nothing more than a façade? "Roger," Laura began weakly and paused. A chill came over her, reaching deep into her until even her bones ached. Her vision blurred, and she fought the tears as panic closed around her. She cleared her throat and sat up straighter, but a wave of dizziness hit her, followed by the feeling that she might throw up. But somehow Laura willed herself to ride out the panic, and as it finally subsided, she spoke. "Do you know a man named Todd Skinner?"

At first Laura thought Roger was going to smile, but then she realized that his mustache was twitching. He had a nervous tic. "Yes, Todd Skinner is an employee of mine."

Laura grasped one hand with the other to keep both from shaking. "I have reason to believe," she began, astounded at the new steadiness of her voice, "that Mr. Skinner has been following me."

Roger sat up slightly. "Yes, he was following you at my instruction."

Laura's mouth dropped open and she stared at him. "Why?"

The attorney swallowed hard. "Your aunt was a headstrong woman—some people even called her controlling. She didn't want your parents to take you away. After all, you were heir to the estate. At first, she wanted to make sure you and your mother were okay. That's why we enlisted a private investigation firm to keep an eye on you both. She had a genuine interest in your lives, and she was sure you would all come back to Buford's Bluff after a few years. But when your father refused to return, it became an obsession for your aunt. She began to wait anxiously for the private investigator's reports. After your father's death, Laura thought for sure that your mother and you would return to Buford's Bluff. She was terribly disappointed when that didn't happen."

"But why did Skinner keep spying on me after Aunt Laura died?"

Roger hesitated. "That was for me. I was afraid you'd refuse to come back and claim the estate when you found out about the three-year residency. I wasn't exactly sure what your mother had told you about Bufordville. I thought perhaps she'd poisoned your perceptions of us."

"But what did it matter to you?" Laura asked. "It would have been easier for you to just sell the place and give the proceeds to charity. You wouldn't have had to go through all of this with me."

He smiled. "You don't know me very well, Laura. Your aunt meant a great deal to me. We had become good friends over the years. I promised her that I would bring you back here, that I would make sure that Buford's Bluff remained in the family. And I'm a man of my word."

Laura sighed and leaned back in her chair. "Do you know how much that detective scared me? He followed me everywhere, and I think he broke into my house!"

Roger looked startled. "Are you sure of that? Skinner mentioned nothing about that to me, and I see no reason why he would do something so blatantly illegal. In fact, he was so good that I actually hired him away from a PI firm." Roger sighed heavily. "Anyway, a year ago Skinner was assigned to find out how you were dealing with your mother's death. Your aunt didn't feel that it was the right time to approach you about coming back here. She wanted you to have time to get over your mother's death. When your aunt died, I had no choice but to get you back here. I asked Skinner to see if he could find out what your feelings were on the matter."

"So why didn't you just ask me? And how did you think a guy following me around would find out?"

He frowned. "I suppose I didn't really give it that much thought. He'd always given us such detailed information before." Roger stood and walked to the door, then opened it and stuck his head into the hall. "Skinner!" he bellowed.

Laura heard a door opening down the hall, and a moment later, footsteps progressing up the hall. She froze instinctively. Roger stepped away from the open door, and a moment later *he* came in.

Gasping, Laura stood and staggered backward, then braced herself and looked into Skinner's deep-set eyes. But the moment her eyes met his, she knew he was no danger to her. He'd been hired to do a job, and he was simply doing it. Laura stifled a chuckle as she realized Skinner probably wasn't thrilled that he'd had to follow her for the past year.

Skinner took a step toward her, his hand reaching for hers. As his cold fingers closed in on her hand, she hesitated. Then he smiled crookedly and vigorously shook her hand. "I'm so happy to finally meet you, Miss Laura," he gushed, the pitch of his voice higher than Laura had expected. "I know so much about you. I feel we've know each other for years, and yet we've never met until now."

He released Laura's hand, and she let out a long breath, feeling as if a heavy weight had been lifted from her shoulders. This was her terrifying stalker? "After your mama died," Skinner continued, "your aunt became mighty worried about you. All that mattered to her was making sure you were safe and happy."

Laura glanced at Roger, and he smiled. "It's true."

Tears filled Laura's eyes. "I guess I've made some misjudgments, but you had no right to go in my house."

Skinner's face turned red. "I'm sorry. I—I—uh . . . was under a lot of pressure to find out." He glanced at Roger, and Roger's face reddened. "I tried not to leave any signs that I was there, so you wouldn't get scared, and—"

"We'll talk about this matter later," Roger interrupted sternly, then nodded his head toward the door.

Skinner headed for the door, then paused. Turning toward Laura, he said, "I *am* sorry, Miss Laura." Then he walked out.

Roger took a step toward her and grasped her hand. "Laura, I'm hoping we can put this misunderstanding behind us. I would like to represent your legal interest just as I did your aunt's. And I would like us to be friends."

Laura smiled. "I would like that too."

27

By Friday evening, the caterers had decorated the reception hall with fall colors. Orange tablecloths draped each table, adorned with arrangements of red and yellow flowers. Strategically placed corn stalks were surrounded with pumpkins and squash, and bright streamers hovered over serving tables covered with food. Julie had arranged the entertainment, which included a local concert pianist playing Chopin and Lizst on the grand piano at the front of the reception hall, and later on, a local singer's performance of several solo pieces.

Laura took her place at the front of the reception hall, wearing an emerald satin evening dress from Julie's shop. The two-piece ensemble featured a top with a pooling neckline and a long skirt with a chic, slanting hem. Julie said the vintage outfit was worn in the 1930s. Since Laura hadn't had time to bother with clothing, she was grateful that her friend had thought to bring the fancy dress. As Laura smoothed the front of her skirt, nervous for the first guests to arrive, Julie approached with Roger Ballister on her arm.

"Laura," Julie said, "Mr. Ballister has agreed to play host tonight. I mean, someone has to introduce you to everyone."

Roger released Julie's arm and stepped forward, then took Laura's hand and kissed it. "Thank you, Roger," Laura said as he took his place beside her. "You have no idea how much I appreciate this."

Within half an hour, a long reception line had formed, winding its way around the dining tables and then out the door and onto the lawn outside the stables. Laura's stomach began to churn as she realized that almost everyone in Bufordville had come out to meet her. Courteously and with flair, Roger introduced Laura to each individual as he or she shook Laura's hand.

After smiling at a young couple from Lakeside, Laura looked to the next guest and saw Hattie O'Donnell's friendly face. Hattie grinned at Laura, but her sister Lettie grimaced.

"Oh, my, Laura, this is such a fine open house," Hattie declared. "Of course, it's nothing like the parties your aunt used to throw, but it's an admirable beginning. Your dress is beautiful, dear—it matches your eyes exactly. And where did you get that wonderful brooch? Is that a real emerald? You look so striking that no one will notice that gigantic bandage on your arm. "

With one arm, Laura hugged Hattie. "I'm glad you could come—it's a relief to see a familiar face."

Hattie's smile widened. "I was relieved to hear you survived your little accident. It was a terrible thing! I do hope you're able to remember your past, Laura."

"Me too," Laura sighed, patting Hattie's hand.

"Hattie, move along," Lettie growled, pushing at her sister. "You're holding up the line."

Hattie chuckled. "Lettie's hungry, Laura. I'd better get her over to the refreshment table before she throws a fit."

Laura waved good-bye as Hattie beamed and Lettie scowled.

Roger introduced Laura to some of his legal colleagues, and Laura shook each of their hands firmly. Glancing over the last attorney's shoulder, she caught a glimpse of Julie and Aaron moving forward in the line. After four or five more introductions, her two friends approached her.

"Laura," Roger began, "I believe you know Miss Julie Morgan, our local antique connoisseur, and Mr. Aaron Farr, one of Bufordville's bright new attorneys."

"That's the best introduction I've ever had," Julie burst out as she pushed forth her ring-clad hand. "Most people call me a junk dealer."

"I beg your pardon!" Roger said teasingly.

Julie stepped closer to Laura and whispered, "Laura, this is so exciting!"

After shaking Roger's hand, Aaron turned toward Laura, who smiled and looked into Aaron's eyes. "Thank you for coming. I really mean that."

"I really believe you." His eyes twinkled as he grinned and squeezed her hand.

Aaron had arranged for two off-duty deputies from the sheriff's office to help with security at the festival. Laura wasn't sure what he'd told them, and she didn't really want to know. She was just glad that they had agreed to the plan: one would watch the front of the house while Aaron watched the back of the house, and the other deputy would be positioned in Laura's aunt's bedroom at the top of the stairs. Laura, Aaron, and each deputy carried a small two-way radio. If anyone entered the house after Laura did, Aaron or one of the deputies would know and would immediately notify the others. A small tape recorder had been placed in Laura's room, and if she was able to get something on tape, that would be a bonus. Either way, the deputy stationed upstairs would nab anyone who tried to harm her. And if the murderer didn't confess, they would at least have a prime suspect.

As Aaron and Julie walked away, Laura glanced over at the serving tables to see Agnes supervising the caterers with an iron hand, while George collected trash and moved chairs. Looking at the guests gathering around the serving tables and then socializing as they sat to dine, Laura decided that at least the party was somewhat similar to the festival her aunt had hosted twenty years before.

An old woman stepped forward, her magenta-colored hair stacked haphazardly on top of her head, and bright blue eye shadow covering each eyelid. The whites around her eyes were bloodshot. "Laura McClain," Roger began his rote process, "it is my pleasure to introduce social columnist Marsha Prestwich."

The old woman's blue evening dress was draped over her heavy form like a sheet over an arm chair, and she wore a pink feather boa around her shoulders. Pulling a notepad and pen from her bag, she looked at Laura and said shrilly, "We'll have to make this quick, young lady. I've got a deadline. Now—"

"I'm afraid the interviews will have to wait until later," Laura interrupted with a smile.

Ms. Prestwich gave Laura a cold stare. "Well!" the journalist retorted, tossing her boa over her shoulder and marching away. Laura glanced at Roger, who shrugged and rolled his eyes.

Just then, Leonard Davis approached. Laura could feel his shrewd eyes on her, and she noticed that his brows were raised into two tufts.

"Miss Laura McClain," Roger began, "let me introduce you to Bufordville's most brilliant attorney, Leonard Davis."

Laura put forth her hand. "Mr. Davis and I have met."

"It seems you've met the most prominent residents of the town already," Mr. Ballister remarked.

Leonard took Laura's hand and declared, "Miss McClain, Oliver Wendell Holmes once said, 'Where we love is home. Home that our feet may leave but not our hearts.' May I use his sentiments as my own and add to them a hearty welcome."

"Thank you, Mr. Davis. That was lovely."

"Please call me Leonard."

"Thank you, Leonard."

Roger patted his mouth as he yawned. "That's Leonard for you, always ready with an appropriate phrase."

Leonard Davis walked toward the food tables, and Roger introduced Laura to more local citizens in what seemed like an endless line. Before long, Louise Lawrence moved towards them with her mother's wheelchair.

"Miss McClain, I wouldn't have missed this for the world," Gertrude said in a hoarse whisper. "I see Agnes is still here. All I can say is watch the silver, young lady! I'd be surprised if there's any left after all these years. Hope you don't mind that we invited the missionaries. It was our night to feed them, and I figured they'd get all the food they wanted here."

"All are welcome here," Roger stated warmly.

When the two young men in dark suits stepped forward, Laura shook their hands and said in a conspiratorial tone, "I have some work for you two to do. See that woman over there at the reception table? The one with the red hair who jingles as she walks?"

"Yes."

"Well, she thinks Mormons wear bonnets and ride horse-drawn buggies. Why don't you go enlighten her?"

The two missionaries dashed over to Julie and introduced themselves. Julie looked over at Laura and made a face, then turned back to shake the two young men's hands.

"Mama, the food line is getting longer," Louise complained loudly.

"Oh, all right, Louise. I suppose a bit to eat wouldn't hurt." Gertrude gave Laura a little wave as Louise pushed her toward the serving tables.

Emily Smith stood next in line. "I don't know what you hope to prove by all this, Miss McClain, but I wouldn't miss it." She marched away, her blond hair bobbing with each step.

After Laura shook several dozen more hands, she felt quite tired, thinking she might not have to fake a headache if this went on much longer. She slipped off one shoe and rubbed her foot against her leg.

"Are you okay, dear?" Roger asked.

"Yes, just tired."

The old man from the drugstore approached Roger. "This is quite a jamboree you've got going, folks."

Roger smiled. "Miss Laura McClain, this is Joe Webster, our local druggist. We'd all be dead if it wasn't for old Joe here." The two men laughed dryly. Laura smiled and extended her hand, remembering how cold Joe had become that day in the shop when she'd mentioned her father. Did he think her father was a murderer?

"Laura!"

Laura jumped as she realized that Julie had crept up behind her and was now whispering in her ear.

"We've got to get rid of these two guys from your church—they're ruining my cover! How can I investigate Ruby's murder with these guys following me around?"

"Hello, Julie," Mr. Webster greeted.

"Oh, hi, Joe. Enjoying yourself?"

"Well, I haven't made it to the food yet, but the music's nice."

"Well, don't just stand there, Joe. Get over to the serving tables before everything's gone," Julie urged.

"I think I'll do that," he responded, heading toward the serving tables.

Laura pulled Julie closer and whispered, "Why don't you tell the missionaries this isn't the proper place to discuss religion and invite them to your shop to talk this week?"

Julie smiled. "That's a great idea." She turned away and then shot back, "Wait a minute."

"What?"

"I don't know, but I think I've been duped."

Laura crossed her arms and smiled. "Well, Julie, it's like that Hitchcock movie, *Vertigo*. You know, the one with Jimmy Stewart and Kim Novak. Jimmy follows the beautiful, mysterious Kim around for days, and then she kills herself. But she doesn't really kill herself. At least not the Kim that Jimmy's been following around, because Jimmy wasn't following the real Kim. But he doesn't realize it until he starts chasing after the new Kim who is really the old Kim but not the real Kim."

Julie's frown deepened, but her eyes sparkled. "I don't understand what that has to do with the missionaries."

Laura smiled. "Now you know how I feel."

Julie walked away, perplexed.

"We ain't going to stand here all day waiting to be acknowledged, lady."

Laura turned. The pit bull appeared ready to pounce. "Hello, Roscoe."

"Hello, Cousin Laura," he exclaimed. Grinning with self-satisfaction, he scanned the hall. "I was mighty surprised that we didn't get no personal invite, seein' as how we're kin an' all."

Roger leaned toward Laura. "He's playing to the gallery."

"Well, the festival was thrown together at the last minute," Laura explained. "But I'm glad you could make it."

"Roscoe! Roscoe!" His haggard wife, Ellen, hurried past the line, pushing Jackson Buford in his wheelchair. "Why didn't you wait for us, Roscoe? Don't you have no manners?"

Roscoe's brow furrowed. "Don't you be embarrassin' me, woman. You shut your mouth and stay out of my way tonight, you hear?"

Ellen stopped the wheelchair in front of Laura and patted Sheriff Buford on the shoulder. "You hear how your boy talks to me, Daddy Buford? You see how he treats me? Look how he tries to put on airs for these high an' mighty relatives of his."

As Roscoe stomped away toward the serving tables, Laura studied Jackson Buford. He wore an old uniform—badge, ranger-type hat, and all. His bulky form slumped in the chair, and he seemed to have trouble breathing under his own weight. "I've been thinking about what you said the other day," he said to Laura, looking her in the eye, "and I think you might be right."

"What do you mean?" Laura asked.

He cleared his throat with a growl. "I think Ruby Davis might have been murdered. Don't forget the stain on the carpet—that was somebody's blood. So I'll be keeping my eyes open tonight, cousin. History has a way of repeating itself, you know."

"Come along, Daddy Buford," Ellen said, fluffing her overbleached hair. "The food looks real good." Ellen ploughed through the crowd with the wheelchair, then stopped abruptly in front of a serving table.

"Poor Jackson," Roger commented. "You can't take anything he says at face value. The poor man's insane."

"He may be the sanest person here tonight," Laura mused.

Roger shrugged and turned again to the guests. Dr. Preston stepped forward, his hair looking as disheveled as it had on Wednesday.

"Miss Laura McClain, this is Dr. Levi Preston, our local healer, but I suppose you've already met the good doctor."

"Yes, I have," Laura affirmed with a smile, but she noticed a frown on Roger's face.

Dr. Preston walked away, and Roger introduced Laura to the mayor of Lakeside. As Laura spoke to the mayor, she heard a commotion and looked over at the serving tables to see Roscoe and Leonard in a verbal standoff.

"You think we're trash to be used and thrown away? Is that what you think?"

"Get away from me," Leonard ordered.

"It's a free country, lawyer man. You hear me? I'm not a doormat. You can come down off your high horse now. Everyone knows you treated Ruby like she was a pet dog on a leash. Everyone in Bufordville knows you made her life miserable."

Laura rolled her eyes, realizing that an actual migraine was coming on. How ironic.

"You're a drunken fool," Leonard barked loudly.

"I may be a fool, but I'm not drunk yet. Just give me a little time. The night is young."

Agnes stepped toward the two men. "No alcohol is being served on these premises. You'll have to go elsewhere for that. Now please leave."

"Don't worry about me, woman. I've come supplied." Roscoe pulled a liquor flask from his pocket."

"We'll call the police if you don't remove yourself from the property immediately," Leonard insisted, then added under his breath, "Have you no respect at all for your cousin?"

Roscoe made a fist and staggered forward. "Respect? Did you say respect? You're a good one to be talking about respect, you hypocrite. You didn't respect your sister or me. We were in love, an' we wanted to get married. You messed up my life an' hers. She'd be alive today if it wasn't for you an' your high an' mighty ways. You think you're such an important man in this town. Well, you ain't nothing but a laughin' stock. You hear me, Davis? You're a joke."

Leonard stepped forward. "You're drunk, Roscoe Buford, as always. Ruby may have thought she loved you, but she quickly recovered from that delusion. She told me herself that you were nothing more than a backwoods drunk with no talent and no future."

Roscoe's heavy jaw fell open, and he clenched the fist that wasn't holding his booze. Then he suddenly burst into tears, turned, and ran from the reception hall.

"You nasty old man. What've you done to my poor Roscoe?" Ellen spat out, then chased after Roscoe, leaving Jackson sitting alone by the serving table.

"This is turning into a pretty good shindig," Jackson exclaimed before stuffing a cheese cube in his mouth.

The piano music had stopped, and the hall fell silent as everyone stared at a red-faced Leonard Davis. Pulling at his mustache, he spun on his heel and marched out into the dark.

Aaron stepped behind Laura and whispered, "It looks like the game has begun."

Laura frowned, scanning the room as the guests all looked at her as if requiring some direction. Suddenly, she swooned, falling into Aaron's arms. A gasp and then murmuring rose from the crowd while Aaron picked Laura up and headed for the door.

Julie snapped her fingers at the piano player, who began playing again. "Everyone," Julie called, "please mingle and have a good time. There's plenty of food." Then she ran after Roger, who was following behind Aaron and Laura, and grabbed his arm. "Mr. Ballister," Julie said dramatically, "you can't leave. Please! You're the host. Don't worry—we'll take care of Laura."

Aaron carried Laura out into the cool night air. She lifted one eyelid. "How did I do?" she whispered.

"It was overacted, but I think it'll do the trick."

Laura frowned. "Well, I never claimed I was going for an Oscar. Is Julie doing her job?"

Aaron chuckled. "By now the whole town knows you've had a terrible walk down memory lane and are on your way to your room to rest. And they'll all know exactly where your room is located in the house. Actually, the impromptu scene in there made this whole scenario halfway believable."

"Good. Now let me down."

"Wait a minute. I haven't carried you across the threshold yet."

"And you're not going to. Now let me down!"

He laughed and carefully placed Laura on her feet, then quickly kissed her on the forehead. "Remember," he assured, "I won't let anything happen to you."

"I know," Laura replied and started climbing the stairs.

Aaron made his way to the back hall where one of the deputies was waiting. Laura had given Aaron a key so that the deputy could get into the house and make sure everything was locked except the front and back doors. The deputy would guard the back door until Aaron brought Laura through the front door and took the deputy's place of watching the back door. Aaron would hide behind some trees in the back lawn, and the deputy he replaced then would wait in Aunt Laura's room. The other deputy was positioned on the front lawn where he could watch the main door.

The stairs creaked under Laura's weight, and she stopped midway up, turned, and gazed down to the floor where Ruby Davis had rested in death. Cringing and turning away, Laura grasped the rail, noticing that her hands were sticky. The house felt hot and stuffy, and Laura longed to return to the fresh air. By the time she made it to the landing, she was fighting a strong urge to run back outside into Aaron's waiting arms. It would be so much easier to not face what could happen tonight. But it was too late, and she still had a whole scene to play.

The mansion was submerged in darkness except for the dim hall sconces and the bright moon piercing through the half-moon window.

The gloom nearly made her turn back, but then she remembered a scripture: *Fear thou not; for I am with thee . . .*

Taking courage at the thought, she crept down the hall to the nursery, then breathlessly turned the doorknob and flung open the door. The room was buried in blackness, so Laura switched on the light casting ghostly shadows across the room. She waited by the door until she saw the deputy appear at the top of the stairs. They nodded to each other, and then she went into her room and closed the door. After checking the two-way radio to make sure it was on, and pushing the RECORD button on the tape recorder, she closed the door and sat on the bed to wait.

28

Waiting in her room for the killer to appear, Laura glanced at the dollhouse that resembled Buford's Bluff. Trying to calm her anxious nerves, she knelt on the floor and rearranged the miniature furniture. The replica of the mansion even featured a nursery with tiny toys. Painted on the outside walls of the dollhouse were miniature trees and flowers, and someone had even painted pyracantha bushes under the nursery window. Even as Laura thought about it, her heart skipped a beat. She began searching her memory, but she was so tired she had trouble making the pieces fit. Pyracantha? She reached deeper inside, trying to will it to come back to her. *Pyracantha and poison ivy.*

Tracing her finger along the outside of the dollhouse from the pyracantha to the miniature nursery window, Laura looked from the window to the hall. "Of course!" she exclaimed. Then she looked at the first floor of the dollhouse, moving her finger from the back hall to the foyer. "A rabbit's foot," she mumbled. Slowly, the pieces of the puzzle began to fall into place. She'd found the one piece that connected the rest. She knew who had murdered Ruby Davis.

* * *

Aaron concealed himself behind a massive oak tree, noting that the harvest moon hung in the sky like a big pumpkin, not quite full but close enough. He had a perfect view of the back door, and for a brief moment, he felt a little foolish playing this game. But as he thought back on Laura's hospital visit and the reason for it, he realized this was anything but a game. Someone had tried to kill her, someone who thought she knew too much.

Hearing the rustling of leaves nearby, Aaron knew someone was approaching, but he saw nothing as he peered into the darkness. Suddenly, a twig cracked directly behind him and he turned just in time to see a large object coming toward him in a downward arc. He had no time to react, and it hit him with great force on the top of the head. His body struck the ground with a dull thud.

* * *

Sitting in a chair just inside Laura Buford's dark bedroom, Deputy Graham heard the stairs creaking and knew someone was coming, but since he'd had no radio contact from either of the lookouts, he knew it must be Farr. Graham chuckled, thinking that Aaron was so worried about that girlfriend of his that he couldn't sit still and wait. *He'd sure make a lousy cop,* Graham thought with a grimace. He had left the bedroom door cracked slightly, so he moved closer to peek out. Suddenly, someone slammed the door into his face. He fell back, grabbing at his gun, but was unable to reach it before something hard hit him in the forehead. Then everything went black.

* * *

The creaking of the stairs had started the hammering of Laura's heart, but when she heard the banging of a door and a thud, she felt full-blown panic. In her terror, her first impulse was to hide in the closet, and her next was to crawl under the bed or jump out the back window and run screaming. But now she heard footsteps in the hallway and knew it was too late. There would be no escape now.

Paralyzed by terror, she heard the footsteps coming closer, and her mind raced. Could it be Aaron? He was watching the back door, and he wouldn't let anyone in to harm her. Maybe he thought the plan too dangerous and had come to get her.

"Aaron? Is that you?"

An eerie quiet was the only response to her query. Whoever was in the hall did not speak. What had happened? A cry of panic rose to her throat and died there.

"Who's there?" Laura finally managed to ask, her voice hoarse and dry. The blood thudded so loudly in her ears that she wondered if she'd missed the answer.

She ran to the door, but before she could lock it, someone grabbed the handle from the other side and pushed it open. She stepped back.

"George?" she whispered.

George moved toward her, as silent as a sleepwalker, holding a bloody shovel in his right hand. Moving close to her, he stared at her dazedly.

"Miss Laura," he said gruffly, "you should have kept your mouth shut about what happened to Ruby."

His eyes looked like dark empty holes. "I don't know what you mean, George. I saw someone in a hood push Ruby down the stairs. I never saw the person's face."

George moved closer to her, and Laura backed away. "You lie," he barked agitatedly. Laura glanced at the shovel, and a wave of panic rose up in her. Then the memories came rushing back like a great wind, and she could see Ruby falling down the stairs. She could see the hooded person hovering over Ruby, but she still couldn't see the murderer's face. Yet, all the pieces had come together tonight. She already knew George had murdered Ruby.

Laura backed up against the dollhouse and listened, but she heard nothing except the ticking of the hall clock and her pulse pounding in her temples. Aaron wasn't there, and neither were the deputies. Then she remembered the radio and glanced at it on the bed, then back at George's empty expression.

Perhaps she could distract him, grab the radio, and call for help. Of course, by the time anyone came, he would have already hit her with the shovel. Perhaps she could keep him talking, sidetrack him. Eventually, Aaron and Julie would come to check on her. "I can't prove anything," Laura insisted. "I really didn't see who pushed Ruby."

"It's too late for that now, Miss Laura. You should have stayed back in St. Louis." He raised the shovel and came at her. She ducked, holding her hands over her head in a protective manner.

"George!"

Laura looked up, and George jerked around. Agnes Hayes stood in the doorway, holding a handgun. "I won't let you do it again. I should have stopped you years ago. I should have told the police."

"Agnes, you stay out of this," he ordered, "or I'll tell the police what I know about you. They'll put you away for what you've been doing."

Agnes's arm straightened as she walked forward and raised the gun higher. "I don't care. I've been imprisoned all these years anyway." Then she glanced at Laura. "I won't let you hurt her. I've heard you lurking about the house at night like a predator, and I know you rigged her car."

A chill shot up Laura's spine as she realized she'd been living so close to Ruby's killer. George stepped toward Agnes. "Put the shovel down," Agnes ordered firmly.

Suddenly, George swung the shovel at Agnes, hitting her arm. The gun fired and flew from Agnes's hand across the room, banging on the wood floor. "No!" Agnes yelled as she dived to the floor, reaching wildly for the gun. George grabbed Agnes and pulled her back, then dropped to his knees and reached for the gun, but Agnes started hitting at him.

Laura roused herself from her shock. *Do something,* she screamed internally. *Do something before it's too late.*

George and Agnes still fought over the gun, and now they both had hold of it in a desperate struggle. Laura ran over and grabbed the shovel from the floor. With a swift swing, she brought it down on the back of George's head. He collapsed to the floor, and Agnes jumped up with the gun.

"Drop it!" commanded an armed deputy in the doorway. Laura dropped the shovel and heard it clatter to the floor, and Agnes gently set down the gun.

George began to moan. With his gun pointing down at George, the deputy walked slowly toward him. "Don't move, old man."

Aaron came into the room, blood trickling down his forehead and onto his white shirt. Laura rushed to him.

"Aaron! Are you okay?"

"Laura! Aaron!" Julie dashed through the door. "I screamed for the police—oh, there you are, deputy. Is everyone okay?"

"It looks like Laura's okay, but the deputy down the hall is injured. I'd better get help," Aaron stated, then left the room.

Laura slumped onto the bed. "Julie, we've caught our killer."

"Oh, Laura, it's like that Hitchcock movie, *Rear Window.* The killer almost got Jimmy Stewart, but they saved him in the nick of time."

"You and your movie comparisons—I couldn't live without them anymore." Laura smiled at her friend.

The sheriff's deputy arrested George and handcuffed him, then pulled him to his feet and pushed him out the door of the nursery. Laura, Julie, and Agnes followed them down the hall. Dr. Preston knelt in Aunt Laura's room examining the other deputy. As they descended the great staircase, Laura saw that the gunshot had drawn a crowd. Sheriff Buford rolled forward in his wheelchair, declaring loudly, "Looks like we can close this case."

29

Laura sat on the mahogany couch in the parlor, Julie next to her. Aaron brought Laura a glass of water, and she carefully cupped it between her trembling hands and took a sip. Looking around, she saw anticipation in each face. The sheriff sat across from her in a large chair, and next to him was a deputy with a notebook poised on his knee and a mini tape recorder in his hand. By the fireplace, Roger Ballister stood looking up at the portrait of Laura Buford, and farther to the right, Leonard Davis leaned forward with his hands resting on the back of a chair.

"Are you ready to make a statement, Miss McClain?" the sheriff asked softly, as if any loud or sudden noise would shatter her. "We can clear the room. We don't normally allow an audience for these things."

"No," Laura affirmed. "If you don't mind, I'd like them all to stay."

Roger Ballister removed his gaze from the portrait and approached the group. Sensing that he was indeed welcome, Leonard Davis stepped from behind the chair and came forward. Aaron sat down next to Julie on the couch.

Movement at the door drew every head in that direction. A deputy stood there with Emily Smith, and the sheriff turned expectantly to Laura. "Let her join us," Laura said as she wiped her eyes with a tissue. Miss Smith came forward and sat in a nearby chair.

"This is a little out of the ordinary," the sheriff commented.

"I don't want to go to Bufordville," Laura stated with resolution. "And all these people deserve to hear the story."

"She's been through too much tonight, Sheriff," Julie interjected, grasping Laura's hand. "Can't this wait until tomorrow?"

"I suppose so, but Miss McClain, didn't you say you wanted to get this over with?"

"Yes, Sheriff," Laura answered quickly.

"But having all these people here is not really protocol." The sheriff sighed.

"I realize that, but I don't want to have to tell this story more than once," Laura explained.

"Do you want a statement from her tonight or not?" Julie asked.

The sheriff nodded, and the deputy turned on the tape recorder.

Taking the cue, Laura began. "At the Harvest Moon Festival twenty years ago, Bobby and Marshall ran into each other carrying trays of hot chocolate." Laura cleared her throat and took a sip of water. "George took Bobby and Marshall to the cottage to get new uniforms."

"That was around seven forty," Julie interrupted.

The sheriff frowned at Julie, who quickly covered her mouth with her hand. She looked at Laura apologetically, and her friend smiled.

"Go on," the sheriff prodded, looking intently at Laura.

"Well, Bobby and Marshall may not have noticed, but George was upset about Ruby's engagement to Edward Smith. You see, George and Ruby had been carrying on a secret affair."

There was a gasp from Leonard, and everyone's head turned toward him. "Sorry," he muttered, and they all turned their attention back to Laura.

"The whole town knew Ruby had run off with Roscoe Buford when she was nineteen," Laura continued, "and some thought she'd secretly resumed her relationship with him when she returned. But Roscoe and Ruby stopped dating when she came to Buford's Bluff. In fact, Ruby was secretly seeing an older man."

"Your father," Miss Smith uttered in a hoarse voice, then looked down at her hands.

"*No*, Miss Smith, it wasn't my father," Laura corrected her. "That was only a rumor. Thinking back on it, I should have caught on that George knew Ruby pretty well. George told me about Ruby's relationship with her brother and about how Leonard didn't approve of her dating the locals. He knew a lot about Ruby. He even stated she didn't love Edward Smith. How would he presume to know that?"

"And he was how old back then?" Roger asked. "Forty-seven or forty-eight?"

"At least," Leonard affirmed. "When I heard the rumors about an older man, I confronted Ruby. She admitted that there was an older local man, but she refused to tell me who. I expressed my displeasure—I was worried about her."

The sheriff cleared his throat loudly and frowned at the two seasoned lawyers. Leonard folded his arms and lifted his chin, while Roger nodded acquiescently at the sheriff.

"That night," Laura started again, "after Bobby and Marshall went back to the party, George decided to try to talk to Ruby. He knew I was afraid of storms, so he knew Ruby would come in to check on me. He threw on a rain slicker—it had started raining by then—and ran to the work shed to get a ladder. I heard the ladder hit the side of the house, and I was terrified. I jumped from bed and ran to the closet to hide. The pyracantha bushes grew thick below my window, and the red berries stained George's shoes. He jimmied the window open but saw no one in my room, so he went out into the hall and walked to the top of the stairs."

Laura paused and looked around the room. She had never been the center of so much attention in her life, and she suddenly felt self-conscious. Speaking more quickly now, she resumed the story. "George heard Ruby talking with Roger Ballister down in the front foyer. George told me he had seen Roger going toward the house as he returned to the party, but Bobby saw Roger going to the house when he returned to the party, and he left before George, so the timeline didn't match up. Roger should have already been in the house when George came along. The only way George could have known that Roger was in the house was if he were in the house with him."

"I made a mistake," Leonard interrupted, glancing briefly at the sheriff. "I had him offer Ruby a trip to Europe and a new wardrobe. I was going to finance the whole thing. It would've been tempting for most young women, especially Ruby. She wanted to travel, but she was in love—not with George but with Edward Smith. George was older, and this may have seemed exciting to Ruby at first, but she must not have loved George."

"Yes," Laura averred. "George must have figured this out as he heard Ruby and Roger talking at the bottom of the stairs. When

Roger left and Ruby started up the stairs, George confronted her on the stairs. That explains the pyracantha-berry stains on the carpet. Anyway, I must have recognized Ruby's voice, so I got out of the closet and ran down the hall. I could feel water under my feet, water that had dripped from George's rain slicker. I peered through the banister. George was wearing the rain slicker with the hood up, and since I was behind him I couldn't see his face. George and Ruby argued, and he pushed her down the stairs.

"George must have gone down the stairs to make sure she was dead, because Sheriff Buford told me there were red stains near the body. When George did that, I must have cried out. George chased me to the nursery, where I hid in the closet again. He started to open the closet door, but someone called my name. It was Agnes Hayes. She'd been in the kitchen, returning the silver spoon she had stolen earlier. Her confrontation with Ruby shook her up. She was afraid Ruby would tell Aunt Laura and that perhaps Aunt Laura would call for a silver inventory. Agnes couldn't take the chance. She had to return the spoon."

"Agnes must have heard Ruby and me talking from the kitchen," Roger added.

"Yes, Roger," Laura said with a nod. "Once you left, George started arguing with Ruby. Agnes probably crept into the hall to see for herself, and she saw George push Ruby down the stairs. When George chased after me, Agnes ran into the foyer to check on Ruby. She dropped her lucky rabbit's foot, leaving the only clue other than the pyracantha stains. Finding that Ruby was already dead, Agnes wondered if I was safe, so she called my name. George heard her and climbed out the window, closing it behind him. Agnes Hayes saved my life."

"Twice now," Roger added.

"Well, Agnes did make some mistakes that night," Laura explained. "She ran into the nursery but couldn't find me, and she saw that George had fled. I don't know what went through her mind at that point—perhaps she was afraid she'd be blamed for Ruby's death. After all, the entire staff had heard Ruby accuse her of being a thief, and everyone knew Ruby and Agnes disliked each other. How would she explain being in the house? Perhaps she feared the family would find out about her sickness. So she decided to distance herself from the situation."

Julie clicked her tongue and shook her head.

Laura went on. "She was probably going to leave then, but she must have realized if George were caught, he would tell them she was there too. Maybe Agnes sympathized with George—after all, she'd seen his encounter with Ruby. I don't know. But I believe that Agnes grabbed a toy from my toy box and planted it on the stairs to make Ruby's death look like an accident. Like George did, she returned to the party as if nothing had happened. Meanwhile, I was left on the closet floor."

Julie squeezed Laura's hand tighter.

"And then there was the poison ivy." Laura chuckled. "George and Agnes went to Dr. Preston's to be treated for poison ivy. You see, it's really the poison ivy that gives the whole thing away. I know a thing or two about poison ivy. I studied the subject when half my class had contact with poison oak one year. Both poison ivy and poison oak contain a skin irritant somewhat like carbolic acid, and even tiny amounts of the oil can cause irritation. Scientists have found traces of the oil in dried poison ivy leaves over a hundred years old. The oil is normally transferred to humans when they touch the plant. But when the plant is burned, the oil escapes into the air and can cause lung, skin, and eye irritation.

"One child in my class unknowingly came in contact with poison oak, and the oil brushed onto his skin. Then he made contact with another student and the oil was transferred to him and so on. And that's really what gives George away."

"Tell us how," Julie begged eagerly.

"Leonard, Ruby, Edward, and Emily were standing by a bonfire by the river around seven forty-five when a careless worker fed the flames with logs laced with poison ivy. Luckily the fire was far enough from the reception hall that only the four were initially exposed. Edward and Emily returned to the reception hall without realizing they'd been exposed. Around that time, Roscoe Buford showed up drunk. He stomped to the bonfire, where he confronted Ruby and was exposed to the poison-ivy fumes. My father, John McClain, came over to throw Roscoe off the property, so he was unknowingly exposed as well. He got rid of Roscoe and returned to the reception hall.

"At that point, Ruby heard thunder and hurried to the house to check on me. After Ruby left the bonfire, the worker realized his mistake and cried out. It was around this time that Leonard's eyes started burning, and he ran for help.

"It began to rain, which doused the fire and cleaned the air. You see, I can explain everyone's poison ivy except George's and Agnes's. Agnes was serving in the reception hall and George was at the cottage with Bobby and Marshall, far from any poison ivy.

"So how did he get it?" Julie asked excitedly, ignoring the sheriff's glare.

"When he grabbed Ruby's arm on the stairs, the oil from her skin was transferred to his. And Agnes surely touched Ruby's body to see if she was dead, so that's when she contacted the oil. They didn't notice it until the next day because the oil usually takes some time to penetrate and do its damage."

"How do you know Agnes didn't kill Ruby?" Julie asked.

"The berry stains," Laura explained, "plus the water on the floor, the ladder, and George's poison ivy. It all adds up. George murdered Ruby Davis. But he almost got caught when Edward Smith came snooping around early Saturday morning. He knew Ruby had been murdered. He was hunting for clues, and he found them. In George's haste, he left the ladder on the side of the house. Maybe he planned on removing it the next day when no one was looking. He probably figured no one would notice it there on the east side among the bushes and trees anyway.

"When George saw Edward climbing the ladder on Saturday morning, he scared him off. Edward had been drinking the night before, so he wasn't in a clear mental state, and anything he told the police would have been considered a drunkard's rambling. At that time, George could do nothing but blame him for the ladder on the side of the house. Since the entire staff saw Edward on the ladder outside my window, it was easy for George to accuse Edward of wanting to come inside to harm me.

"When George went with Agnes to Dr. Preston's office, the doctor probably told him that Emily and Edward Smith had come by. Perhaps the doctor even told them he'd heard Edward tell Emily he was going home to sleep for the remainder of the day. So George had his opportunity. After he dropped Agnes off at her sister's, he drove to Edward's apartment. He jimmied the door open—being a handyman, he probably had the tools in his truck. Edward was sound asleep in the bedroom, and George went into the kitchen and turned on the gas."

"Laura, you've built quite a case here," Aaron said, reaching behind Julie to squeeze Laura's shoulder.

"Most of what you've told me is just your opinion, Laura," the sheriff indicated. "But your story certainly makes sense to me, and it gives us enough information to do a thorough investigation. You've already identified the witnesses we need to speak to, and you've given us an idea of the kind of information they can provide. Once we've gathered their statements and organized all the facts and evidence, we can press charges against the appropriate parties."

"I knew we could solve this case," Julie remarked, her face beaming.

30

Spring had come to Buford's Bluff. The daffodils and crocuses were blooming, and tulip leaves had begun to push their way up through the soil. The forsythia bushes were in full bloom all across the lawns, and birds could be seen returning to their nests high in the trees, where tiny green buds were appearing.

Once again, Laura found herself standing in a reception line in the great banquet hall at Buford's Bluff, yet the circumstances were quite different from the Harvest Moon Open House months before. This time she wore a flowing white wedding dress, and it was brand new. Though she had determined that the wedding dress in the attic was indeed her mother's, and though it actually fit Laura quite well, the fabric was yellowed beyond repair, so wearing it for her own wedding wasn't an option. Laura had decided it was for the best anyway—she would wear a new dress for her new beginning, and she would keep her mother's dress in memory of her.

The reception line was quite long for a bride who was new to the area and a groom who was also a relative newcomer. In fact, it seemed that the entire community had turned out on this warm spring evening to congratulate Laura and her new husband, Aaron Farr. Aaron stood next to her in a black tuxedo with a silver vest and cravat, and next to him were his mother and brothers. They had accompanied Laura and Aaron that morning to the Washington DC Temple, where Laura and Aaron were sealed for all eternity. Representing Laura's family in the reception line were Megan, Julie, and Roger.

Laura smiled when she saw Hattie O'Donnell approaching with the ever-frowning Lettie. "Oh, my, Laura, this is such a fine reception. Your dress is beautiful, dear," Hattie gushed.

"Thank you so much for coming! It means a lot to me," Laura responded with a tear in her eye, hugging Hattie and then shaking Lettie's hand.

As she spoke with Aaron, Hattie momentarily took her eyes from Lettie, who immediately headed for the buffet tables. With a shake of her head, Hattie excused herself and followed her elderly sister.

Laura looked across the reception hall and saw Louise Lawrence pushing her mother's wheelchair. Walking with the women were the two missionaries who had been teaching Julie the gospel for the last few months. Dr. Preston, Emily Smith, and Joe Webster sat around a table chatting. Someone had even brought Jackson Buford, but luckily Roscoe and Ellen were nowhere in sight.

Refilling a large bowl with peach punch, Agnes must have seen Marsha Prestwich walking towards her, notebook and pen in hand, because she suddenly scurried back to the kitchen. As part of her punishment for not coming forward about the murder, Agnes was under house arrest for eight months, and she was required to wear an ankle bracelet that allowed the police to monitor her location. While Laura didn't press charges against Agnes for the many instances of petty theft to which she had confessed, Laura did insist that her employee complete an addiction recovery and rehabilitation program. Because Laura believed that Agnes wanted to overcome her kleptomania, she paid for her to attend the best private program in the area.

Agnes had agreed to testify against George, but there would be no need for that. George had pled guilty to the second-degree murder of Ruby Davis and the first-degree murder of Edward Smith. He would serve the rest of his life in the state penitentiary, but he commented at his sentencing that it would be no worse than the prison of guilt he had been in for over twenty years.

Leonard Davis approached Laura and Aaron with a smile. He kissed Laura on the cheek and shook Aaron's hand. "Well, Aaron, my boy," he began, "Tennyson said, 'In the spring a young man's fancy lightly turns to thoughts of love.' I guess we can't fault you for falling in love with such an enchanting creature."

Laura blushed.

"But, my boy, your mind will need to return to more serious matters a week and a half from now when you return to the office."

"Yes, sir," Aaron replied with a hearty laugh.

Leonard turned toward Laura. "Well, my lady, I hear you plan to settle down at Buford's Bluff. Your aunt would be pleased."

"Well, Mr. Davis, I'm not too sure about that." Laura chuckled. "You see, Julie and I are planning to diversify."

Julie approached them. "Tobacco stinks!" she declared. "We're talking about turning this place into an orchard, aren't we, Laura?"

Laura felt her face grow warm. "Yes, we are."

Roger came up behind Julie. "Well, the stipulations in your aunt's will indicate that you have to stay here for three years and keep the place going. There's nothing that forbids you from using the plantation to grow something other than tobacco."

Imagining the plantation's rolling hills covered with blossoming fruit trees, Laura looked around at her new friends and smiled. Aaron grasped her hand and pulled her closer to him, then kissed her soundly. For the first time in her life, she felt confident that whatever came her way, she could face it with courage and faith.

ABOUT THE AUTHOR

J. Michael Hunter was born and raised in the Blue Ridge Mountains of Virginia. He received a BA in history and a master's degree in Library and Information Science from Brigham Young University. He received a second master's degree in humanities with an emphasis in history from California State University, Dominguez Hills. He has worked at the Church Historical Department, Salt Lake City, and is currently the Chair of the Religion and Family History Department at the Harold B. Lee Library, Brigham Young University. Mike lives in Lehi with his wife, LeAnn, and his three children, Victoria, Elizabeth, and Cody.